Praise for Detroitaphobia

In true Afrofuturist fashion, Keith Owens's stories offer rare and intriguing perspectives on the African diaspora of tomorrow. With clarity, vision, and enchantment, Owens superbly weaves an alternative reality for Detroiters who just happen to have ancestors from The Motherland. Call it sci-fi with a Motown edge and a beat that's out of this world.

Denise Crittendon

"It has been a long time since I've read a collection of stories composed of such pure, simple, unadorned horror and eeriness. There is not a speck of guile herein, no frill, no cliches, no parlor tricks, no fakery. Keith Owens' stories are long, gray, cobwebbed hallways that walk us straight into phantasms, nightmares, broken realities, and the appalling misfortunes that suffuse all of our hopes and desires. Keep your lights on, check over your shoulder, take out the ear buds, and give one more good listen to the still night. Mr. Owens ain't playing."

Reginald McKnight, author of *He Sleeps* and *The Kind of Light that Shines on Texas*

"Like Detroit, these stories are fast, no nonsense, and know how to catch you unexpected. They pull readers into the sidestreets, rhythms, and aspirations of an oasis outside the bounds of 8 Mile but fitting perfectly into the Twilight Zone."

Zig Zag Claybourne, author of *Afro Puffs Are the Antennae of the Universe* and *The Brothers Jet Stream: Leviathan*

Copyright © 2026 Keith A. Owens

Published by Detroit Stories Quarterly

Table of Contents

Corona My Love

Part 1: The Reason

Nobody ever accused me of being a modern man. I am, unapologetically, who I am. And who I am is a fat as hell, single as hell, occasionally employed, 43-year-old Black man living with his mother in a small red-brick house on the West Side of Detroit. A house my father built, which is something you almost never hear of in this city where everyone lives in a structure built by someone else, usually someone else from a long time ago.

Anyway, I don't look like somebody who did a lot of school any more than I look like somebody who did a lot of exercise, but I was actually an art major in college. First in my family to make it past high school, and first in my family to leave Michigan. Shit, I was one of the few to ever leave Detroit.

My mother always said it didn't make any sense for me to go all that way to learn how to draw pictures when I was already better than everybody in my class. Plus, there was a perfectly good art school in Detroit. But the biggest thing from her perspective was the money. Because wasn't no money in art as far as she could see.

"You ever meet any rich artists, Tommy? Me neither. You ever wonder why that is?"

This was a few months before I graduated high school, when we had that mother-to-only-son 'discussion' about my future plans.

Why pursue a major in something I was already good at, *and* was gonna keep me broke like everybody else, when I could learn how to do something that would improve my lot in life? And hers. And the rest of the family's …

"That scholarship you got is an opportunity. It's an opportunity to do something nobody else in the Banks family ever did. You're not just representing yourself, you're representing all of us. So it's not just an opportunity, it's a responsibility."

Yeah, well… I didn't agree. Because what was the purpose of having a wonderful opportunity if it had *chains* attached to it? That would be called a fake opportunity, Mom. Maybe it was selfish, but I refused to accept that I was supposed to sideline my desire to be an artist because I might not make enough money to support the entire Banks extended clan. If Dad had still been alive when I made my choice, I know he would have understood. But a drunk driver snatched that understanding out of my life at the age of fourteen.

And actually, I *did* know a rich artist. Maybe he wasn't rich like Michael Jackson rich, but he had enough money to own a nice home in Bloomfield Hills. He was a white guy named Oscar Peters—how I got to know him is a long story, but he was the one who encouraged me in my art. He was the one who helped me to get the scholarship and encouraged me to get out of the city.

"One of the most important things for a creative is *experiences*," he said. "The more limited your experience, the more limited your creativity. The two go hand-in-hand, Tommy. So you need to see something else besides this city, powerful as it may be. You need some more colors for your brush, young man."

Oscar's advice sounded better to me than my mother's, so I took it. And even though things didn't work out as planned—which would explain why I've been back living at home in my mom's basement for the past couple years—I didn't regret it. I took that leap of faith, and for a while, I managed to float and even fly a little bit while navigating the South Side of Chicago in a small Hyde Park flat I shared with a small-boned, olive-skinned, and dreadlocked woman named Gail. Gail, who was phenomenally talented, eventually headed off to New York and made a name for herself as a wildly unconventional sculptor—she designed these open and free-flowing creations out of wrought iron. As for me, I ultimately came crashing down, Icarus style. Nothing to do with getting too close to the sun, though. I just failed, plain and simple.

But I was nothing if not stubborn, and being a successful artist was the only dream I'd ever had. I wasn't going to let it go without a fight. As long as I was living in the basement, I was going to fight until I was the Black Da Vinci, or, was at least making enough to move out of the dungeon.

Weekdays, I spent stocking shelves at a nearby grocery store, and that damned sure wasn't putting enough in the bank account for me to be able to move out. It seemed like every day when I got home from work, I would walk in the door, and Mom would be sitting there on the couch, not even lookin' up at me or smiling. She never asked how my day went—not that there was much to tell. She would just shake her head and sigh.

Why can't you aim for something higher?

But I *was* aiming higher. Just higher in a different direction. I know she tried to understand my way of thinking, but she just couldn't. The only way I was going to get her to understand was to succeed, so, after that first year, I decided to quit my job at the grocery store and spend all my time painting and sketching.

"You ain't makin' no money over there anyway, so you might as well," she said.

"I know you can't see it now, Mom, but this will work. I promise you that."

"Shouldn't make those types of promises," she said.

That was the last time I actually saw my mother.

Part 2: The Cocoon

It was a good thing that Mom let me have my privacy in the basement. I don't like to say anything is a blessing, because I get tired of folks saying every damned thing is a blessing, but it probably was close to that. She didn't even come downstairs to do laundry anymore once we agreed I would take care of it each week if she would just let me have that small space, uninterrupted, as my own.

Once the updated living arrangement was finalized between my mother and her failed, grown-assed son, I began rearranging the basement into a makeshift studio. That was when I went into self-imposed quarantine—all I really needed was my imagination, my easel, some sketching paper, a canvas, some brushes, and my charcoal pencils. The rest of what I had during that relatively brief shining moment of borderline survival-success in Chicago, I could do without. All I needed to ascend to my rightful place as a world-renowned artist was to strip back down to the basics, figure out another angle of attack, and make another run at it.

The results of all that figuring out were scattered around my makeshift studio in piles of canvas and paper on the floor, jammed into congested spots occupying every single square inch of every single wall. There were a few unfinished sketches I'd made of neighborhood scenes with kids playing in the streets and old folks sitting on porches. There were a few other musicians caught in that moment of holiness when I imagined their inspiration took hold, and their solos began to dance around the room.

But mostly what I liked to draw, *loved* to draw, was women. Didn't matter if they were Black, white, brown, or whatever corner of the rainbow. It was the sheer variety of colors and shapes that made women so beautiful. I didn't care if she was so heavy her footprints left craters, or so thin that you couldn't see her sideways. Busty and ripe, or straight up and down like a cliff face.

Didn't matter.

Even though I never had a girlfriend, to me, women represented all the beauty there was left in the world. I remember one day in Chicago, when I was taking a break from a particularly difficult sketch I was trying to bring to life, I was moaning and groaning about my inability to 'get lucky.' Gail, who was a lesbian, asked me why I thought *luck* had anything to do with it as she sat across from me at the kitchen table, sipping coffee. One eyebrow was arched high and sharp like a steeple, and I knew I had stumbled myself into a conversation—by sheer accident or carelessness—that I was in no way ready for. So, instead of engaging, I retreated with an apology and was about to head out the door to get some summer air when…

"Coward."

My hand was on the doorknob, mid-turn, and I froze.

"What did you call me?" I said, feeling a level of threat inside my voice I barely recognized. Gail must have heard it too, because what she said next contained a note of caution, perhaps weighing the potential consequences of her next words.

"Nevermind," she said. "That was mean. I shouldn't have said that."

"But you did."

The level of discomfort in the atmosphere was thick, and I wondered if I should let it go and step out the door without another word. When I returned, everything would be at least forgiven, if not forgotten, and both of us could re-enter our lives as two artists who shared a flat without sharing a life. It wasn't an accident that Gail was a lesbian.

"But you did," I said again, turning away from the door. So much for walking away.

"Yes. I did."

"And?"

Gail shrugged her shoulders, then took another sip of coffee.

"Like I said, it was mean. You didn't deserve that."

"No, I don't think I did. And if that was an apology, then I guess I accept. But I'd still like to know what was going through your mind when you said it."

Gail sighed, then lowered her cup to the table. She stood up and walked over to me, her eyes holding me gently. She raised one small hand and stroked the side of my face, tilting her head.

"*You* were the one who apologized, Tommy. And that's why I called you a coward. You don't finish things. And until you finish something, you'll never really get started."

"I don't know what you mean…"

"I said luck has nothing to do with why you don't have a girlfriend. I don't have a girlfriend either, but I know why. It's by choice. And when I feel like I want to dive back into those waters again? I will. But at least I'm not lying to myself. So when you apologized and started to walk away? Yeah, I got a little pissed. Because I thought after all this time being roommates, we might actually be on the verge of having a real discussion about something that mattered."

We stared at each other for a long while, and then I grinned. Gail frowned.

"This is funny to you, Tommy?"

"Not at all. I was just thinking something."

"Thinking what?"

"That it's too damned bad you're gay, because otherwise I could swear you and I just had an argument like an old married couple."

She may not have wanted to, but Gail couldn't help but laugh. She knew it was true. We both laughed together, and it felt good. Really good.

And then I walked out the door into the summer weather, and we never talked about the purpose of luck, or why I needed to finish things, ever again.

We never talked about *anything* that mattered again, but it stuck with me what she said about finishing things. All the evidence Gail would have needed to prove her point was scattered around my studio in an army of aborted works. The discarded canvases on the floor, the sketches stuck to the walls—all of them were missing a conclusion. Some of them were only half done, while others, inexplicably, were just a dash of color or a few added strokes away from being done. But for some reason, I could never bring myself to add those last few strokes. I could run right to the edge of that cliff, but I couldn't let myself look over for fear of falling.

Until you finish something, you'll never really get started.

I thought about Gail and how she had gone on to a famed career in New York, and here I was still in my mother's basement with nothing but bits and pieces. There was only one way to *get started:* I had to destroy. Everything.

I began gathering up all the canvases off the floor and tearing down the unfinished sketches from the walls. I felt like I was peeling away dead skin. *My* dead skin. Exposing the real flesh underneath.

I stuffed everything into a mountain of Black garbage bags and hauled them out back to the dumpster. When I came back, I stood in the middle of the floor with my hands on my hips, like my father used to do, and looked around at all the emptiness. I felt lighter, and it was easier to breathe. Once again, I had stripped my life down to the studs to make way for rebuilding and rebirth—but this time I could see a light at the end of the tunnel. This time, the butterfly.

"Fuck you, Gail."

Part 3: The Sketch

The door squealed open at the top of the stairs.

"You OK down there, Tommy? I haven't heard anything outta you in a month."

"I'm OK, Ma. I'm fine. Just working."

"Thought you mighta died or something."

"That's nice. Good thing you checked then, huh?"

"Boy, don't go gettin' smart. Just 'cause you grown don't mean you *grown,* hear? This is still my house. And you know what that means, right?"

"Still your rules," I muttered, clenching my jaw.

"Couldn't hear you," she said.

I squeezed my eyes shut as I leaned back in my chair and looked up at the ceiling. I took a deep breath.

"*I'm fine, Ma.* I'm fine. I got that mini-fridge down here now, so I don't need to be bothering you all the time going up and down the stairs to get something to eat. Just trying to be considerate."

"You call not seeing your mother in a month considerate?"

Jesus.

"If the weather's good tomorrow, maybe we can do something. Go out to the park or something like that. OK?"

"I'll have to check my calendar, but that could be nice. I haven't been to that park in a while."

I shook my head as I opened my eyes.

"All right. You let me know, OK? Just send me an email, though. I'm really trying to work on something, and it's kinda hard when you interrupt. I don't mean to be…"

"Fine, I'll let you know. I'll send you one of those secret encrypted things."

The door closed. I could hear her footsteps making their way towards her bedroom. The sound of the TV upstairs was muffled, but I liked the sound of it as background noise while I worked. When I was in Chicago, I would put on some of Gail's classical music while I stood on my feet at my easel, sometimes for hours, trying to create something that always seemed out of my grasp, like a butterfly teasing overhead. Here, I just had that steady, inane hum of disconnected voices and commercials that came from the upstairs TV. I liked it better than strict silence.

I think *she* liked it better, too.

I still hadn't come up with a name for her yet, probably because each time I thought I had her face just right—I liked to draw faces before anything else—I realized there was something missing, so I had to erase and start all over again. The face was full and almost ripe, but the lips needed to be full, too. I wanted her to be smiling, but I couldn't seem to get her lips' fullness right when I made her smile. If they were too full, she looked almost minstrel-like, and that was nothing short of a sin. But if they were too thin, then she looked like she had white girl lips, and that wasn't going to work either.

Damn.

All these years, and I'd never had this problem before. Not with any woman I had ever sketched or painted, and that amounted to quite a few. But with this one, I had a deep feeling of something special. This was the one. I *had to* get her right, because otherwise she…

She *what?* What the hell was I thinking?

Maybe Mom was right. Maybe I *had* been down here too long without taking a break and needed to get outside for a while. Decompress. She wasn't going anywhere without me, and I would probably have a better shot of getting her right if I stepped away for just a little...

"Don't."

Her lips were incomplete, yet still trying to smile. Her eyes, the shape of almonds, were lookin' directly at me.

Was that the way I drew them?

I didn't think so, but now I can't remember. As for what I may have heard her say, I refused to process it, so instead I looked around the room.

"Don't."

Her eyes brought me back. They looked insistent, but also pleading. What was happening to me? I scanned the room once more as my heart started pumping so hard that I thought I might have an attack. I wasn't in the best shape, so it wasn't out of the question.

My eyes returned to hers. Hers blinked.

This shit is not happening.

"There has got to be an explanation for this," I said out loud, because I desperately needed to hear a voice of reason. Maybe Mom put acid in my oatmeal. Maybe I was dreaming longer and harder than usual and only *thought* I was awake. Maybe I was...

"You're not crazy, Tommy. It's me."

Jesus...

I lowered my head and closed my eyes. Started rubbing them with my fists. Maybe if I rubbed them hard enough…

"That won't work either, so you might as well open up those beautiful brown eyes of yours and finish me."

I stopped rubbing and made myself look up. Her eyes looked gentle, almost seductive. Same as her voice, which was soft and a little raspy like the wind through trees in the fall. I felt something twitch inside that made me feel embarrassed.

She winked.

"So let me ask you this," I began cautiously. "If it's you talking to me, and this is supposed to be real—which it's not—then how the hell are you talking without lips? How am I hearing these words you're saying when you don't have any lips yet?"

She chuckled.

"Well, in fairness, I *do* have some lips, Tommy. They're just half erased, which I guess means you haven't figured out how you want them. But still, it's a fair question. The answer is, I don't really know how this works either. I *do* know I've been watching you work on me ever since you finished my eyes."

"I started with your eyes."

"Yes! Yes, you did, and I am very happy with them. *Very* sexy. And I have wanted to have this conversation ever since I could see you, but I was afraid that if I spoke too soon, I might spook you. You've been in a wonderful sort of rhythm of creation, and I didn't want to interrupt."

"So, then why did you? Interrupt? And you *still* spooked me, by the way. Just so you know, there's no good time for a sketch to start talking to the artist."

She laughed.

"You're probably right. But to answer your question, I felt like I had to say something when I saw you were about to leave. I got scared."

"Scared? Why would you... hey... your lips... your *lips!*"

"What about my lips?"

"Shit, look at them! They're... they're finished! And they're *moving...*"

Her eyes rolled down, but she still looked confused.

"I can't see them, Tommy. Do you have a mirror? I want to see my new lips. Do they look OK?"

"They look fantastic! Just like how I was trying to get them to look... but hold on: you said before that your lips were half erased. How did you know that if you couldn't see them?"

"Because I can feel them, Tommy. And I've been watching you work. I've seen how frustrated you get when the creativity isn't coming like you want it to, and I've seen how your eyes light up when it's all coming together. I only wish you could see it for yourself, how happy you get. I think maybe if you could see what I see, then you would feel more confident about what you do. About that gift you have in those stubby little fingers of yours."

"Gift? You think I have a gift? For real?"

She smiled with those beautiful, full lips, her teeth whiter than a Colgate commercial. She nodded.

"I *know* you do. But it doesn't matter what I know if you don't know it yourself. Nothing matters in this world if you don't know who you are, Thomas Augustus Banks."

Hearing that made me stand up real slow. I had started to let my guard down, but this brought it back up higher than that wall Trump swore he was gonna build.

"How do you know my full name? I *know* I never said anything about my full name while I've been down here working, and my mother never calls me by that name."

I could tell she was a little worried now, which I thought was a good thing.

"You need to tell me *your* damned name! *Who the hell are you?*"

"Tommy, you created me. You dreamed me up. I'm whoever you want me to be."

I shook my head.

"Naw, it's not that simple. You know it's not. If I really did create you, then how did you get those teeth? And how did your lips finish themselves? You say you don't know how any of this works, but if it wasn't you and it wasn't me, then who the hell was it?"

"Calm down, Tommy..."

"Don't fucking tell me to calm down!"

Shit. Mom's footsteps. The upstairs door swung open hard.

"Tommy?"

I didn't answer, hoping against hope that my mother would let the silence hang there for a bit and then shrug it off. But this was my mother, which meant…

"Tommy."

I glared at this nameless woman I had created. She mouthed "Sorry," and shrugged her shoulders.

"I'm OK, Ma. Everything's OK."

"Then why you yellin'? And who is it you got down there with you? You know what I said about—"

"Ain't nobody down here, Ma. And I know what you said."

Even though I'm over 40 and a grown man.

"Boy, I heard you tell somebody to don't bleeping tell you to calm down. Now you tryin to tell me you down there giving that advice to *yourself?"*

I squeezed my eyes shut and didn't say anything for a really long, stretched-out moment.

"Why is she so upset all the time?" the woman asked in a semi-whisper.

"I heard that, too!" my mother shouted.

Shit. *Shit.* I mouthed for her to shut the hell up as emphatically as I knew how without yelling at the top of my lungs. She looked disappointed, but she nodded.

"That was me, Ma. I was just wondering why it is you're so upset all the time since I've been back. You didn't used to be like this."

"Uh-huh. Sure didn't sound like you, and I've known you a *very* long time, Tommy. Maybe I should come down there and see…"

"*No!* …I mean, I'm sorry for raising my voice, but that's not what we agreed. Look, everything's fine, Ma. I'm sorry if I'm bothering you. This is a temporary arrangement anyway, just until I get back on my feet, and I'm thinking that won't be long. Then I'll be outta your hair. For good this time."

Mom sighed deeply, which made me ache inside. I hated being the disappointment, and I heard that embedded in her voice.

"You and I both know I ain't got much hair left, Tommy. Or that many years left either. I'm not tryin' to kick you out. I'm just so tired of worryin' about you all the time."

"But Ma, you don't have to worry about... "

The door clicked shut, and I could feel the silence coil tight around my neck. I would have felt better if she had slammed it.

Part 4: My Name is Corona

As Mom's footsteps retreated toward her favorite cushion chair in the den, I stood in the middle of the floor staring straight ahead at nothing at all and wondering if maybe nothingness was my future. I felt both calm and numb at once, which isn't the best state of mind for an artist. An artist is supposed to feel things, and right then, I wasn't feeling much of anything except utter exhaustion with this life, and a growing anger at my own creation. I turned on her.

"I'm gonna ask you one more time before I light you up and toss you out back with all my other failures. What's your name? And don't try and say it's up to me because I sketched you, because ain't nothing normal about you. I thought maybe I was crazy, but now I know my mother can hear you too, so it's not just me. It's my whole world that's gone fucking nuts."

"Tommy, if I could just get you to understand..."

"I don't bluff. Either you tell me your name or—"

"My name is Corona."

I tilted my head to the side and squinted like the sun was in my eyes. She couldn't be serious.

"Like the Mexican beer? Or like the virus?"

She shook her head.

"No. Like that's the best I could come up with right now to keep you from throwing a match on me. I don't want to die, Tommy. And neither did those other women you tore up and threw away. Just thought you should know that..."

I felt a chill run through me as I took a step back.

"What in the blind hell are you talking about? Ain't no way you can die, *Corona,* and there is no way those other women... *sketches...* felt anything at all. They weren't flesh and blood, OK? It's not like I had American Psycho going on down here. Look, I don't like being surrounded by my failures. It's kinda hard to get inspired when all you see around you is what you can't do. So, I tossed them out so I could start fresh. Artists do that all the time."

Corona stared at me blankly.

"OK," she said.

"What does that mean when you say OK? I don't understand..."

"I'm saying OK, Tommy. That's all I'm saying. You don't need to make this complicated. If that's what it was, then that's what it was. I was just telling you what they told me, is all."

"But I didn't even *start* working on you until after I'd thrown them all away. How do you know how they felt if you didn't even exist when they were around?"

"All you destroyed was canvas and paper, Tommy. They're still here. That's why I said you have a gift, baby. Once you create something? It's almost like how God does it, because what you create comes alive. *You are a giver of life, Tommy Banks.*"

"Stop that shit right now. I ain't no kinda God, and I don't want him pissed at me for you saying I am. And if those other women were in such pain, then why didn't they say something to me? Why are you the first one to get the nerve to speak up?"

She started to say something, but then decided against it. That just made me angrier.

"Tell me the truth about your name. I don't want to throw you away, but I swear I will leave you unfinished just like you are and throw you in a dumpster way on the other side of town, which something tells me would be a lot worse than dying.

Or going to whatever dimension your friends are trapped in."

"They're not trapped, but you're right. Leaving me unfinished would be uncomfortable. But you left my friends unfinished and uncomfortable, too, so I really wouldn't be any worse off than they are. I would just be another ghost in your basement studio, watching you keep trying to get it right. And failing."

I smiled, but didn't really mean it.

"But *you* want me to get it right, is that it? You're my friend in all this? That's what I'm supposed to believe?"

"We can be friends if you want, but more importantly, the answer is yes. I want you to get it right. I *need* you to get it right. We all do. If you get it right with me, then that's a victory for all of us that you threw away."

We stared at each other for a long while, each waiting for the other to speak first.

"So is Corona really your name?"

She sighed, then closed her eyes. This was the first time I noticed how beautiful her face really was. More gorgeous than any one woman had a right to be. How could someone that beautiful be created by someone like me?

"In Spanish, one meaning of the word 'Corona' is a halo. Another meaning has something to do with astronomy—a circle of light made by the apparent convergence of the aurora borealis. At least that's what it says in the dictionary."

"Dictionary? How do you have access to a dictionary?"

"I don't. But you do. Are you starting to understand now?"

I felt that chill coming back, but hoped it didn't show. Did I really want to understand?

"No, not really," I answered. "But let's keep going."

"My name is closer to the Spanish meaning. Close, but not quite."

Part 5: The Beautiful Flesh

For the next two weeks, Corona and I got to know one another as I drew the rest of her, which was kind of an erotic experience. I'm not sure an artist should ever feel the things I was feeling for their art, but I would be lying if I didn't admit I felt myself getting a little stiff in the joint every so often as I perfected a curve in her hip, or indulged myself by making her breasts just a little bit heavier, her hips just a little wider.

Corona only smiled; sometimes she winked. She said she was glad that I was enjoying myself because my joy made her more complete. It was joy that was making me finish what I'd started.

Occasionally, she would instruct me on what needed to be done—or corrected—about certain parts of her anatomy, reminding me that we were a team. But mostly she relegated herself to the role of observer and conversationalist. The real joy came in watching her witness her own creation so approvingly.

Mom called down the stairs to check on me twice; the first time, I told her again not to worry, but the second time, I didn't bother to answer. She sounded sad, almost forlorn, but I shoved that guilt as far underneath the clutter in my brain as I could. I just didn't have time for her right now.

Then came the dawn of my third week with Corona. I woke up like I usually did, in a bit of a fog. I still remember how Gail used to wake up at our place back in Chicago, as if she had never been asleep. She would pop off her bed like a well-done piece of toast and get straight to work.

Not me. It usually took somewhere between a half hour and forty-five minutes before I was fully present in the so-called Real World.

It was sometime during that lengthy waking-up phase, still caught in my customary tug-of-war between worlds, that I heard the chattering. Voices that didn't sound like complete voices at all, but more a combination of whispers and dry, guttural utterings spewed from a record player. It seemed to come from the direction of my easel, standing alone against the far wall of the basement.

Then, in the midst of all that noise, I heard Corona's voice. Unlike the rest of the disconnected chattering, her voice was sharp and almost venomous, so contrary to the soft and soothing tongue that had been putting all sorts of erotic imaginings in my mind.

"In time. No sooner, no later."

The chattering grew louder, like a flock of angry birds.

"Hush! The man is mine. It is settled."

The volume dropped to a dry whisper. I was afraid to open my eyes, but I had to see for myself what was going on. Peeking out from under my sheets, what I saw at first wasn't clear—like looking through a thick, dirty piece of glass. When I fixed my blurred eyes on my easel across the room, what I saw looked like a face formed from a Black plastic trash bag, shoving itself out of the canvas toward a group of swirling Blackish-gray shadows struggling to hold form. Briefly, it looked as if a misshapen hand, more of a claw, was trying to push its way out as well, but then it withdrew back into the canvas. I closed my eyes, shook my head, and then took another look. This time, the swirling shadows were only clearer, and I could feel my heart pounding as I realized this was no dream.

"My God!"

The head swiveled to look over at me as I began to pull myself out from under the covers of my bed in the corner of the basement. The expression on that twisted face was both alarmed and viciously angry. Or at least that's what I thought I had seen—it was there and gone so fast that I briefly doubted the evidence of my own eyes. The burning red eyes cooled to dark brown, and the contorted mask of rage swiftly reconfigured to an image of intense worry and concern. The swirling shadows collapsed into dust and then blew away in an ice-cold breeze that rushed past my face. Corona tilted her head gently.

"Tommy…"

"What was that, Corona? What the *fuck* was that?*"

"I thought you were asleep. I didn't mean to wake you."

"Me being asleep isn't the issue. Don't play me for stupid. What were you *doing* just now, and what were those *things* that were just here? What's going on?"

Corona stared at me for a moment, then began to step out of her canvas as she kept her eyes focused on mine, holding my gaze tight, not allowing me to look away. The brief return to gentleness in her eyes was burned away by something much more volatile.

"You aren't ready yet, Tommy, but I suppose you're going to have to be. I tried to keep this at a pace I felt you could handle, but because you're a man, you feel you have to push and push and push until you make something yield to your will. I'm sure you're aware of the saying, be careful what you wish for…"

"…because you just might get it…?"

Corona smiled, but there was no warmth behind the upward curve of her lips.

"See how good it feels to finish something?"

She was standing in front of me, totally nude, as I sat on the edge of my bed. Her legs were spread far apart in what resembled a warrior's stance, both hands clamped firmly on the roundness of her hips. Her skin coloring was coffee and cream with hints of cinnamon and gold; her thick locks, now long, stretched down nearly to her knees. Around her neck were three multi-colored chains containing a variety of stones and other objects I couldn't quite identify, which seemed strange, since…

"I still don't understand how it is that I created you, since so much of what you are I don't recognize…I mean, I *do* recognize you, but there's just so much…more…"

Corona threw back her head and laughed, and her laughter sounded like the tinkling of small glass bells.

"Do you remember what I told you about your gift? How was it God-like?" she asked, once her laughter had faded away.

"I don't suspect God liked that, but yeah. I remember."

"God is fine with it, Tommy. We are all God, and God is us. If you understand that, then you can understand how it is that you created me. And how I created you as well."

"What do you mean?"

"We are what we imagine, Tommy. Our imaginations are living things, and they shape who we are. You imagined me, and so there you are."

I felt like my mind was being pulled into a pretzel.

"But what about *them?*" I asked.

That blood redness flashed behind her eyes.

"*Them?* You mean my sisters? The ones you threw away?"

"I thought they were just drawings! How was I supposed to know they were anything more than what I intended them to be? I'm just an artist, Corona! Not a monster. That's all I've ever been, and that's all I ever wanted to be. If they're alive, then…"

"They are not alive. They are incomplete, which leaves them in between."

"So then what do they want? What do *you* want? What is this all about?"

"They want the same thing that I want, the same thing that any being wants; they want to be complete. Is that such a terrible thing, Tommy? To want to be whole and not spend eternity as an unfinished thing, not wanted in either Heaven or Hell?"

I put my face in my hands as I began to rock back and forth. All I ever wanted to be in life was a successful artist. How in the hell did that bring me *here?*

"It's not a terrible thing, no," I muttered.

I felt the slender fingers of her hand wrap themselves softly around my left wrist as she pulled it away from my face.

"Look at me, Tommy Banks."

"Why?"

Look at me.

This time, her voice spoke inside my head. I looked up, my heart starting to race all over again.

"What did you just do?" I asked.

Corona smiled, shaking her head slowly.

"Don't worry about that. But if you really believe it is not a terrible thing for my sisters to desire completion, then I will need something from you."

"What, to paint each of them all over again? From memory? How am I supposed to do that?"

"No. *Not* that. Even if you did, that would not help them. No matter how closely your new sketches resembled my sisters, they would be new sisters unto themselves."

"But they weren't complete for a reason. No offense to your sisters, but every single one of them was another failed attempt to try to create *you.*"

"They may be failures to you, but let me ask you this: have you ever seen a child with a deformity?"

I nodded.

"Of course, but—"

"*Shhh.* I know what you're about to say, but you are wrong. It is exactly the same thing. We don't all have to be perfect to deserve life. And as a giver of life, this is something you have an obligation to understand."

She reached out and stroked the side of my face, and I saw a warmth in her eyes that I had never seen before in any other woman who had ever taken the time to really look at me, not even my mother, and I broke.

"What is it that you need?"

Part 6: The Halo of Breath

"I need your breath, Tommy Banks."

My heart squeezed tight inside my chest like a fist.

"My *breath?* What do you mean you need *my breath?*"

"There won't be any pain," she said. "I promise. You'll be fine, and you will be loved. But most importantly, you will be remembered."

"My mother loves me, and that's good enough. But what do you mean, I will be remembered? Are you asking me to give up my life?"

"I would never ask you to give away your life, Tommy. I am asking you to share it, to *expand* it. Isn't that the purpose of art? To expand life beyond its boundaries? And you will be remembered as the artist who brought Corona to the world, so that the world can truly see!"

"But *you're* Corona—why are you talking in the third person all of a sudden? And what is it you are supposed to help the world to see? How is this supposed to help your sisters?"

"We are all Corona. While yes, they are my sisters, we share one name and one being. One divine purpose. You are meant to be a part of that purpose, but I can't force you. It has to be something you want."

Just then, I heard my mother's slow footsteps making their way toward the basement door. For the first time since I had moved back home, I was so relieved to hear that sound.

"What are you going to tell her?" whispered Corona, lookin' just the slightest bit concerned.

I shrugged my shoulders.

The door squealed open. I heard a deep breath, and then a sigh.

"Tommy? Please tell me who this is you're talking to down there, will you? I know you're grown, but I still worry. And when you lie to me, that makes me worry even more. And whoever you are, I can hear your voice, baby. Every time you speak. So you don't need to whisper. Every whisper that happens in this old house, I hear about it. My husband built this house for me and Tommy, and that means it can't hold a secret for too long without me finding out."

Corona seemed about to reply, but I shook my head.

"It's OK, Ma. Really. It is. I know I've been down here a long time, and I probably need to get out, at least to see you again, and to get some outside air, but I've just really been hard at work on this sketch, trying to get it right. I'm just afraid to break my routine, that's all. Sometimes quarantine is a good thing."

"I don't see how, but I guess you're the artist. Still wanna know who it is you got down there with you and how they got down there. These steps are the only way to get to the basement where you are, and I ain't let nobody in this house for more than a year."

"Everything's fine, Ma. Everything's gonna be fine. I promise. Soon as I finish this work, I'm gonna take a break, and you and I are gonna get outta here and take that trip to the park. OK?"

It took a while for her to answer, and for a moment I worried she was going to come downstairs. How would Corona react to that? But then I heard her sigh again, and could almost see her shaking her head in the way she always did when she was either frustrated or disgusted.

"Just take care of yourself, Tommy. That's all."

"You know I will, Ma."

"Um-hmm..."

The door closed quietly, and Corona and I looked at one another.

"Close your eyes," she said softly. "I'm going to give you a kiss."

This time, I didn't resist, and the feeling was almost pleasant. Not in a sexual way, but more like being submissive to a degree I had never experienced. Even though I was vaguely aware of my breath being inhaled out of my body through lips that I had helped design, I also felt a growing sense of euphoria and freedom. I felt like I wanted to cry.

…until the chattering.

This time, though, the sound didn't give me chills or make my heart race. Instead, I smiled as Corona's kiss grew more forceful and she extended her snake-like tongue into my mouth and around my own tongue before it stretched halfway down my throat. It seemed like I should be choking. Except I wasn't.

Meanwhile, the chattering had evolved into a sound that was less dry and raspy, and more…

… human…

Although I didn't understand what was being said, I could sense the joy as the chorus grew in size and volume. I could tell that Corona and I were no longer alone, that her sisters had returned. And that it was my breath that had brought them to the fullness of completion. *My* breath!

Maybe I really was created in the image of God after all, the Great Artist Himself.

And then the long, passionate kiss was over.

"You can open your eyes now, Tommy."

Part 7: The Unveiling

A loud screaming noise echoed as the laughter around me grew in volume. Corona's sharp, corrosive laugh was the loudest of all as she pointed a long, withered finger in my direction. Her eyes once again burned a hellish red. They looked nothing like the almond-shaped beauties I had made for her.

"Behold! Our Creator!"

That's when I realized the screaming was coming from me. My mouth was stretched open to what felt like twice its normal size, making my jaws ache and contorting my face into a mask of pain. But that wasn't why I was screaming.

Part 8: A Mother's Love

Upstairs, Gwendolyn Banks had finally had enough—plus, there was the guilt. For more than three months, she had abided by Tommy's request (he had practically begged her) not to come downstairs, no matter what. He was trying to create something beautiful, he said, which was all any artist ever wanted. But as a mother, she knew his true motivation was to create something that made him feel *worthwhile*. And all she had ever wanted him to know was that he didn't need to paint the damned Sistine Chapel in her basement to be that. He was her son, and that made him the most beautiful work of art ever created simply by being who he was.

But now, clearly, something was terribly wrong. Every time she had listened to her gut, or heard that woman's sinful voice, Tommy's calming tone would offer another excuse for Gwendolyn to ignore her mother's instinct and wrap a muffler around it. And, the longer she ignored it, the easier it became.

Until today.

Just as she turned away from the basement door and started to walk away, she heard that voice again, this time telling Tommy she was going to kiss him. There was something seething and hungry woven into the corrupted tone of that offering—a purposeful sound warped by an evil that felt ancient and outside of time. Why couldn't Tommy feel that, too? Why couldn't he hear it? Gwendolyn couldn't understand why he didn't heed that same warning that was flashing so insistently inside her spirit.

There was that wretched chattering again. It was a sound she had heard before, lifeless and cold—but then, the indecipherable noise became words. Hysterical laughter, which seemed to echo at a steadily increasing volume throughout the house, danced around the horrible screams that she knew were coming from her son.

Then his screaming stopped.

"This is our body. This is our flesh. This is our time."

"This is our body. This is our flesh. This is our time."

"This is our body. This is our flesh. This is our time."

Gwendolyn ran to the door and turned the handle. As she made her way down the creaking steps, the chanting stopped, replaced by a pregnant silence. She stopped a third of the way down, still only able to see a part of the basement.

"Tommy...?"

There was no reply, and she swallowed hard. She squeezed her eyes shut for a moment before opening them again and taking a deep breath. The air in the basement tasted stale and dead.

"Tommy."

She continued her descent, pushing past her mounting dread. Her hand still clutching the wooden rail, she looked across the room into the corner where Tommy's mattress lay. The thing that Gwendolyn saw hovering above that mattress defied description: a three-dimensional, vaguely human form constructed out of twisted Black garbage bags. Everything about it was perversely wrong and out of place...

And yet, she knew it had once been her son. A tear escaped the corner of her eye, trickling down her cheek.

"My baby. *My baby.* What they do to you?" she moaned.

An icy breeze worked its way slowly around the room, as if taking inventory—or maybe saying goodbye. It blew right through Gwendolyn's frail body on its way toward the stairs, and she felt the chill take anchor deep in her bones.

"Damn you," she muttered.

Gwendolyn could see the breeze taking a vague, pulsating shape as it paused its progress. She sensed it lookin' at her, taking measure before it spoke.

"I am damnation's origin star, Gwendolyn Banks, and I am here to claim what's mine."

"But you didn't need to kill my boy."

"He's more alive than he has ever been. The flesh of the willing provides the most fertile soil, and his willing flesh provided the womb for our rebirth. As a mother, you should understand."

"As a mother, I understand you ain't nothing but a filthy murderer and a thief. Talk pretty all you want, but I know whose and what you are. You are an unholy beast."

The breeze flashed gold, then a molten red.

"If you truly know whose and what I am, then you understand the necessity of who and what I am. We are Corona. We are the cycle of both life and death. We are the world within worlds."

Gwendolyn's shoulders slumped as her gaze dropped to the floor beneath her feet. More tears flowed.

"But you didn't need to kill *my* boy. Not *my* boy."

The pulsating breeze shifted again from molten red to a near-blinding white as it unfolded to expand its shimmering size. An opening appeared in its front, and far away inside its distance, Gwendolyn could see Tommy lookin' back at her, waving, a broad smile creasing his face.

"Oh baby..." she murmured. "What have you done... ?"

But Tommy only kept waving and smiling, not saying a word. She wondered if he could see her at all.

"Come."

Gwendolyn shook her head, not wanting to trust the corrupted voice of this shapeshifting thing that had invaded her home. The request came again.

"Come."

Again, Gwendolyn shook her head.

"Then let this be goodbye, Gwendolyn."

"Wait..."

Dread

Part 1: The Interview

Every Black person I know has seen this look from a white person interviewing them for a job at least once. It's a look that lets you know they're about to say some really dumb shit, and all you can do is smile about it.

It's the look I'm getting right now.

"You know, that's a very interesting name—I mean, for a Black person. I hope you don't mind my saying…"

"Yeah, I get that a lot. Mostly from white people, though. If you don't mind *my* saying."

I gave him my best 'It's all good, bro' smile, thereby releasing the tension I already knew was starting to tie his stomach up in knots. Besides, he wasn't wrong; not a whole lotta Black folks named Jack Frost. Probably even fewer with a head fulla dreads and cowry shells hangin down their back like mine—even here in Detroit, where pretty much the only folks who ain't Black are the ones who just moved here. Like this perky little guy interviewing me for this magazine writing job.

His name was Drake, which I thought was kinda hilarious because of the rapper with the same name. He returned my smile as confidently as he could. I think he was trying to match my 'It's all good, bro,' but it didn't quite work as planned. Drake looked like the geeky white guy in a *Saturday Night Live* skit who always laughs at the wrong things at the wrong times and just can't seem to get it.

Drake was holding—no, *caressing*—my resume in one hand, in a perverse kind of way, like he knew he held a symbol for my life at this point in his hands, because I really did need this job. I know he was trying his best to be polite, but his smile really did irritate the fuck outta me.

"Have you tried anywhere else?" he asked, his smile starting to look a little forced.

Like…where?

The Free Press and the News had shut down a year ago, and the Metro Times was only selling ads and paid stories these days. There weren't a whole lotta options for someone like myself, who wanted to become a professional writer. I'd had some pretty decent success freelancing—selling pieces outside the city and to some online 'zines. But freelancing is a hard way to go to make a decent living. This new magazine, 'D-Lite', was the only place offering any full-time slots.

I gave Drake one of my carefully curious, non-threatening looks: eyes squinted just a touch, head cocked to the side. It was a look that said, 'What in the hell are you talking about?' in such a way as not to push those hair-trigger white people buttons. Strange to have to walk on eggshells in what was still the Blackest big city in America. But when they said this was the 'new' Detroit, a whole lotta redefinition and recalculation came with that.

Anyway, Drake wasn't too swift, so he didn't quite catch the meaning of my non-verbal response—swooped over his head like the last bird headed south.

"Hey, it's perfectly OK if you have!" he said. "I was just curious if we were your first choice. I mean, your writing samples are excellent. It's obvious to me that once you get some more experience under your belt, you could probably land a job anywhere you wanted. Seriously, *any* magazine would be lucky to have you."

"Once I get the experience…I see."

Drake nodded. Yeah—his smile was definitely starting to look a bit strained.

"Right. Well, did you get a chance to read any of the clips I sent you? Or did you just kinda glance at them? Or…I mean, I'm only asking because I think I've written some pretty interesting stuff—the kind of stuff I think your audience would be interested in. Not that more experience isn't a good thing? But my copy is usually pretty clean, and I've already got a lot of good sources here in the city, so I thought…"

"I'm sorry, Mr. Frost. I just don't think we're ready to…what in the…oh my God…*what is going on with your hair?"*

Shit. I was so busy getting pissed at the geeky guy that I wasn't paying attention to the dreads. I probably should have warned him, but it was too late now. The dreads had picked up on Drake's funky attitude throughout the interview, and they weren't having it. A few of them began to hiss—something I kept asking them not to do because I wasn't trying to be the Black Medusa. But the few ropes in back that had started to growl weren't helping matters much either.

Still, since it was obvious I wasn't getting this job anyway, I figured it might be more fun to play

ignorant and really fuck with the guy's head. So I
gave him the Black man frown.

"Dude, you got a problem with my hair?
Seriously? You know you in Detroit, right?"

Drake was already out of his chair and backing
away. His eyes were big as a character from a Looney
Tunes cartoon, and he was mumbling: "Something
isn't…your hair is…how can your hair be *alive?* This
doesn't make any…oh my God, I have to go."

"Hold on, *what?* Drake, you tellin me you ain't
never seen a brother with dreadlocks before? *You're
tellin' me you're scared of locks, bro?"*

I couldn't see myself in a mirror, but I could
feel what the dreads were up to. I had a pretty good
idea of what Drake was seeing before he turned and
ran out of the interview room. The boy was quick.
Quicker than I would have imagined.

Part 2: The Schoolyard Incident

My dreads weren't always so aggressive.
Matter of fact, I didn't even know they were *special*
until I was seven years old. That was when the
'incident' happened in school, and my parents had to
sit me down and explain a few things to me about

what to expect the rest of my life. I still remember the look on Mom's face when she came to pick me up at the principal's office.

Mom was a short woman with a warm brown face; she rarely spoke unless she had to, but she always had this aura about her that let you know this was not a woman you wanted to fuck with unless you didn't care what happened next.

But on that Friday morning at the principal's office, she looked more exhausted than anything else. I felt sorry for her, because I knew somehow this was all my fault—even though I had no idea how I could have prevented it.

I was as confused and terrified as everyone else, but then maybe not as scared as my teacher, Miss Cane. Or Tommy. I remember Tommy couldn't stop screaming, even after Miss Cane started shaking him. When I walked over to say I was sorry—that I didn't know how it had happened, that it had never happened before— Miss Cane just yelled for me not to come any closer.

"You've done enough, you little freak!" she screamed, making me stumble backward a few steps.

As young as I was, I could hear more fear in that yell than anger. My own elementary school teacher was scared to death of me. Maybe I should have been proud of scaring her. I truly hated that woman.

As for Tommy—I didn't even know Tommy's last name. I wasn't interested in knowing anything about him. He was short, fat, greasy, and specialized in being a bully—that was all I needed to know. Whenever we had recess on the playground, it was like Tommy got unleashed. None of the teachers ever paid any attention to what he did to the rest of us. They just let him run around and push, shove, and kick the rest of us to his little fat heart's delight. The one time I approached Miss Cane about Tommy's behavior, she looked down at me disapprovingly before she wagged her finger in my face, cautioning me not to be a tattle-tale.

"But Miss Cane! He…"

"What did I just tell you, Mr. Frost!"

And for a slow procession of weeks and months, that was how recess went.

Until that one day…

It was late in the school year when you could feel winter starting to get restless, wanting to take its turn. A couple of my friends and I were seeing who could kick the ball backwards over our heads the farthest. Just being able to do this had already set us apart as being recognizably cooler than some of the other kids, like Tommy.

Anyway, I was busy focusing my concentration on kicking this white soccer ball so hard that it would wish no kid would ever kick it again. My friend James had just kicked the ball the farthest, and I was determined to outkick him if it was the last thing I did. None of us had been paying any attention to Tommy, because why would we? But Tommy was on his way to changing all that as his rotundness bore down on us like an angry bowling ball set on exploding a bunch of hapless pins. James tried to warn me about the oncoming train headed my way, but it was too late.

"Jack, look out!"

"Huh…?"

That was the last thing I said before Tommy suddenly appeared in the corner of my eye. I felt him crash into me, knocking the air out of my lungs and slamming my body into the dirt. As he landed on top of me, he started swinging at my head for no apparent reason other than that he could. I drew myself up into a tight knot and started hollering for him to stop. For a while, it seemed like the beating would go on forever.

Until it didn't.

First, there came a stinging sensation in my scalp that kept getting hotter—then I heard the screaming, which sounded like it was coming from far, far away. What was such a big deal that it could make Tommy stop swinging on me?

The screams got louder in a rush, and somehow I knew they had something to do with me. I pulled my hands away from my face and opened my eyes real slow. That was when I saw Tommy, all covered in bloody tears. I couldn't make any sense of it, but he was all wrapped up in these thick Black ropes, squeezing and tearing at him. He was writhing and kicking, his eyes all bugged out and wild. lookin' back, I'm guessing it was denial, but at the time, I couldn't figure out the origin of those things that were squeezing him.

My eyes found James again, but James turned and ran—and I mean he was running away *fast*. Most of the other kids were running away too, or just stood there dumbstruck, staring at Tommy writhing on the ground. Miss Cane and the other teachers in the yard were trying to order the kids back inside the building, but this was hard for them to enforce—they seemed afraid to take their eyes off me. Miss Cane pointed with one of those long, bone-white fingers of hers and commanded me to stop what I was doing to Tommy. She tried to keep her voice stern, but it was cracking and shrill.

What did she mean, what *I* was doing to Tommy?

Meanwhile, two of the Black ropes had pried open Tommy's puckered little mouth and slithered down his throat. Several more had wrapped themselves around his body so tight that he couldn't move. Miss Cain was still shouting for me to stop hurting Tommy.

But hadn't she seen what happened? It was *Tommy* who had run across the playground to blindside me. It was *Tommy* who had knocked me over into the dirt and knocked the wind out of my lungs. Did she have any idea how much that hurt? Or did she just not care?

As I felt my anger toward Miss Cane intensify, the ropes seemed to lose interest in Tommy, slowly unwrapping themselves from around him. The Black, hairy tentacles retracted from his throat, and he coughed and spluttered uncontrollably.

They were refocusing their attentions on Miss Cane.

"Oh my God…" she squeaked, as she backed away.

"*What the hell are you?*"

Part 3: Back Home with the Folks

"You must never call yourself that! Do you hear me? *Never.* There is nothing wrong with you, Jack. *Nothing.* You are our beautiful boy, the best thing to ever happen to your father and me, and you are *perfect.*"

Mom's eyes were red from crying as she sat beside me on my bed, holding me so close I could hardly breathe. She was rocking me back and forth slowly, and for the past half hour, she had refused to let me go.

Dad was sitting across from us in a small wooden chair. He'd stare at me hard, and I thought that maybe he was mad at me, but then his gaze would sink to the floor, and he just looked defeated. I noticed his eyes were red too, and his large hands were clasped together real tight in his lap like he was trying to crush something.

"You are not a monster, son," he said, his voice almost like a whisper.

"But Dad, if you coulda seen what those things did to Miss Cane and Tommy. *And it was my hair that did it.* I never even liked Tommy, but…Dad, what's wrong with me? Something's wrong with me, isn't there?"

"Jack! What did I just tell you! Jonah, tell this boy he isn't…"

"Marie."

"Jonah, please, you've got to—"

"*Marie.* We knew this day was coming. We've known it for a long time. It's time to tell the boy who he *is,* not who he *isn't.*"

"Dad…?"

Part 4: Jonah Remembers

A lot of my friends ain't sold on this wonderful "new Detroit" everyone keeps talking about. They wanna go back in time and remember the way Detroit used to be before the riots (or rebellion, or whatever you wanna call it, because either way our neighborhoods still got tore up). They remember the neighborhoods when we had our own stores and shops. *Our own.* They remember when Motown was poppin, and anybody who wanted a job at the auto plant could get one. Didn't matter if you hadn't finished high school because high school wasn't gonna help you none inside those factories—especially not with the jobs they had for Black folks. How much education did you need to sweat yourself to death inside a blast furnace?

I was there during those days, just like my buddies, except maybe you can tell I don't remember it all the same rosy way they do. Maybe it's just harder for me to forget those uglier memories. Memories of white cops who beat the shit out of young Black men for sport when they got bored. Or whenever they wanted to "blow off some steam." Or whenever they figured they could get away with it—which was whenever they felt like it.

Some of those memories are my own memories. They happened to me once upon a time—a once upon a time that may as well be right now. They come to haunt me whenever they feel like it, just like the way those cops beat us any time they damned well pleased. Those scars will never heal.

But I deal with it.

Anyway, when me and Marie had Jack, all I could think about in the hospital was how small he was. So small, defenseless, and Black. Is there anything worse you can be in this world?

The doctor said that Jack was a perfectly healthy baby boy, which made Marie smile so wide, and I tried to smile too. We decided to give him the name 'Jack' because of my last name (out of a shared sense of humor). Plus, we wanted to see how a name like Jack Frost might shape the way a Black child might navigate the world.

Long after we took Jack home from the hospital, I'd have these ugly flashbacks of my own childhood whenever I looked at him for too long. It was painful, because as a new father who only had the one child (we weren't able to have more), all I wanted to do was to look at him forever. I didn't even know my heart could get that big, or hurt so much.

When Jack turned four years old, he was still small for his age. I asked the doctor if he thought Jack would remain small as an adult. I was a pretty big guy—230 pounds on a good day and not quite six feet. Marie was just a couple of inches shorter than me. She had always been thick and shapely in the way that made Black women a whole other standard of beauty. It was that standard that white folks could never let themselves acknowledge publicly—even though all those high yellas who started poppin up in slavery time were proof we weren't the only ones who couldn't resist.

But that's another conversation. Marie always said I spend way too much time talking race. "Ain't nothin you can do about it noway," she'd say. "Might as well focus that brain of yours on somethin' you can do something about."

Which, in a meandering kinda way, brings me back to Jack and me being nervous about how small he was. The doctor asked me if there was anyone in the family who was smaller than normal, and I told him not that I knew of. The doc told us that Jack might not get any bigger, but he wouldn't be a dwarf or anything like that. He didn't see any signs of malnourishment or anything. He said that overall, Jack looked like a "healthy, happy kid" and that we shouldn't worry.

Except that I couldn't help worrying. I told Marie that I couldn't help it when I got home that day. Jack was outside in the backyard playing, making up games he could play by himself (which he was getting pretty good at). I remember we were sitting at the kitchen table drinking coffee.

"So what do you think we should do about it?" Marie asked, giving me a look that let me know that my worry was getting contagious.

"Is there anything we *can* do about it?" I said. "I mean, there really isn't any way we can make the child grow if his body is telling him that this is who he's gonna be, right?"

I shrugged as I watched Jack through the window. It was true what the doctor said—he seemed like a happy kid, and maybe that should have been enough. But still, I couldn't let it go out of my mind. I kept thinking that there had to be a way to provide him with some extra level of security. Something just for him, so that he'd be protected when we weren't around.

That thought was still stomping around inside my head when I was out on one of my early morning walks through the neighborhood. The sun was just making its way up into the sky, and it looked like there was a chance this would be one of those deceptive kinds of Michigan winter mornings. They'd look beautiful in a way, because the sky would be all clear and the sun would be out, but it was still cold as the wrong side of hell.

I shoved my hands deeper into my pockets as I watched my breath puff out, and that's when I saw this funny-lookin' house. It was a couple of empty lots down from the corner, and it was strange seeing it there because it didn't look like it belonged.

It wasn't just the fact that I didn't recognize the place that made it stick out, but this little blue house was something different—and I mean *really* different. For one thing, Detroit wasn't the kind of place where you saw a lot of sky-blue houses. Matter of fact, I don't think I had *ever* seen one, and I had lived in this city my whole life. Over on the west side where we lived, most of the houses were old, sturdy brick, and they were dark red or maybe grey.

So when I saw this blue house, I slowed down my step and stared at it. It was the oddest thing—it didn't look like it was made of any kind of material that I recognized. The outside was *smooth* and rounded, like a giant teakettle. The whole thing was maybe two stories tall, with windows that weren't quite right somehow and seemed to change shape the longer you looked at them.

"Good morning!" said a cheerful voice in my ear.

The voice came from directly behind me, and I'm pretty sure I jumped high enough that a car could have passed under me, and all I woulda felt was *whoosh*. When I landed, I had turned all the way around somehow, like a cat, and I was facing a short, stocky little guy wearing a torn red jacket. His jacket was too thin for the weather, and oddly bright. The brown plaid cap he wore was pulled down over his long, snow-white dreadlocks—all of which let me know he didn't much care about fashion. He looked Black, but he was mixed with something else. Maybe Spanish? Asian..? But then hell, we're all mixed with something, so whatever.

Anyway, he was smiling so hard I thought it might break his face, and his hand was extended in my direction. I noticed he wasn't wearing gloves, which seemed strange for as cold as it was.

I reached out to shake his hand, and his grip was *way* stronger than I would have imagined for his size and build. His face practically glowed with gratitude, and I wondered if most folks chose *not* to shake his hand for some reason.

"Morning…" I said, warily.

"Yes, it is!" he said, still pumping my hand.

After what I figured was a polite enough interlude, I pulled my hand away and looked over at the house.

"This you?" I asked.

He tilted his head to the side.

"Sorry?"

"The blue... house. This you?"

His face brightened all over again. His head began bobbing up and down.

"Ahhhhh! Yes! This is me! You want to come in?"

Now I *knew* this guy wasn't from the city.

"Are you new here?" I asked, trying to steer past the invitation. "I don't remember seeing this house before."

"It hasn't been here long. A few hours, maybe."

"Wait...what?"

He laughed, then motioned for me to follow him to the house.

"Don't worry, I'll be glad to explain. But you should come inside. I have something for you."

"OK, hold up. Look, man, I don't know who you are..."

"Actually, it's not for you, Jonah. It's for your son, Jack Frost. "

I froze. I didn't know whether to be mad or scared. You hear about that animal instinct thing called fight or flight, and right then, my mind couldn't make itself up about which made the most sense. Who the hell was this guy?

"Please. I know you have been worried about your son, and I'm here to make those worries go away."

I opened my mouth to try and respond, but no words would come out. All I could feel was my heart starting to pump real hard, like it was trying to jailbreak outta my chest.

The little man started to nod, his smile now lookin' a bit more concerned.

"I probably should have introduced myself first. Especially since I already know who you are. My name is Ned."

"Ned…?"

"Yes. I don't have a last name. It's always been just Ned. And I come from a long line of Neds."

"So what are you about, Ned? What do you do exactly?"

"I guess you could say our family has always been in the service industry."

"That doesn't really narrow it down for me, Ned."

"Right. And it's true, we're actually quite specialized. But usually when I explain our particular specialty, that's when people stop believing. And once the believing is gone, then that creates a problem for what comes next. The good part."

"The good part?"

"You know, I really do wish you'd come in so I could explain. If you don't like what I have to offer, then you are free to leave at any time. For goodness' sake, I'm not here to hurt you! Look at the size of you, and then look at me! What kind of threat do you imagine I might pose?"

"Out here on the street? Right now? Probably not much. Inside that all-wrong blue house? That could be a whole other story..."

Ned tilted his head back and started laughing so loud I was surprised the local canines didn't start barking in response. When he was done, I could see his dark eyes sparkling, almost like there was a light shining from inside his head.

"Yes, we probably should have chosen a less intrusive design. As a matter of fact, I believe I mentioned that as a concern to my associates before agreeing to take this assignment. But nobody ever listens to me—"

"Well, if nobody ever listens to you, then why should…"

"…until it's too late, I was going to say. Now please. Come inside. You will be doing your son a favor."

And with that, Ned turned and walked inside the house. If I hadn't followed, I'm pretty sure our lives would have gone on as they were. Ned would have gone on to his next assignment, and I would have done my best to forget all about him.

But I did follow him, and nothing was ever the same again.

* * *

If the house looked all wrong from the outside, on the inside, it looked impossible. No way could a little blue house with funny-lookin' windows have that much space and that many rooms on the inside— but here it was. What looked like a teapot house from a fairy tale from the street looked like a Palmer Woods mansion on the inside.

"You live here by yourself? Or…"

"I don't actually live here. This is just for travel. But it's pretty nice, right?"

He spun around with his arms outstretched in the middle of what must have been the main room, inviting me to take it all in: the chandeliers, the deep wood paneling, the artwork. Hardly what you'd expect to find inside a blue teapot house.

"I'd say that's an understatement. So who are these associates you mentioned? Are they here with you?"

He shook his head firmly.

"No. I am here alone. So are you ready to get to the good part?"

Ned invited me to sit down in a small room near the front door. Or at least I think it was the front door. I couldn't quite remember after wandering in and out of so many rooms for the past…well…it had been a while.

"Are you familiar with the story of Samson?" he asked.

I had read pretty much everything in every library I could get to by the time I was twelve, so when Ned asked me that question, I had to laugh. It was one of my favorites. But Ned wasn't laughing at all. He was dead serious.

"After you give Jack this medicine, you must never let anyone cut his hair. *Never* again—that includes you and your wife. Not even Jack himself. This is extremely important."

"But if we don't cut his hair *ever*…."

"Do you want your son protected?"

"Of course I do. But you're asking me to believe that once he takes this stuff, it's gonna be his *hair* that protects him? Look, man, I don't mean to be laughing this off, but this is Detroit—and in Detroit, folks got somethin for you if you weak. Hair spray ain't gonna…"

Right then, I thought his locks moved in a kinda way that—well, in a way they shouldn't have.

"Hey…what's going on with…?"

"Hit me," Ned said suddenly. "In the face."

"Are you crazy? Why would I want to hit you…?"

The smile on Ned's face was so serene that it kinda scared me. He looked like a little brown Buddha with powdery white dreads, and they were starting to float up all around his face. I wondered if maybe he had slipped me some acid when I wasn't paying attention, but I hadn't eaten or drunk anything…

"Punch me. I'll be fine—do it for your son, because he needs this. Ball up your fist and punch me in the face. I believe it is the only way we will be able to finalize our transaction."

Now, please understand that I ain't never been anybody's idea of a pacifist, so this wasn't the first time I had cocked my fist back to take a motherfucker's head off. I don't think I knew anyone who hadn't been in that situation at least a few times—just outta plain survival and living in the city. But when my fist got to be just a few inches from Ned's face, I saw my hand get swallowed up all the way to my shoulder by a swarm of hissing white ropes. They were squeezing my arm so tight it made me grit my teeth, and the locks felt more like steel cables than anything made of hair. Then, slowly, they moved my fist to the side.

There in front of me, still smiling as calm as a summer day on Belle Isle, was Ned's face; it was framed dead center in the middle of all that chaos.

He began to chuckle, and my heart started doing the jailbreak thing again.

"Ned, these things hurt, man."

The dreads relaxed themselves and fell away from my arm, which was starting to throb from lack of blood circulation. Ned reached over and squeezed my hand.

"Now?" he asked.

Slowly, I nodded my head.

"Yeah. OK."

Part 5: Back to Jack

I will never forget what my father said that day:

"It's time to tell the boy what he is, not what he isn't."

Sure, I still have questions about why he made that deal with Ned. And why Mom co-signed. After all, this was a guy that Dad met on the street, and Mom *never* met—not even once. She had to take my father's word about the blue teakettle house, because when Dad practically dragged her down there to see for herself, there was nothing there.

But Mom knew Dad wasn't in the habit of lying—not about anything. If he said a thing happened, then the odds were good that it happened, and it happened the way he said it did. Mom also knew that the only reason Dad did what he did was out of love. He knew he wouldn't always be around to protect me, and when he saw I was always gonna be a little guy, he figured what Ned had would keep me safe.

And for the most part, Dad was right. After that day on the playground, when Ned's elixir finally kicked in, and I wound up scaring the whole school to death, there weren't many times when I ever had to worry about defending myself. Those who knew me were scared of me, and those who didn't know me learned real quick how to *be* scared the first time they made the mistake of giving me any trouble.

But as I got older, the problem wasn't that nobody messed with me—the problem was that no one wanted to be around me. I didn't have any real friends because nobody wanted to be buddy-buddy with a circus freak. Same thing with the girls. Except for those few times when I got *lucky,* most girls didn't have much interest in fucking a midget with killer dreads.

And so, I spend most of my time alone at home with my locks, who are really the only friends I have. They understand what it is to be a freak, because they're the ones who made me this way. I really do think they care about me, and they like my stories. Sometimes they even give me ideas.

Oh, I know the folks care about me, too, although I haven't seen them in a while. But that's OK. They do what they need to do for each other in their house, and I do what I need to do for me and my dreads in mine.

My beautiful blue teakettle house.

Hell Delivers

The day before I was fired, I figured, what the hell. I already knew the answer I would get to the question I was gonna ask Charlie because there was only one answer anymore. Didn't used to be that way, but things change. God, how they change...

Still, I guess it's the human nature in me that wants to keep hope alive, like Jesse Jackson says. At least my human nature is still intact.

"So what did he have this time?" I asked.

"Same."

"Doesn't it just make you wonder? C'mon, doesn't it?"

Charlie just shrugged, wet brown eyes regarding me suspiciously through the bulletproof thickness of his perfect oval frames. He was standing in front of my desk, all 300-plus obscene, greasy pounds of him, lookin' as if he had been planted there in rock-hard soil by an angry hand of God as punishment. Punishment for being too fat, punishment for desecrating God's temple at every available opportunity, punishment for so many other things I could name. But that would be judgmental.

So, mostly I think Charlie is being punished for shrugging whenever I ask him that question, which is the same question I have asked him almost every day for what seems like forever. And every day, at least in the beginning before things started to go bad, Charlie would give me that same look, the same answers, and then he would shrug. And then he would keep staring at me, never blinking, his grease-stained brown paper bag clutched tightly in his bear-sized paw like a velvet purse full of diamonds.

Waiting.

During that interminable 60 seconds (not 59, not 61), it's like all else has faded away and there is just the two of us, damned for all eternity to repeat this perverse little drama in a tiny, barren cubicle, stuffed between a thousand other tiny barren cubicles, all swallowed whole by the echoing expanse of The Office. Some say this is what hell is like, and they may be right. Hell is the endless repetition of meaningless activity.

So what is it that Charlie is clutching so tightly in that brown bag? The exact same thing that he has been clutching every day at the exact same time during the noon break ever since the lunch truck started coming. But more on that later.

Charlie used to sometimes bring his lunch from home on those days when his mother felt like making him feel special - or whenever she wanted him to bring her back a pint from Dirty Joe's Market We Stay Open 24 Hours. If his mother (her name was Roseanne, I think) didn't feel like making her baby whale of a son feel special that day, or if Charlie simply couldn't shake her awake from an alcohol-drenched stupor, then those were the days Charlie would actually leave the office and go out for lunch. Sometimes with other people.

Those were the days when Charlie would smile. Maybe we would all be at Dirty Joe's Diner, laughing, telling jokes about The Boss, and Charlie would just sit there lookin' comfortably amused. He never said anything, never even so much as cleared his throat, but he was smiling, you know? Smiling. And sometimes he might order the fish. Other times, he might just settle for a burger. No fries. With a small orange juice. Couple times I remember he tried the Reuben sandwich, which took more guts than I ever had. But he *tried* it, and that's the point. Charlie *tried* the Reuben, Charlie *tried* the burger, and he *tried* the salad.

All of this, of course, was before the lunch truck.

It showed up on a Wednesday, one month ago today, and I still don't understand how the guy knew to be there precisely at 12:01 pm. And I don't know why he chose a Wednesday, the middle of the week. Why not a Monday? Wouldn't that have made more sense? I remember asking a few other folks around the office if they knew who the guy was, or if they had ever heard of or seen the Bite On This lunch truck before. No one had. And no one much cared. I shoved my hands in my pockets and peered down through the shades from the second floor at the sparkling white truck, which was parked almost carefully in front of our building, the engine purring like a tomcat in a porn star's lap. Through the windshield, I could see a man's vague, shadowy outline.

Several moments later, there was a slight crackling noise, followed by the crystal bell voice of Pauline, the receptionist, reaching out through the loudspeaker, politely informing us that "Ladies and Gentlemen, we are happy to announce the arrival of the Bite On This lunch truck. The Bite On Us people promise good eats and good sweets for the busy working man and woman, and they will be here every day from now on at the beginning of each lunch hour. Those of you who occasionally find yourselves too busy to step away at lunchtime might find the Bite On Us lunch truck a pleasant and healthy alternative to the vending machines in the lunchroom. Those horrible things."

A few of us chuckled, knowing how much the motherly Pauline always exhorted us to stay away from the candy and pop machines because they would kill us. She was probably right, but so what? Simply confronting each day was a risk.

"Have a nice day," she said, followed by another harsh electric crackle, then silence.

Charlie was the first to go. Not more than 10 seconds had passed before he shoved himself away from his desk, the overburdened wheels of his chair squeaking in vain protest, then hoisted his immense bulk up to standing position, where he first steadied himself, then adjusted his pants. Grunted. He offered me an anxious smile, like a small child preparing to go downstairs on Christmas morning.

"Gonna check it out, eh?" I asked.

He nodded briskly.

"Tell me if they have anything good. I think I'm gonna go out. Nice day, you know? Spring's almost here."

He nodded again, then waddled out from behind his desk and proceeded toward the stairs. I shook my head, then returned my attention to my computer screen to finish up my task before heading down the street to the Sandwich Factory, where you could actually watch your sandwich being constructed on a miniature assembly line. Only in Detroit, the manufacturing capital of the world, would you ever find a restaurant like this.

About a minute later, Lois walked by, her pudgy chocolate face twisted into a cute scowl as she dug around in a purse big enough to comfortably carry a dead body.

"You gonna try it out too, huh, Lois?"

She nodded absent-mindedly, a polite grin tugging at the corner of her lip.

"Might as well," she said. "And I do have a lot of things to get done today. This kinda makes things easier, right?"

"Guess so."

Before I even had a chance to finish my last few minutes' worth of pre-lunch workload, at least six or seven others – about a third of the staff – had made the decision to sample the lunch truck. What kind of person would come up with a name like Bite On This, I wondered. And how hungry do you have to be to eat at a place with a name like that?

On my way out the door, Bob, one of the guys who worked in accounting, asked me where I was going for lunch, then asked if he could join me. I said sure. As we walked past the lunch truck, Charlie was paying for whatever was wrapped up in the brown paper bag. The smile on his face was gone, and I noticed a pattern of sweat beads adding an unhealthy shine to his forehead. The man he was giving his money to had his back turned to me, and he wore a plain brown UPS-lookin' jacket with the words "Bite On This" inscribed in bright white cursive lettering across the back. He was average size and height, no more than six foot, with near jet-black shiny hair combed back tightly in straight lines across his perfectly shaped skull. From inside the cab of the truck, you could hear just the slightest strains of classical music, which I never would have associated with anyone who drove a lunch truck.

"You have a good day, buddy," I heard him tell Charlie. "Enjoy. Next?"

Charlie grunted as he stepped aside so Lois could place her order.

"Hey there, pretty lady! What can I get you?"

Not even a blind man would have ever called Lois pretty, which probably explained why she suddenly dropped her purse. lookin' painfully startled and embarrassed, she started to stoop down to pick it up, when…

"Here, let me get that for you! You must not have seen this handsome gentleman standing here!"

Lois started to giggle, then she looked inside the back of the truck. For a brief moment, so brief I might have missed it if I'd looked the other way, she looked like she wanted to either scream, run, or both. Then her eyes went flat, like what you'd see on a dead fish in the market. She quietly placed her order, offered her money, accepted her brown paper bag, and stepped aside.

You have a good day, sweetheart. Enjoy. Next?"

Bob and I exchanged glances, but said nothing. We headed off to the Sandwich Factory in silence.

* * *

For the next three days, it was only the original group of lunch truck fans who would dutifully march out every day at the same time to retrieve their brown paper bags, and each one of those days, Charlie was always the first to go, followed by Lois. Then Jerry. Then Fred. Then Horace and Loretta. Marsha. Lou. First would come the announcement from Pauline, and then there they would go. They never spoke to one another, and they always looked straight ahead. When they came back into his office, they came back the same way – and in the same order.

I decided maybe it was time Bob and I talked about what was going on. Maybe there wasn't anything we could do. Then again, maybe there was. Like maybe we could try and talk to some of the other holdouts who still resisted the lunch truck, see if we could figure this thing out. If nothing else, at least we could keep each other company. You know, safety in numbers. That sort of thing.

"I dunno," said Bob, still chewing on a rather large bite of his stacked ham and cheese tower sandwich. "I mean, maybe it's one of those things we oughta just leave alone."

"Leave alone? Bob, c'mon. It's not like this is something dealing with national security or anything like that, right? Hell, it's just a lunch truck!"

Bob swallowed, then took a long swig from his Coke, all the time keeping his rather large brown eyes locked on me like he was worried I might jump over the table at him.

"Well, there you are, then. It's just a lunch truck. What are we supposed to do? Report the thing to the police?"

"Maybe. That might be a start."

Now he was lookin' at me like I was his seven-year-old son.

"OK, OK, so maybe it's a little soon for that. You're right. But hey, we both know something's wrong with that truck, Bob. We both know something ain't right. You remember the first day, the way Charlie started sweating? The way Lois almost screamed? And the way that guy talks? The things he says? For Chrissake, calling Lois a pretty lady? *Lois?*

Bob grinned.

"Yeah, that was pretty strange. But maybe he was just being nice. I mean, the man's trying to sell his food, right? Flattery is probably worth more than a week's salary to a woman like Lois, who I'm guessing hasn't been laid since the Ice Age."

"OK, you score again. Lois probably *hasn't* been laid since the Ice Age, and maybe the guy's astute enough to pick that up. But I don't think it's just so he can sell her a box lunch, Bob, and neither do you. Why is it the same folks go out to get that lunch, and why is it they always go and come back in the same order? What kind of sense does that make?"

Bob finished his lunch, then didn't say anything for a long time. Just stared out the window at the passing traffic. I figured it was best not to push him too hard. After all, if I got Bob pissed off at me, then I was pretty much alone in this deal. It's not like we were buddies, but he was definitely the only one of the remaining holdouts who I could approach with my concerns.

"So do you have a plan?" he asked finally, his voice kind of distant, still lookin' out the window.

"Well, I think the first thing we need to do is find out what's for lunch that's so good it keeps bringing the same folks back for more. Then we need to find out some more about this Bite On This lunch truck company. You know, where they're based out of, who their clients are, that sort of thing. Do some homework."

Bob started to chuckle.

"And how the hell are we supposed to do all this? Put some kind of tracking device on the lunch truck when nobody's lookin'? Then run around behind him during lunch break? I think you've been watching too many movies."

"I've got five sick days left. How many you got?"

* * *

The day after Bob and I had agreed to investigate, I was standing in front of Charlie's desk with my hands in my pockets, trying my best to look like I was just asking an innocent question on my way to the men's room.

"Looks like meatloaf," I said. "Say, doesn't he give you anything to go along with that? I mean, for what he's charging, I figure he'd at least..."

It looked like mealoaf, but I don't think that's what it was. And there weren't any vegetables or any other side dishes. No ketchup. Nothing. Just that grayish brown chunk of pockmarked meat covered with a thick, sickly green sauce, which I watched Charlie unwrap from a thin piece of wax paper.

"Only five bucks. Not that much. And it's not meatloaf. Don't know where you got that idea. Chicken. With mushrooms and carrots."

"Chicken...?"

I started to say something else, maybe to point out that no matter what you did to a chicken, there was no way it could wind up lookin' like what was squatting there on his plate. You just can't do that to a chicken. But the way Charlie was lookin' at me made me decide otherwise. It was like something inside him was getting hotter and hotter and was about to boil over. Just that quick, I could see his breathing starting to come quick and deep, and I knew my time wouldn't be long if I pushed much harder, so I just put my palms up in surrender, nodded, and backed away.

"Enjoy your ...uhhh...chicken. Really. I mean it."

But Charlie didn't even take a bite until I was all the way down the hall and completely out of his field of vision. I know because I kept lookin' over my shoulder making sure he wasn't getting up to come after me. Jesus, I thought, who gets that mad when you ask them what they're having for lunch? And who in their right mind would call that gray glob of mystery meat chicken?

After I came out of the men's room, I figured I'd check up on Lois, who was a few cubicles down. More importantly, her desk couldn't be seen by Charlie. I noticed the brown paper bag resting on top of some of her paperwork, and I guess I was a little surprised she hadn't already started digging in. Instead, she was gazing at her computer screen as if it had the answers to life displayed in big bold letters.

"Hey! Lois! How's it going there?" I said. forcing a grin at her over the top of her computer terminal, wishing I could figure a way to keep the conversation going long enough to move my way around beside her and catch a glimpse of whatever it was she was worshipping on that screen.

Normally? If I had popped up on Lois like that all sudden, asking how she was doing? Through the ceiling. Just like that. Matter of fact, it used to be a kind of fun prank when she first got hired last year to sneak up on her just to see it happen. I was the only one twisted enough to do it, but I have to say I think a good time was had by all. Well, except maybe for Lois. But she got used to it after a while, and pretty soon it wasn't as much fun, so I left her alone. We even started to get along pretty good as co-workers, which showed me she was really more of a good sport than I had imagined.

But this time, Lois wasn't a good sport at all. She didn't jump out of her chair, and she didn't even look up from her computer screen. If it hadn't been for the way I noticed her eyes heat up and narrow into slits, I wouldn't have even been sure she'd heard me. I felt a bit of a chill.

"Lois...?"

Slowly, she rolled her eyes up just enough to meet mine. I almost wish she hadn't, but I worked hard to keep the grin attached to my face. My mother was always telling me how folks just couldn't resist my smile. Mom wasn't always right.

"What?" said Lois, almost like she was spitting out a piece of rotten meat. I took a deep breath.

"OK. Slow down, all right? I'm not the IRS. Just a little friendly conversation. That's all we're having here."

She kept staring, and I could feel my foolproof grin starting to falter.

"So, hey, what did you get off the lunch truck. Anything good?"

Loretta, who was the only truly attractive woman in the place, sat across the aisle from Lois. Kinda quiet, a bit too serious, but would always crack a grin whenever I used to tease Lois. The guys used to say she had a face by Ford but a body by Rolls-Royce. I used to say she was the kind of woman who put the 'wet' in wet dream.

But right about now, the look she was giving me would have turned anybody's wet dream to ice.

"You don't have to show him, Lois, you know," she said. "If he wants to know, let him order his own lunch instead of wasting time at that Sandwich Factory down the street. Not all of us have time to leave the office, but I guess some people..."

Lois was nodding, which made me think I wasn't going to get an answer about the lunch. But then she surprised me, and very carefully reached into the bag to pull out the contents.

"Wow," I said. "Meatloaf."

Lois had stopped nodding and was giving me a look as if I were some delirious person just stumbled in off the street. Her eyes burned, and when she spoke, her voice sounded more like a hiss belonging to something that slithers than to any female human being. Then again, when I start to think about some of the women I've dated...

"I know you think you're being funny, but you're not. Funny. You know good and well this is perch, with peas and carrots."

I did my best not to let my face change expression, and I'm hoping I pulled it off. Besides, I was sort of expecting this after my experience with Charlie, who, I noticed with a growing sick feeling, was headed in my direction, wearing the face of an axe murderer.

"You're right. Bad joke. Enjoy your meal. I'm outta here."

Later, when Bob and I were walking down to the Sandwich Factory, I asked him if he'd had a chance to check out what everybody was having for lunch, the ones who bought theirs off the lunch truck. He chuckled, but I noticed he wasn't smiling.

"Looked like meatloaf to me. But..."

"Yeah. I know."

We made it to the end of the block in silence before Bob turned to look me square in the face, which was something he didn't normally do.

"What the hell's going on?"

"That's what we need to find out, Bob. That's what we need to find out."

* * *

Within another week, Bob and I were the only ones who still weren't getting their lunch from the swell folks at Bite On This. Sometimes we'd go to the Sandwich Factory, sometimes we'd go someplace else, but we always made a point of getting as far away from the office as we could during the lunch hour. Even on the days when we had a lot of work to do, days when we normally might have gotten something to go and brought it back to the desk, we made sure to take up every ticking minute of the one-hour break we had coming to us. But one thing we also made sure of was that we were never late coming back, not even by 30 seconds.

Normally? That's another thing that wouldn't have been a big deal so long as you didn't come strolling back more than five minutes over and it didn't happen more than once or twice a pay period. We got paid every two weeks. But things were far from normal these days, and judging by the looks everyone was starting to give us on the job, sometimes for no reason at all, it just didn't seem like such a good idea to push our luck - if that's what you'd call it. I could be sitting at my desk, minding no one's business but my own, and next thing you know, there would be Charlie, or Loretta, or maybe a group of three or four of them just gathered not more than a few yards away, glaring at me like I'd just bragged about having sex with their mothers over the loudspeaker.

And speaking of the loudspeaker, that's another thing. Now that it's only me and Bob who refuse to patronize the lunch truck, Pauline doesn't even have to announce that it's arrived anymore. They all just know. Then again, I guess it's not that hard to figure out the schedule when the damned vehicle gets there at exactly the same time each and every day. I stopped asking what folks had ordered when Fran, a soft-spoken but devout vegetarian with huge saucer-shaped brown eyes, told me that she was eating a filet mignon with some kind of specially prepared asparagus. I know there may be a few different ways of preparing meatloaf, but this really was getting to be ridiculous.

"I saw another truck today," said Bob later that day, forcing himself to sound casual. We were just a few steps away from opening the door to Burnin' Billy's BBQ, a really popular rib shack - and I do mean shack - about a five-minute walk past the Sandwich Factory if you're headed away from the office down Woodward toward downtown.

I felt something seize up in my gut. Stopped just before reaching to pull open the door.

"Truck...? What kind of...?"

"You know what kind of truck. One of those lunch trucks. Saw it on my way in to work this morning. It was over there near Harbortown, just about to pull in to that little strip mall they have there. Said 'Bite On This' right along the side, just like the one in front of the office.

"Are you sure?" I said.

Of course, he was sure, which was why he gave me the blank look. He was refusing to register, let alone process, what this could mean.

"Sorry," I said, as I watched a broken-down Ford Taurus screech down the street, the head of the driver bobbing viciously from side to side to a thunderous beat that should have exploded the wreck he was driving.

"There's something else," he said.

I nodded, not at all sure I wanted to hear what it was.

"I caught a glimpse of the driver. Actually, it was more than a glimpse, because I was driving alongside him for a bit before he turned into Harbortown."

"It was him?"

"No, it was *him.* Same guy. Same slicked back hair, same everything."

"Jesus...well, I guess we had to know he was delivering to more places than just the office."

"Well, yeah, except for one other thing."

"What other thing?"

"About five minutes later, when I was going through downtown? I saw another truck. Same logo. Parked in front of the Penobscot Building with the flashers on. And our guy? He was opening up the back of the truck. Line of folks waiting on him must have stretched all the way down to the corner. No bullshit."

"But that's..."

"What? Impossible? Yeah, you'd think so, wouldn't you?"

I nodded, feeling an overwhelming need for a cigarette - or a joint. Sure, I quit last year, but these were special circumstances.

"You smoke, don't you, Bob?"

He shook his head.

"Quit last year. Same time you did."

"Shit. OK, well, guess we might as well have ribs then. While we still can."

Bob grunted.

Once we got inside, it hit like a Mack truck going 90. This just couldn't be right. Not at Burnin' Billy's...

When I say that Billy's was popular, I mean you couldn't buy a seat in the place at lunchtime. An average wait was at least 15 minutes, and that was on a good day. So when we looked around and saw only three tables occupied, I started to feel a chill, even though the summer heat and humidity made it hard to breathe in that little, cramped-up joint.

I heard a cough coming from the rear and looked over toward the back exit where Billy was sitting in an old rickety chair, leaning back on two legs against a grease-stained wall. His chef's hat was all crumpled up in his lap, and he was smoking a cigarette, lookin' back at us with a confused stare. A moment later, he let the chair fall back down onto all fours. He cleared his throat.

"Y'all want some ribs?" he asked. "Have a seat. Let me fix y'all some ribs. Got the best ribs in the city right here. Everybody knows that."

He shook out his chef's hat, then stood up with a loud grunt. Tried to smile, act like everything was same as always.

"Billy...Billy, what's going on here, man? Where's the crowd? I mean, usually..."

Billy just shrugged, but he stopped lookin' at me. I could see his face tightening up as he waddled toward the kitchen, fastening his apron around the continent of his waist.

"Some days just slower than others, that's all," he muttered, like he was talking to himself. "Have a seat."

From the time Billy brought the ribs to our table, two plates stacked high with meat smothered in a blood-red sauce surrounded by a half-moon fortress of home fries, until the time Bob and I managed to plow our way through it all, not one more customer came through the door. Two of the three occupied tables had emptied, without having uttered a sound throughout the entire meal. I knew because the jukebox had never been turned on, so the only noise in the whole place was the street noise filtering in from outside and the lonely hissing sound of Billy's grill.

"Time to go," I said to Bob.

"Yeah."

"Say Billy! We're outta here. Ribs were great as always, man. And don't you worry, those crowds will be back. They can't stay away but so long, right?"

It warmed me up to see the old man grin, even if it was a weak one. He waved from behind the grill.

"Y'all come back here tomorrow. I'll fix you up some more ribs. Make 'em special. Special sauce and everything. Y'all come back."

"OK, Billy."

On the way back was when we saw him. Bob and I had silently agreed not to even talk about the strange scene at Billy's, so instead we started talking about last night's baseball game, even though neither one of us was what you'd call a great baseball fan. With the Tiger's losing streak it seemed pretty hard to get into the spirit of the thing. Still, it was a lot easier to handle than everything else that was going on. Bob was in the middle of ragging on one of the newer players when something cut him off mid-rant. I was the one walking closest to the street, so at first I thought maybe he saw a car heading my way. But he just kept walking and staring, and the look in his eyes was just as much curiosity as it was fear.

"You know that guy?" he asked.

"Who?" I said, turning my head to see who he was talking about.

"Him," he said.

There wasn't any need to clarify which 'him.' Even though there was a crowd of winos across the street, pretty much the same crowd that was there each and every day in front of the party store, rain or shine, only one of them was lookin' at us like he wanted to do us some damage. He wasn't that big, probably not even six foot, and he wasn't the type that would have caught anyone's attention. Just a wino, and winos never bothered me. All they ever wanted was to get that next bottle and be left alone – unless you had some spare change. Winos were harmless. So what was the deal with this one?

"Why would I know any of your family members?" I asked.

"I'm serious. You know that guy? I mean, like maybe somebody you went to school with back in the day who maybe didn't turn out so well?"

We were walking even slower now, neither of us even trying to pretend we weren't talking about the guy as we stared back at him.

"I don't know him, Bob. And I don't know what his problem is either."

"Yeah, that was going to be my next question."

I decided maybe it was time to find out just what this guy's problem was, which was precisely what Bob did *not* want to do, but I couldn't help myself. Everything was getting too damned strange, and I was needing some answers. But even if I couldn't get answers, I was feeling a need just to confront this thing, whatever it was, face-to-face. Whatever happened would just have to happen.

Once he saw me crossing the street, I could tell right away he didn't expect it. He backed up a few steps, and for a moment, he even looked a little bit scared, like he might cut and run. But then something dark and unholy came over his face like a cloud's shadow sliding down the side of a building. The other winos were checking me out, too, but mostly they just looked confused. Wasn't every day when somebody dressed like me crossed the street to talk to one of them.

"You think this is a good idea?" mumbled Bob, who was tagging along about two steps behind me.

"Don't know if it is or not, but this guy is pissing me off."

"Right," he said, still not sounding convinced.

Up close, the man looked even smaller and more shrivelled up than he had at a distance. His skin looked like link sausage that had been in the frying pan too long. He wore a pair of blue and white-striped pants that looked slick with grime, and he was wearing a sleeveless parka that might have been green once upon a time, pulled over the top of a white t-shirt. He had a full beard that had spread like a riot over most of his face, and a wild thatch of Black, matted hair was pressed tightly against his skull by a Black knit cap. He was shorter than me, definitely weighed less than me, and in every way resembled the worn-out scrap of life that he was – except for those eyes. They were so Black I couldn't even see the pupils, and yet they were still somehow incredibly bright, as if drawing on some other source of energy that couldn't possibly be his. Once I got close, he cleared his throat with an awful sound that resembled something clawing its way back up out of a garbage disposal, then spat a foul greenish mass of whatever had been clogging his throat directly at my feet. I stepped aside just in time.

"You don't know me, I don't know you, so what the fuck? Why the crazy stare, man? And why the hell are you spitting at me?"

His eyes went from me to Bob, then back to me again. The hatred was so intense I could almost feel the heat coming off of him like off a Blacktop in July. Then he grinned, and that's when my heart started to race.

"You think you're clever, don't you?" he asked. His voice sounded like someone who gargled with razor blades. "You think we don't see. Or perhaps you think you are special, that you are somehow better than the others. But soon it is you who will see, and then you will know. And when you know you will partake. Because you are just the same, Donald Frazier. *You are just the same.*"

Against my better judgment, I took a step closer to him, trying to show I wasn't afraid.

"The same as what? What the hell are you talking about?"

His grin stretched a little wider, and I could see the stained ruin of his teeth. He nodded, chuckled, then turned around and started walking away. I made a move to follow him, but Bob grabbed my shoulder. Maybe he was right.

"Hey. *Hey!* The same as *what?"*

He just kept walking.

Every day after that, it kept getting worse, and it got worse quick. It got to where my neighbors would stop whatever they were doing outside when I got home and just stare at me until I was inside. If I spoke to them, they refused to reply, as if I hadn't said a word. I'd lived in this same neighbourhood on the west side of the city for nearly 15 years, and most of my neighbors had been there just as long, if not longer. It wasn't a close-knit area, but we all knew each other, and most of us spoke when we saw one another. It was a nice place to have a home. But now, within a matter of days, I was starting to get a glimmer of how it must have felt when Black folks moved into all-white areas back in the day. Only thing was, this was an all-Black neighbourhood. Hey, it was Detroit.

On my way in to work every day I started seeing more and more of those trucks out and about. Once, when I was at a stoplight on Wyoming near 7 Mile, I noticed one of the trucks parked on the street outside a CVS drugstore. When I pulled up alongside the driver's side window, which was rolled down all the way, there he was. He was just sitting there, and it looked like he was writing something down on a notepad in his lap. Then, as if someone had called his name, he looked up from whatever he was doing and turned to face me. I swear he had the same eyes as that bum I'd confronted just a few days earlier on the street; pitch Black and shining, and burning with a heat that could have melted cast iron in a matter of seconds. Whenever I saw him outside the office, he was always smiling and joking with his customers, even though I don't ever remember any of them smiling back. But now, as he stared back at me, and as I prayed for the light to turn green, there wasn't even a hint of a smile. His lips started to move, but I shook my head, indicating I couldn't hear him. My stereo was cranked, and I wasn't about to roll down my window.

I didn't have to. He leaned his head outside, then mouthed the same words over again. This time, I didn't have a hard time understanding him at all.

"You are just the same."

The light turned, and I stomped on the gas like I was trying to shove it through the grille. When I got to work, I was still shaking. As I walked up the stairs to the second floor, I began to wonder where all this was headed – and how much worse it could get. Were me and Bob going to end up the last two normal folks on the planet? Would *I* wind up the last normal person?

I sat down at my desk, doing my best not to look at anyone, even though I could feel all the gazes tearing at me like invisible claws. Ever since the lunch truck had started coming, it had been much quieter than usual at work, everyone just punching away in front of their terminals and not doing much else, but today something was way more wrong than usual. Just something I could feel. I wondered if any of *them* could still feel anything, sense anything, or if they were just husks harboring something unnatural. Maybe this was like that body snatchers movie…? Then again, maybe I'd been watching too many of those damned sci-fi movies, and that was the problem. It had only been yesterday when I'd made the mistake of asking Charlie what the lunch truck had on the menu.

"Same," he'd said. Just like I knew he would.

After about five minutes of just sitting there, I knew it was no use trying to get any work done because there was no way I could concentrate. I decided to ring Bob to see if he'd made it in yet, but I only got his voicemail. I decided against leaving a message. He'd be in soon enough, or at least I hoped he would. Instead, I decided to take a trip to the men's room, but once I opened the door, I noticed a sign in front of all the stalls saying "DO NOT USE". Considering the sudden urgency of the situation – my bladder had never been quite right – this was going to be a problem.

I went back to my desk, trying to figure out what to do.

"Hey, Charlie. Any idea what's up with the men's room? I just went in there, and there's all these signs posted up. This just happen last night or something?"

Charlie kept right on typing and staring into his terminal as if he hadn't heard a thing. Given the way things had been going around the office the past few weeks, normally I would have left Charlie alone. But my bladder was screaming, and discomfort like that can seriously affect a man's mood.

"Hey, *Charlie*."

I could see the beginnings of a storm front taking shape on his face, and I admit it did bother me.

It bothered me a lot. But I needed an answer about this men's room situation, and quick.

"C'mon, Charlie. Help me out here, all right? I know I've been a pain in the neck about some things here recently, and I'm sorry about that, but if you could just...."

I swear I have never heard a sound like that come from any human being in life. It wasn't a scream, and it wasn't a yell. It was more like the kind of roar you might hear one of those creatures make on the Sci-Fi channel. The noise was totally unrelated to anything even remotely human, and it was so loud I had to cover my ears. But even when I did that, it was like my ears hadn't been covered at all, and the sound just kept getting louder and louder. Before I knew it, I was on my knees rocking back and forth, screaming for Charlie to stop. But he wouldn't stop.

"Charlie pleeeeeze!"

When it finally did come to an end, my whole head was ringing. It felt like an army of small men was running rampant inside my head, banging pots and pans with hammers, and I don't know how long I stayed on my knees even after everything had gone quiet. When I finally did look up, I noticed my desk was surrounded by a crowd of co-workers, and they were lookin' at me like I was the one who had been making all the racket. Nobody said a word. They didn't have to. Slowly, I got to my feet and looked around at all the enraged expressions. I was breathing hard as if I'd just finished sprinting a mile.

"It…it wasn't me though," I said. "Charlie. It was Charlie…"

I'm really not sure what he hit me with, but if it was his fist, then Charlie should have the thing registered as a deadly weapon. It came so fast there was no time to react, and it crunched into the bones of my face like a cinder block. Nothing made out of human flesh could possibly be that hard or heavy. I was knocked clean over my desk without touching so much as a sheet of paper, then landed flat on my back, blood gushing out of my nose and mouth like a warm red fountain.

"What the fuck is this?" I yelled.

Nobody said a word, and their expressions all looked the same. Then somebody kicked me in the head. Then in the ribs. Legs…

"*Hey…*"

* * *

Nobody ever told me why. All anybody told me, after I finally managed to scrape myself up off the floor, was that I had been fired. The boss told me that after kicking me twice in the stomach with his brand new cowboy boots, then leaning down and punching me in the face so hard the back of my head bounced up off the floor.

"You are a disruptive influence, Mr. Frazier. You have been a disruptive influence ever since you began working here, which is why I am relieving you of your duties here at the company, effective immediately. I would advise you to have all your things removed from your desk and to be gone by the end of business today. Any questions?"

I had a hell of a lot of questions, actually, but they could wait. If I opened my mouth now, either somebody was going to close it permanently with another well-placed kick, or the pool of blood already in my mouth was going to spill all over the sparkling clean floor. Either way, it was gonna be a mess if I tried to say anything, so I shook my head and groaned.

"No questions? Very well, Mr. Frazier. OK, everyone. Nothing else to see here. Back to work."

Where the hell was Bob?

* * *

It took me almost a week of either lying in bed or lying in a bathtub full of hot water and Epsom salt for me to get to the place where I felt like I could walk outside without lookin' like too much of a cripple. By then, my head still throbbed a bit, but nothing like the excruciating pain that wouldn't let me sleep more than a few hours the first couple of nights. But most important, at least I could finally walk upright all the way from my bedroom to the refrigerator. This was a major accomplishment in my book, and even though I still wasn't 100 percent, I figured it was about time for me to try and put the pieces together on this thing once and for all. Maybe there wasn't anything I could do about it, and seeing as how I still hadn't heard a word from Bob, maybe I was in this thing all alone. Still, I at least had to get some answers for myself. Sometimes it helps just to know *why* you're going crazy.

After lying in bed for most of the day, I had to tell my body to move a couple of times before it paid me any mind. I threw the sheets over to the side, then propped myself up on one elbow before dragging my feet over the side of the bed. On purpose, I got up on the side of the bed that didn't face the mirror because I didn't want to take the chance of seeing how bad I knew I looked. I glanced at the clock beside the bed and noticed it was about time for the news, so I reached for the remote and flicked on the TV. A thought crossed my mind that maybe there might be some report about what the hell was going on, but then I had to laugh at that. If it was important and relevant, why in the hell would it be on the news? Those days were long gone. Besides, if it hadn't made the news by now…

Someone was knocking at the door. I started to obey my reflex and check to see who it was, but then I sat back down. All this time, I'd been home recuperating from a gag beating delivered courtesy of my own co-workers, and all this time, nobody had so much as called to see how I was doing, if I needed anything, or bothered to drop by. Bob wasn't answering his phone, and he wasn't returning messages. After I'd called and told my folks what happened, they said that was "really too bad," then asked if I'd heard anything from my sister lately. She had started this "really great job" at an accounting firm, and they were sure she'd want to tell me all about it. My 24-year-old baby sister. The same one who only two months ago had been working as a cashier at the neighbourhood Ready Mart and still had dreams of making it as a rock singer – a Black rock singer – in some band called The Furious that she kept telling us was about to get signed any day. *That* sister?

Whoever it was at the door knocked again, only harder. Even though my car wasn't out front, somebody was pretty convinced I was home. I got up and walked around the side of the bed to peer through the side of the curtains to see if I could get a glimpse. Turned out I didn't have to. I recognized the green truck parked in front of the house. It belonged to Bob.

I went to the door, looked through the peephole, then stepped back. He was alone, which I guess was good, and was wearing a faded pair of jeans and a red Hendrix t-shirt – on a workday. That was almost enough for me to open the door, but when I took another peek and saw how scared he looked, that's what finally convinced me he hadn't gone over to the other side. None of those folks ever looked scared of anything. For that matter, they never looked happy or sad either. They either looked angry or they just looked.

"You really need to work on your timing, buddy," I said. "You might wanna check to see if somebody stole your phone, too."

"Get your clothes on, then come with me," he said, his voice almost a whisper.

I didn't say anything for a minute while I sized him up. He was getting even more nervous, if that was possible.

"Where the hell have you been, Bob? Do you have any idea what…"

"Yes! I know! I know what happened! That's why I'm here, all right? Now just get your clothes on because there's something you've gotta see."

"OK, fine. You wanna come inside while I change, or you wanna stay out there lookin' like the cops are after you?"

Bob almost knocked me over on his way in.

"I wish it was the cops, I really do."

"*Where the hell have you been, Bob??*"

"Get dressed."

We'd been on the road for almost 10 minutes before Bob said so much as a single word. Several times, I started to break the silence, but something kept telling me to wait.

"They want to see you," he said.

"What the hell did you just say?"

"They want to see you. I think they want to make you an offer of some kind."

"An offer of some kind? Jesus, man, do you know how that sounds? And who the hell are 'they' and why do they want to make me any kind of offer?"

"OK, calm down. All right? I mean, I know how this sounds, but it's not as bad as it sounds. Well, it is, but then it's not, you know?"

"You're sweating, Bob. The AC is on full blast, and you're sweating like you're sitting on a hot pad. But you're telling me it's not as bad as it sounds. Yeah. OK."

We were passing a broken-down strip mall right then, and Bob made a sudden decision to veer across traffic and pull into the nearly empty mall parking lot. He parked across several parking spaces, but left the car running as he stared straight ahead through the windshield for several moments. Once again, something told me to wait, to let him say whatever it was he had to say when he was ready.

"They just don't understand you, Frazier. Us. They don't understand us. I guess they thought they had it all figured out, but then we kinda screwed up the works for them. And these folks, or whatever they are, they're not accustomed to things not going as planned. Not one bit. To be honest? I think it kinda scares them. They don't know how to handle failure."

"Just because we didn't want any meatloaf, this counts as some kind of monumental failure for a whole race of space aliens? And how did you get to know all this about them anyway? You guys go out for a beer or what?"

"Well, I'm not so sure they're from space, Frazier. Could be, I guess, but I'm not so sure. They never mentioned anything about another planet or anything like that. You asked…? Oh. Right. That same day you got beat up, that evening, the guy from the lunch truck showed up at my place. Just walked up and rang the doorbell. Don't ask me how he knew where I lived, but then I guess it wasn't that hard to figure. Anyway, when I saw who it was, I was pretty damned scared. Then he told me to open the door because we had to talk. I didn't figure I had much of a choice.

"So he comes in, still wearing that 'Bite On This' lunch truck uniform. Looks all around the house. I don't mean he walked all through the place. He just looked with his eyes, like he was making mental notes or something. Like he was *studying* everything, you know? Gave me the chills. I asked him what this was all about, and that's when he tells me to have a seat on the sofa. I mean, this is my house, right? But this guy, who I don't even know is telling me to have a seat *in my own damned house.*

"So I take a seat. Then I asked him if he was gonna sit down too. He said sure. I asked him again what this was all about. He didn't say anything for a while, and I don't think he ever blinked. Now that I think about it, that's something else that made me nervous. He just sat there across from me, never blinking, like he was waiting for something. And he looked kinda tense, too. The whole time, he was sitting on the edge of the couch, like he was afraid to lean back. Then, all of a sudden, he asks me this really crazy question….

"He asks me, 'What is it that you want?' I told him that's the same question I wanted to ask him. Who the hell were they, and why were they messin' with everybody like this? What did *they* want?"

"Well, that was the only time the guy smiled, and even then, he didn't smile all the way. Kind of a half smile. Then the smile disappears, and he asks me again, only this time it's starting to sound more like a threat than a question. *What is it that you want?'* he says. I tell him I want him and his people to leave us the hell alone and to get the hell out of here and to take their lunch trucks with them. And to set the other folks back on normal. The guy just stares at me for a while, then he nods. 'You mentioned hell,' he says.

"All I said was for you guys to go back to wherever in the hell they came from, I said. Why is that important? 'Because hell is exactly where we are from,' he says. 'And I have an offer that you and your friend may be interested in."

My stomach felt like a large block of ice was sitting there, refusing to melt. This was all way too crazy.

"So what do you think?" he asked.

I just shook my head. How do you respond to a proposal from a demon who drives a lunch truck full of magic meatloaf? I had always heard that hell was supposed to be so damned scary with lakes of fire and blood, people screaming and getting pitchforks jabbed in their ribs. That kind of thing. But now come to find out that you never really go to hell. Hell comes to you. Hell delivers.

What kind of insane shit is this?

"You're gonna have to give me a minute on this one, Bob. It's all a bit much to digest, if you know what I mean."

"Sure. Right. It's just that we're gonna be there pretty soon and these guys, you know, they're expecting..."

"Just give me a minute, Bob, all right? Just a minute."

"OK, but just let me say this and then I'll shut up. You know, when you consider the set of circumstances that we're faced with, I mean with this being hell and all? It's really not such a bad offer. Could be worse is all I'm saying. Just a thought."

"Could be worse, huh? Hmmmm. Interesting thought, Bob."

"Just saying."

* * *

The next day I woke up around 5 a.m. Felt downright perky, just the way that Katie Couric woman always looked on that morning talk show. I've always hated Katie Couric, but you could never say she wasn't perky. Anyway, I switched on the lamp next to the bed, swung my legs over the side of the bed, and jumped in the shower. *Man* that hot water felt great! Before I knew it, I was whistling an old Commodores tune.

"Cause I'm, eeeeesehhhh, I'm easy like Sunday mooooooanin…"

It was funny because normally I would have slept until at least 9 or 10 if it wasn't a workday, and even then it would have taken me another 15-20 minutes to finally drag myself out of the bed. But this was a new day! There were places to go and things to do, and I had to get started early. That was the agreement, and besides, people hated to be kept waiting.

People need their meatloaf.

Open Fields

Scene 1

A smell like that would wake anybody up. I say that because my mother always said I sleep like the dead. By the time she managed to wake me up to get me ready for school when I was a kid, she was already worn out, face tired and angry from all that yelling. Usually, my little brother, Felix, would be standing next to her with this crazy wide grin on his face.

"It's just so cool how you can always do that," he'd say sometimes, after Mom had left and I was managing to find my way back to the land of the living.

But that was long ago and far away. I haven't been a kid for more decades than I'd care to remember, and Felix doesn't think much of anything I do is that cool anymore. He works downtown at some major law firm that I might actually know the name of if I gave a damn. Me and Felix, we haven't spoken in quite a while. Mom died back in 2025, in March.

But yeah, I was talking about that smell. Because when you got an odor like that pricking up your nostrils first thing in the morning, it's kinda hard to talk about much else. I was surprised Maryanne hadn't woken me up to maybe go check and see what it was all about, since she was a much lighter sleeper than I ever was. And she had a sense of smell that made me think she must have been part dog. I know how that sounds, but it's not what I meant. Trust me. It's just that no human being should be able to pick up scents the way she can. It's not normal.

I reached around behind me to shake her, but that's when something shook the whole house. Like some huge person had just pounded our block with a hammer the size of, well, the entire block. Our house wasn't that big, one of those small wood frame types you see all over the East Side, but it was big enough that it shouldn't have shook like what I'd just felt. This wasn't Los Angeles after all. Or what was left of it, anyway. Detroit still had its share of problems, but earthquakes weren't part of the deal.

Maryanne wasn't there. I started patting around on the bed behind me, where she normally was always curled up so tight like only someone that small can do, before my eyes shot open and I rolled over to confirm with my sleep-deprived vision what my hands had been trying to tell me for the past few moments.

"Maryanne…? *Maryanne.*"

" I'm in here," she said with that husky voice that sounded like it belonged to someone at least twice her size.

Between her name and that voice, nobody ever believed she was Black when they spoke to her over the phone, which was probably why she got hired on that call center job in the first place. They didn't want anybody who sounded like a Chantal or a Chiniqua. It was funny in a way, not just because Detroit was still mostly Black, but because if anyone at that job of hers could hear the way she talked around the house, or just about anywhere outside that job, they would have known pretty damned quick.

I rolled back over, squinted, trying to focus on what the clock said next to the bed. It was 4:59, but it was still dark outside, or pretty much so, which let me know this was the morning. For various reasons, I didn't always keep track. One of the reasons being I hadn't had a job in quite a while, so I didn't need to.

Maryanne never gave me a hard time about it, at least not anymore, because she knew this wasn't who I was. We'd been married for six years, but we'd been together for longer than it was legal. She knew me better than anyone, even better than my folks, truth be told.

"What you doin' in there, girl? You see what time it is, right? And you musta felt that…whatever it was…."

Silence.

"Maryanne…?"

"Yeah. Look, you should probably come out here, Raymond."

I frowned, then looked out the small bedroom window, thinking maybe what I was supposed to see would be visible from there without me having to get myself up. But no such luck. Just the darkness of the partially lit back yard and the same stretch of alley full of weeds that had been there ever since we'd bought the place.

"So what is it?" I asked, lookin' at the door, wondering why she was standing on the other side with none of the lights turned on.

"You just need to come out here, Raymond. You know I wouldn't ask this time of night if…"

"Yeah, yeah…OK. Gimme a minute. Gotta put something on."

I rubbed my eyes with my fists, then swung my legs over the side of the bed and sat there for a few counts, trying to get myself steady. Just because my eyes was open, or because I'd carried on a bit of a conversation, didn't mean I was fully awake. That was something always took a while with me. And I was guessing whatever it was Maryanne thought I had to see was something that was gonna require me being full woke.

After a while, I grabbed my robe. Stood up, scratched my head, then made my way into the living room. Mayanne's big almond-shaped eyes were staring at me hard as I came into view, which caught me off guard. Normally, whenever I came drifting into whatever space she happened to be occupying, she was busy doing something else, hardly noticing my existence. Not in a bad way, just in a way like folks who've been together for a while. You know each other is there, so there's no need to keep making a point of noticing it. Married life. But on this morning, in the living room with the outside streetlight being the only light inside the house,

Maryanne was staring straight at me, hard, like she needed to be sure of something. Really sure.

"What is it?" I asked, trying to keep my voice from sounding like how I was starting to feel. "Did you see something?"

She took two slow steps toward me, stopping just far enough away that I couldn't reach out and pull her to me without taking another long step of my own.

"You asked if I heard that sound from earlier? That really loud…sounded like…"

"Well, I mean, I knew you musta heard it. I was only…"

Maryanne squeezed her eyes shut tight and shook her head real sharp two times.

"No," she said.

"No…? Why…"

When she started to speak again, her words came hard and fast, like she had no control. Like the words weren't giving her any kind of choice about whether or not they were gonna get said.

"Do you remember what they told us about those plans they had for that open field across the street? All those plans about how they were going to grow all this food there and then all of us who lived here on this block, we were gonna have all the food we needed, and then after that the value of the neighborhood was gonna go up and all that shit? You remember that, right? Because I do."

I shoved my hands down the side of my thighs, then remembered what I was wearing didn't have pockets, which left me a bit confused about what to do with my hands. Still, I managed to nod, wondering where this was going.

"Yeah…Yeah, sure. I remember. You're talkin about when those folks from the City came over there last summer, had that big shindig with all the media and all that. Everybody was out there. Said this was something they were doing all around the city."

"I sure hope not."

I grinned.

"I remember you weren't too crazy about the idea. And about how you let them know it, too. Gotta say I was pretty proud how you…"

"Thanks, babe. But not now. Because we got a…"

Just then, the house shook again. I heard the neighbor's door swing open, and the image of that fat bastard came into my head and made me grimace. One of the worst things about home ownership sometimes is you don't get to choose your neighbors. And unless you shoot 'em, you're usually stuck with 'em. In a quick flash of fantasy, I imagined what it might feel like to point a gun right up his nose and then…

And then he screamed.

What the…?

"We got a problem."

The look in Maryanne's eyes wasn't something I wanted to see, especially not that time of morning. And especially not after hearing the way Bernard - that's the neighbor - screamed. In this kinda circumstance, most men would rather have it said that they yelled or shouted. But that's not what Bernard did; the man screamed in a way that made the hair on my arms stand up. It wasn't because I didn't much like the guy that I didn't want to go and see what made him scream like that. At least not right away. It was something else. It was that thing inside of me, that thing we all got inside of us, that told me maybe I didn't want go rushing out there just yet.

"Maryanne…how long you been standing out here in the living room?"

She shook her head again, then pointed toward the window like she was making an accusation. The shades were closed tight. Tighter than usual.

"That's not the question, Raymond. That's not the question you need to be asking."

"OK. So then let me ask you this: what brought you out here? And what the hell was that noise?"

This time she nodded, but real slow.

"That's the right question, baby."

She took a step toward me and grabbed my hand, weaving her fingers into mine. Her eyes were scared, but not like how you see those silly-assed white girls in those horror movies with nothing on, kinda scared, when some guy is chasing her around the house with an axe or whatever. This was the kinda scared that would make the guy with the axe run like hell in the other direction.

"Come look."

"…OK…."

Maryanne kept her eyes locked on me as she pulled me several steps toward the shades. The fact that she wasn't pulling me toward the door told me something, and it wasn't something good. With her other hand, she reached behind her and pulled open a narrow view between the shades of whatever was on the other side. But her eyes were still locked on me, I guess to gauge how I was going to react to whatever it was I was guessing she had already seen.

"Come look," she said again.

To be honest, I wasn't so sure that's what I wanted to do, but I did it anyway because I knew my wife needed me to see. We needed to be in this together. So I sucked in a quick, deep breath and leaned forward to take a peek at…

"Jesus."

I jumped backward. Without really meaning to, I snatched my hand away from Maryanne's.

"What the …?"

Maryanne started nodding, as she took two steps toward me in a real careful way, like she wasn't sure what I might do. I don't think she even cared about me yanking my hand away, something that on any other day she would have cursed me out with a string of words guaranteed to melt a stained glass window.

"Maryanne, what…what *are* those things? They weren't…were they even there yesterday? I didn't see them there yesterday. I *know* I didn't see them there yesterday, did you? What the *fuck,* Maryanne…?

"They're growing people," she said.

I cocked my head to the side, like one of those dogs. I knew what I'd seen in that brief moment, and it wasn't what I could have really seen.

"No…."

Maryanne reached out and grabbed my hand again, and she squeezed. Hard.

"They're growing people."

Scene 2

"How you expect me to eat all this?"

"What you mean? Since when you ain't had an appetite?"

"Damn, Maryanne. An appetite's one thing but…I mean, thanks and everything. You know I like it when you cook. But all *this?* There some kinda special occasion I don't know anything about? Shit. You ain't pregnant are you?"

A couple months had gone by since that night, and we were sitting across from each other at the table, which was stacked high with pancakes and all kinds of fruit and a tray overflowing with scrambled eggs and another tray overflowing with bacon and several different kinds of sausages. Then there were all the pastries, the toast, the pitcher of orange juice…

And that was just what was on the table. There was more food on the stove.

Maryanne started laughing. Real slow at first, but then it kinda took hold until she was laughing so hard the tears came. I wasn't so sure how to react at first, so I figured maybe the safe thing was for me to start laughing along with her. I could tell I didn't sound right, but I kept on laughing anyway, watching Maryanne for maybe some kind of cue as to what to do next. Or for why we were doing this, laughing and crying in the kitchen with all this obscene amount of food heaped up in front of us that we would never be able to eat.

After a while, she stopped. Not all at once, but gradually. Wiping her eyes. Sniffling.

She looked at me, her eyes begging me for something that I didn't know how to give. I felt a sudden ache in my chest.

"Seriously, you're not hungry?" she asked, her voice so much quieter than usual.

The ache got worse.

"*Babe.* It's not that, OK? You know how I love to eat. It's just…"

Someone knocked at the door. Once, hard, then three more times. Each time harder than the last, and spaced too far apart. The way they always did. Maryanne and I stared at each other, and I knew that she knew what it was I'd been trying to say. She smiled, and I smiled back.

"Pancakes," I said.

The Beasts of Belle Isle

"OK, so now tell me this again...What was this you think you saw, James, and I mean for real."

Even when we was kids, Fred didn't never believe a damned thing I said, so I don't guess I was surprised at how he was acting now after I told him.

If I was the little brother, then I guess maybe I coulda written it off to that. Except it was the other way around by about ten years. Let's make that ten years, three months, and five days. I could even give you the number of minutes, but Fred being Fred, he would swear I was just making that up to sound impressive. Just because he couldn't do it, and he was supposed to be the more 'reliable' one (according to Mom and Dad who...fuck it, that's a whole other story), then naturally that meant I couldn't *possibly.* Right? Because...

Well, because I'm not Fred.

But just because you're the most reliable one, which I ain't saying he is, who the hell says that more reliable means more smart?

Anyways... in spite of it all, I love Fred. I've always been proud of him. Big time lawyer in a big name firm downtown. I'm pretty sure he loves me too, even if he wasn't always willing to give me the benefit of the doubt. I mean, he had to, right? Blood.

The one thing me and Fred have in common is our love for Belle Isle. Growing up, that park had been something special for us. It was like a whole other world apart, away from the crazy shit that went on in the neighborhood - not that crazy shit didn't happen on Belle Isle too; like that two-headed baby they found climbing that tree that one time a few years back. And it was blue, too? Now that was some crazy shit for real.

Speaking of which, if one of those State Police hadn't seen it, you know damned well nobody would have believed me then neither; because that was wild even by Detroit standards.

But I'm just saying that for the most part, Belle Isle was a refuge, you know? It was a place you could go like kind of a filling station. You could fill up on enough peace of mind to get you through until, hopefully, the next time.

Anyway, so there we were. It was this really beautiful summer afternoon on a Sunday, meaning warm, somewhere upwards near ninety, but not too humid. It's always the humidity that kills you. We were sitting on a bench with our legs crossed, both of us watching one of those really huge ships making its way down the river. We had been there nearly half an hour before Fred finally put the question to me. I guess I coulda been a little pissed that he disturbed such a rare and peaceful moment between brothers, but then again, this *was* why I'd asked him to meet me there in the first place.

I looked over at Fred, letting him see in my face that this wasn't the time.

"I didn't say anything about anything I *thought* I saw, Fred. I don't know what the hell it was, but it was something real. Scared the shit outta me..."

Fred nodded. I knew what he was gonna ask me next, and sure enough, he did.

"I'm not trying to doubt you, James, it's just...sorry. So then just tell me what was this thing you *saw*. And you called me late as hell, so I'm guessing it was...wait. The park closes at ten, and you didn't even call me until practically one in the morning. What the hell were you doing out here? How did you even get past the police?"

I shook my head and sighed.

"Here we go…"

"James, I don't think that's an unreasonable question, right? What were you doing out here so late?"

"To be a lawyer, I swear I don't know how you can ask so *many* wrong questions. *You're asking the wrong questions, Fred.* Man, this isn't about me missing curfew like when we were kids. This isn't about me sneaking out the window to go see that girl. This is about something serious, and if it ain't handled then I think it might be something real dangerous."

Fred's eyes popped open wide as he leaned forward.

"Fucking *dangerous?* Big brother, if this thing is dangerous, then why the hell you telling me first? You need to…"

"*Listen* to me, Fred. Just… *listen…*"

He didn't want to listen, I could tell. Show me a lawyer who wants to stop talking, right? But he did stop talking, and I was thankful.

"They asked me to come get you," I finally said. "They say they need to talk to both of us about what's going to happen."

"Jesus Christ! How could I be so damned stupid? You owe some thugs money or something, and after you swore to me…"

I slammed the bench with my fist so hard it rattled. He looked a little scared of me now, which was probably a good thing since Fred is bigger than me and had always been in better shape. As a matter of fact, Fred is built like he was born with a gym membership. But I had his attention now.

I reached into my pocket to pull out my phone.

"There's something you need to see. Because then just maybe you'll start asking the right kinda questions."

While I was digging in my pocket, Fred kept lookin' at me hard. I knew what was going through his mind. How could I *not* know? We'd been brothers for forty-five years, forty-six in a couple months when Fred had his birthday. Anyway, what he was thinking was whether he gave a shit about what I had on my phone because I had just pounded a park bench like a crazy person. Kinda like the Hulk. But I knew that once he saw what…

"OK, here you go. *Look.* Because I knew you were gonna get like this. I dunno, maybe they knew how you were gonna react too. Watch this."

The phone was set on video playback, and I placed it between us so we could both see. Once Fred let himself glance at the screen, I saw his expression shift. Because there was no way you could see what was on that screen, even before I pressed the 'play' button, and not wonder…

"James…what…"

"Exactly. But you haven't even seen it yet, so hold your questions - the right ones - for just a sec."

I pressed the play button, and that's when you could hear it - that same loud humming noise that I heard last night. The same noise that made me drive deep into those wild woods on the east side of the island, to the part where it looks like you suddenly just left Detroit and disappeared up north somewhere.

Oh, and those cops Fred was asking about how did I get past? Yeah, right. Hadn't been a cop on Belle Isle in three months. Or not an actual cop anyway. Not since what we all called *the incident.* Now all they had was those little roving metallic sensors I call Motor Booties because that's pretty much what they look like to me. Not that you wanted to make the mistake of fuckin with one of them neither, because they were set up to take a brother down with a quickness.

Maybe it's me, but I'm still thinkin we woulda got a whole lot more than Motor Booties to replace those cops if it was mostly white folks hangin out on Belle Isle. We woulda got Black helicopters 24-7 and an army of robocops is what we woulda got.

Anyway, it wasn't the noise that was getting Fred's attention and making him question the reality of what was right in front of him, making him question reality, *period.* What was putting that look on Fred's face was the beast. It was standing there directly in full view of my dash cam, with long scaly arms stretched behind its back, lookin' like it didn't have any bones. It was maybe six foot tall, and its body wasn't so completely different from ours… except that it was. I mean, the shape... two arms, two legs, two feet, one head… all that was the same. But then there was that boneless thing, and there was no sex organ that I could see. And then there were those thick-assed scales covering the entire creature, lookin' more like wood chips than any scales you might see on a lizard or reptile… and they *breathed.* I don't know how to say it any other way, because it doesn't make any kinda sense what I was lookin' at. But I'm telling you, those scales were *breathing…*

And those eyes? *Three eyes?* Seeing it again on the small screen brought back the same chill I felt when I first saw it come walking out onto the road, right in front of my headlights like it did. I jammed the brakes, but it didn't even move to jump out the way. Like it knew I knew better than to make the mistake of running into it. I sat there in the car for what seemed like way longer than it probably was before I made the questionable decision to get out of the car. But OK, yeah, I had been drinking a bit, so there was that.

"James. What's that sound."

"Just wait a minute."

Fred started to protest, again acting like a lawyer, but I shoved my warning finger up in the air, still lookin' down at the screen.

"Just hold up."

So we both watched the replay of the dashcam video as I approached this thing. The beast cocked its head to the side, then blinked all three of its gold-colored eyes in a way that was almost seductive, which really messed with my head. But then, almost like it was reading my mind, it kinda grinned. That made me jump two steps back in a hurry.

"What the fuck are you, man?" I asked. And as soon as I asked the question, I felt like a damned fool, because why was I assuming this thing would speak…

"We are related, you and I."

The way its voice sounded wasn't like any voice I had ever heard, like hissing steam spewing out of a large pipe, and the way its mouth moved didn't look like it was in any way synced up to what it had just said. Even though they didn't look that much different from regular folk lips, which I have to admit was kind of a shocker when you looked at the rest of the creature, there was obviously a difference in the way these lip things worked. Maybe he - she, whatever the hell - ate with that mouth. Maybe it did other things. The more I thought about it, the more I really didn't wanna think about it.

Oh, and the other thing? About that voice? It didn't just go into your ears like a normal sound. Like how you would hear anything else. It…

"James, why is the inside of my head starting to itch?"

Yeah. That. And the thing was, because that itch was on the inside of your head, it wasn't like you could reach it and give yourself any kind of relief. All you could do was just scrunch up your face and handle it the best way you could. Or at least pretend like you were. Because once it started talking, all you really wanted was for it to stop - except you knew you had to hear what it was saying.

"How in the green hell you figure we're related? I got a lotta relatives, and trust me not a damned one looks a thing like you. Some of 'em ugly, true enough, but I mean…damn."

"Hell is not green."

"So how would you…oh shit…"

The thing made a sound that I guessed was supposed to be laughter, judging by how the lips curled up at the sides, and the way the shoulders were bouncing up and down.

"Do not worry, I am not him. And we don't much care for him either. He is not pleasant."

"Yeah, well. You really didn't have to go to hell to find out that the devil is not a nice guy. I coulda told you that for free. So what is it you want? Why did you step in front of my car like you did? Man, if I hadn't seen you in time, I could have run you over. Speaking of which, what are you, anyway?"

The thing laughed again, which gave me chills.

"Many questions."

"If you saw something looked like me pop out into the middle of the road in front of whatever it is your kind drives back on wherever your planet happens to be, wouldn't you have questions?"

"This is our planet, James Thompson. That is a good place to begin. We have always been here. Long before you, and long after you. We are the Tzz. I am called Tzz-Phat. We inhabit the Other Side. We are also known as the beasts of Belle Isle. In your limited context, we feel the term applies."

"The beasts of…? Forget it. The other side of what? The other side of Belle Isle? And why hasn't anyone seen you before if you guys have been here all along? And where is everybody else? How many of you are there? And how in the hell you know my name?"

"Many questions. I will give you answers. But first, we need to talk about Fred. He is a lawyer, correct?"

Right then was when my brother jumped up off that park bench like it was a skillet, and then he started backing away from me.

"James…? How in the…what the *fuck,* James…"

"Little brother, I know, OK? *I know.* How you feeling right now ain't even close to how my head was reeling last night, believe me. But at least you got me here to watch this thing with you. You got *me*. But last night? I was all alone with this shit, man, you hear me? I was all alone, and any damned thing coulda happened."

"But it knows I'm a lawyer!"

"Fred, you gotta sit back down, man. Because this Tzz-Phat guy doesn't just know you a lawyer, hear? He knows a lot more than that. He...no, *they* been watching you. For years. It's what they do, little brother. *It's what they do.*"

"But …the beasts of Belle Isle..? What kind of…"

"*Fred.* You gotta listen to the rest. So sit down, man. OK? Sit down."

Fred gave me a long look, like he was making up his mind to do what I said or take off running. If he decided to do the stupid thing, then I had always been a lot faster than Fred and I would tackle him if I had to.

"Just finish this thing," he said, sounding like he'd just aged by about twenty years. "After that, I'm going home."

"I wish you could, little brother. I really do."

Fred squeezed his eyes shut, massaged his temples with his thumbs, then shook his head real slow. I pressed the button again, and the video started to play.

"How you know Fred is a lawyer? And how the hell you know his name is Fred? Or that I even have a brother?"

"As I said, we were here long before you, and we are here long after you are gone. That is all you need to know for now. You must make the introduction."

"To Fred?"

"Correct. We require his services."

"Require or request? There's a difference. Because whatever the hell you guys are, you damned sure ain't our masters so Fred ain't got to do shit for you, and I ain't got to tell him to do shit. We clear on that?"

The beast smiled, but not in a way that inspired confidence. Was there a way for a beast to smile that would inspire confidence? Something to consider... I held my ground, though. Fuck it. I'd run up against some hard boys in my time and hadn't backed down from one. I never backed down because that ain't what you do. I still remember the day when a group of bullies chased me home from school, and I ran into the house thinking I was safe. My mother looked out the window, saw those bullies still out on the sidewalk, talking loud and stickin their chests out.

"They chase you home?" she asked.

"Yes m'am."

"Stay right there. I'll be back."

"Yes m'am."

Two minutes later, my mother came back with a baseball bat.

"Now you go back out there and don't come back inside until you deal with them. You start running now and you ain't never gonna stop."

"But mom, there's seven of them! This bat ain't gonna be enough, they gonna kill me!"

Mom looked at me real hard, then hollered for my brother to come downstairs. It was more than a year before he ever forgave me, but it also made us closer. And I still to this day don't understand why he blamed me and not Mom.

"Now you got your brother. And a bat. That ought to even it up a little, but remember, you won't always have your mother to make things even for you. Life don't work like that. Whatever life throws at you,

you got to deal with it however it comes. Now get your asses out there, and I'm locking this door."

When it was all over, I have to say me and Fred didn't do too bad. But the point here is that I never backed down from any kinda fight in my life, thanks to Mahalia Thompson, God rest.

So there I was, heart pounding inside my chest like a crazy man with a really big hammer trying to beat his way out, but hoping I still looked cool. The beast kept smiling, and I guess that was when I noticed his eyes didn't blink. At all.

Considering the situation I was in, that was probably going to be the least of my problems.

The beast cocked his head to the side real slow, then stretched its smile a bit wider. He pointed his finger at me, which was really long, and I looked at it real hard, like maybe it was going to fire a shot. This thing was some kinda alien, so who knew what it could do.

But then it threw me a curveball. Kinda.

"We are clear," it said.

"Huh?"

"We are clear, and we request. Satisfactory?"

Damn. Who woulda thought.

"Oh. Alright then. Good to know."

We stared at each other a bit longer.

"Is our request granted?"

"Depends. What you need a lawyer for?"

The beast gave me a funny look. I couldn't figure out whether it was anger or just some kinda curious, but then it told me to wait there while it ducked off into the woods. Don't think I didn't think about jumping in my car and getting the hell outta there. But I was starting to get really curious, and my curiosity was outweighing my common sense.

A few more minutes, and I heard a loud rustling, and then there were four beasts standing in the road in front of me. All of them giving me that same funny look. Wasn't like I hadn't ever been stomped before, so I steeled myself up and got ready.

"So you needed backup for this?"

"Backup…?" said one, which I assumed was the one I had originally been talking to. No way to know for sure because they all looked pretty much alike to me.

"Yeah. Look, I know what this is, all right? I'm East Side Detroit for real. But if you knew what that was, then you'd know I still ain't tellin you shit until you answer my question."

"Which is why we are all here. You thought we were preparing to do you harm?"

I took a deep breath, then let it out slow.

"And you say we're related. That's bullshit. Look, what is it you need with Fred? Why you guys need a lawyer? And whichever one of you is Tzz-Phat, or however the hell you pronounce that name, that's the one I wanna hear from. Keep things consistent..."

They all looked back and forth at one another, then I guess it was Tzz-Phat who stepped forward.

"You cannot tell us apart?"

"Obviously."

"But we can…"

"That's because we don't all look alike. Not to be like white people, but I'm just sayin. In this case? The shit applies."

I'm pretty sure Tzz-Phat shrugged his shoulders, but I wasn't sure if it meant the same thing. I was just gonna have to assume that it did.

"Those of us you see here are not the rest of us. Who you see here are The Council. The Council must always be present when we discuss collective issues, such as we are about to do."

"OK. Got it. But just outta curiosity, how many of you are there over here from that other side you were talking about?"

"Somewhere in the tens of thousands, but we would like to bring more."

"Tens of…but ain't no way this island can even fit…where you keeping everybody?"

"Questions, questions, and questions! Can we please begin with the answers?"

So the beast was getting pissed. I probably should have been scared, but it was actually kinda funny for some reason. He sounded huffy, like those white butlers you see on comedy shows.

"Sure, Tzz. My bad. Go ahead."

"Tzz-Phat," they all said in unison.

They all stared at me for a long moment, I think sizing me up to decide if I was even worth dealing with. But somewhere along that moment, they figured out they didn't have a whole lotta choice.

"You recall the event referred to as *the incident*? The one that took place here on Belle Isle several months ago?"

"Of course I do. Everybody remembers that. How could we not? Nobody could figure out how that shit was even possible, not with Belle Isle being as big as it is. It happened back in April. So what about it?"

"We caused it."

"Ain't no way."

"But you say you don't know how such a thing was possible, correct?"

"Causing an entire island to levitate more than one-hundred feet straight up into the sky without even damaging the bridge? Then keeping it up there for a whole two days? Then easing it back down into the Detroit River like that? And nobody died? Hell naw, I don't know how a thing like that is possible. Except I was riding my bike across the street, down East Jefferson, when that whole thing went down. I saw it with my own eyes, man."

"What did you think?"

"Man, damn what I thought about it, OK? Because if you really did do this thing, then I wanna know why."

"That is fair. It is because we needed to make repairs."

"Repairs…? You gotta be kidding! You all been on that island since the beginning of time but you didn't see when the folks from the State came in and fixed the fountain and all that stuff? I mean, you saw what it looked like before, right?"

"You are talking about changes on top of the island. We are talking about the island itself. After so many years of being your plaything, the island had become ill. Had we not done anything, it would have been dead within a decade. It has been our home for all this time, so we felt obligated to fix the problem since you are not capable. The only way to fix the problem was to disconnect Belle Isle from the river and elevate it beyond your reach so that we could do what needed to be done. Without disruption. A thorough repair of the entire system. We were partially successful. Regretfully, some damage simply cannot be undone."

All I could do was just stare at them for quite a while, with that image back in my head of those long two days when Belle Isle was just hovering above the city like a flying saucer. That whole time, you could hear the folks who got stuck on the island screaming their lungs out. It was the biggest story in the world for a whole month, until another two-headed baby showed up down in El Paso. The press damned near stampeded outta here, and a day later it was like

nothin' had even happened. The sooner I could erase
that from my memory banks, the better.

"Man…what am I supposed to say to that?"

"Actually, it is what we would like to say. To
all of you. We would like to explain our actions to
your city. But to do this, we believe we may need a
lawyer in case there are any complications. Which is
why we need your Fred."

"Look, lemme tell you something; if you think
you all gonna just show up lookin' like you do in
Hart Plaza or …"

"We are not leaving the island."

"Right. So OK. You make this announcement
at the band shell or wherever. lookin' like how you
look? I mean, you been observing us all these years,
so you gotta know at least a little bit about how we
react to things. And something like this? You gonna
need one helluva lot more than just a lawyer. And
when it comes to lawyers, you gonna need a whole
lot more than just one. You gonna need a whole
damned army of Freds, hear me?

"And you gonna have to leave this island
because the courtroom ain't comin to you."

They looked at me for a while, then started to
talk among themselves. For a minute, it got kinda

animated, and I really wished I spoke whatever language it was they were slinging around. Once they were done, the one I was pretty sure was Tzz-Phat took a couple steps forward until he was standing real close. He reached out and put his hand on my shoulder, while his face did something that was like a smile.

"We believe one Fred will be sufficient. We appreciate your concern, and it has been noted. Will you introduce us to your Fred?"

"Man, can't you all just let this thing go? I'm telling you I know Detroiters, and they don't want no long conversation with a group of aliens trying to explain why they hauled our favorite place up into the sky so they could fix it. Plus you didn't even wait until all the people were off the island, man! You even had cops stranded up there! How you gonna explain that?"

"But we did it for them. They need to understand. We have discussed this, and we cannot let it go, as you say. If we wanted to, we could make our case more forcefully. I believe you suspect this already. And quite obviously, we have little use for your legal system, as you call it. But we believe it is the most conventional way to get ourselves heard. We are not completely familiar with your laws, but I have no doubt that doing what we did is in violation of them…"

"That's a good guess."

"…so allowing ourselves to plead guilty will give us the opportunity to explain ourselves before a wide audience. It will also alert your people that we are here. That we have always been here."

"OK, first thing? I think you guys been watching too much Law and Order, because if you…"

"Very good show."

"Yeah. Sure. And it's fiction. Because if you think any judge is gonna let you guys make some big speech in his courtroom about how you only stole Belle Isle to save it? Man, they sendin brothers to prison for stealing lollipops, and you think…? Shit. Your ass goin to jail. Soon as they get you in that building they lockin you up and throwing away the key like you ain't never been…"

"I can assure you that will never happen."

I started to say something else, based on the benefits of experience as a Black man in this country, or as anything that ain't white and blonde in this country, which would for damned sure include Tzz-

Phat and his crew. But something about the way he said what he said made me chill on that one. Because somehow I knew that before any one of his guys spent a minute in a Detroit holding cell, somebody was going to get hurt, and hurt bad.

...

"I'll do it."

"Whoa, hold up. *Fred.* Do you know what you signin up for with this? Just a minute ago, you were all scared and fixin to jackrabbit outta here. You were all bent outta shape because they knew you were a lawyer. You were freakin out that they even knew your *name.* And now you wanna be Perry Mason for these beasts?"

"Yes."

I couldn't see my own incredulous expression because I didn't have a mirror handy, but I'm pretty sure that expression was sending the message of who the hell are you and what have you done with my brother Fred. Because this didn't make not one bit of sense.

"Fred, you got to…"

Fred reached over and squeezed my shoulder in the way he always did ever since we were kids when he knew I was starting to get overheated. He was better at getting me to calm down than Mom or Dad had ever been.

"James, I know you're worried. And everything you just said? You're right. At least pretty much. But you got to see this as a bigger thing, big brother. A way bigger thing. Yeah, sure, I was scared to death for most of the time we were watching that video you took. But then, once I got past that? I got to thinking about what this was that I was really lookin' at. That *we* were really lookin' at. Man, do you have any idea what something like this could do for the city if we pull this thing off right? Not to mention my career?"

"You worried about your career right now? Seriously? We got space aliens with the power to lift an entire island out of the Detroit River up into the sky *and keep it there.* And what you talking about is your damned career?"

"OK, look, first of all, they ain't space aliens. They said right there on your video that they've been here forever. Probably longer than us. Hell, they mighta been running around down here since before human beings were even an idea. But I also didn't just say this was a career move, did I? Naw. I said this could be good for the city, too."

"Oh. Yeah. Right. And how you figure that?"

Fred leaned in as he started tapping his temple with his forefinger, giving me this real intense look that didn't have quite the effect I think he was going for. He was just getting on my nerves.

"You got to *think,* big brother. Because if these things have the ability to do what they did, that means they have the ability to do a whole lotta harm too. If that's what they wanted. But instead, they've just been living their lives out there all this time without nobody even knowing they were there. Until they decided they had an obligation - *an obligation* - to fix Belle Isle because they said it was sick and they knew we didn't have the ability!"

"Sounds to me like they trippin. That's what it sounds like to me."

"Naw. What it *sounds* like is they lookin' out for us. They on our side. Hell, we been tryin to get the State Police outta that park ever since we heard that shit was comin down, and they managed to do it in just a few days. If that's not lookin' out for us then what is?"

I had to admit Fred did have a point. I really didn't want to admit it, but I had to. And so we sat there for more than a minute without saying anything else, which for us is a really long time.

"So you really wanna take this thing to court, Fred?"

Fred smiled so wide I thought his face was gonna split.

"Oh hell yeah, big brother. *Oh hell yeah.*"

…

When it came close to time for the trial, I can't even begin to explain what the whole thing was like. Everything about it was surreal. Detroit had been worldwide news for months as the city with its own aliens, except they weren't really aliens because, like they said, they had always been here. We were more like the aliens than they were.

But anyway, shit was crazy. The closer it got to the date, the more camera crews you started seeing all over town. They were like locusts. You couldn't take two steps without tripping over one. And it got to the point where you really had to get rude to stop them chasing you down the street asking you a damned question everywhere you went. And nine times out of ten they were always stupid questions, like would I let one of them play with my kids or some dumb shit. I mean for real?

And then there were the crazies out in the streets with signs and bullhorns, yelling that the beasts needed to leave Belle Isle alone, leave it to the humans as God intended. As if God had time to be out here settling landlord tenant disputes.

The beasts? You woulda thought all this insanity would have really pissed them off, or even made them decide this trial strategy wasn't worth the hassle. They said they did what they did for us, the people of Detroit, but now here came all these folks - most of them not even from Detroit - makin all this noise about an issue that wasn't even any of their damned business as far as I was concerned. Were we really worth leaving the island for?

The day of the trial was actually a beautiful summer day, but I don't think anyone noticed. Everybody outside was all pushing, shoving and cursing, trying to get a glimpse of the beasts once they arrived via police escort. Normally that wasn't something you would see, but normal had left this city a long time ago. Right around the time Belle Isle was floating up in the sky. But it was funny because once the beasts finally did arrive? Everybody suddenly got real quiet. Like you coulda heard a pin drop.

As for Fred? He was smiling just as cool as East Side should. Shades on and everything as he escorted his clients into the courthouse. Did I mention they made them all wear suits?

Anyway that's where shit got really deep. The basic charges the beasts were facing weren't all that heavy because they hadn't done a whole lot. Not really. But then there was the question of them not being human, so did our laws really apply? And wasn't it a bit more than theft when they stole an entire island? But can you say they stole it when it never left the city and everyone knew where it was? And can you really say it was destruction of public property when they actually made it better, and they did so in the public interest? And when the public isn't even their public, so to speak? And can you actually say someone is vagrant when they are living in their own home, even if that home is an entire island? Or how about trespassing? Because were they really?

And if they hadn't turned themselves in, would there even be a trial? Hell no, because we probably still wouldn't even know they existed. They could have gone back to that 'other side' that Tzz-Phat told me about, but never really explained.

And then it came time where the beasts got to speak for themselves. Anybody who's ever been to a regular trial knows the difference between what really goes down as opposed to what you see in the movies or on Law and Order; ain't no judge got time to listen to any one defendant give any long dissertation in his own defense while mood music plays in the background. The docket is way too backed up for that, and in Detroit the judges have seen it all before and just want to get it over with.

But like I said, normal was out the window with this one. Even the judge knew there was no way to handle this like just another court case because this was definitely not in the category of anything he had ever seen before or was ever likely to see again. The world was literally watching and waiting on what happened in this courtroom today. Far as we knew, the fate of the world might depend on what happened today, and that's for real.

Tzz-Phat had been appointed chief spokesman for the beasts by his clan, but when he stood up, I still couldn't get over how strange he looked in that suit. Then again, maybe it wasn't a half bad idea Fred had come up with. Because they already looked threatening enough with the three eyes and the scales on their bodies that breathed, so maybe the suits made them easier to take. Then again, maybe it reminded everyone how much they weren't one of us.

But who the hell is 'us' in this scenario?

Tzz-Phat cleared his throat before lookin' around at the packed courtroom. I was worried how folks were gonna respond to that weird voice of his that made your ears itch…

But that voice was gone. The beast sounded like James Earl Jones!

"Your honor, I'm sure everyone here is wondering who …*what* we are and how we got here. Why in all these years no one has known that we existed until this very day. And I'm sure the largest two questions your people have is what is it that we want and why are we here now?

"Perhaps those are the two easiest questions to answer; we have always been here and we don't want anything. All we want is to continue to live in harmony with all of you as we have been doing before you knew of our existence. Strangely, I do realize that the very acknowledgment of our existence may pose a bigger threat to this harmony than anything else. But I remain hopeful that this poses a lesser hurdle than it may at first appear. Harmony is not harmful, wouldn't you agree?"

The judge smiled and nodded. I actually knew this judge, and this was probably the first time since he'd been a baby in a crib that he had ever smiled at any damned thing.

"Yes. And so harmony is our only objective. But as to why we are here and why we have not made ourselves known before now? Certainly that is a fair question. And let me first say again, as I told my new friend James Thompson when we first met on the island; we have always been here. We are not from outer space, nor from any other dimension. I see James lookin' at me the way he is right now, and I know it is because I told him about the Other Side. But the Other Side is not really another dimension, it is simply a portal into what Detroit is meant to become that our kind have accessed for generations. It is a creative space where alternate futures are tried, shaped and molded. We have not shared this portal with you because there has never been a need. Possibly until now, but we shall see.

"But we have been here since long before there was a Detroit as well as long after this point in time, which in some ways I suppose makes us the original Detroiters. We are well aware how you like to rank one another in that regard, which we find amusing. But we do understand that sentiment given its context. For not only are we aware of Detroit, but we are well aware of how the world views Detroit. And we know the world is watching even now.

"Which leads to why we did what we did. Certainly Belle Isle was in need of deeper repair than you were capable of, which is no reflection on any of you. You are all limited to this time and therefore limited to its capabilities. We are also all of you, a sort of mirror reflection, even though our appearance may indicate otherwise. But we are not shackled to the baggage of the here and now, nor of the many crippling mischaracterizations and misperceptions that have poisoned your realities.

"In short? We are free. Which is the other reason why we raised up Belle Isle in the manner that we did for all to witness and wonder. Because in truth, we could have performed our repairs in such a way that none except us would have ever known, and all life would have continued on uninterrupted.

"Except that you all were in grave need of disruption. As I said, we were here before it all, and we are here after it all even as we continually shape and reshape future scenarios, which places upon us a grave responsibility that, honestly, we oftentimes wish we could abandon. And yet, if we abandon you then we are abandoning ourselves, which will result in the evaporation of us all. Which will result in a clean slate, as if all that is never was."

Right then the judge got a funny look on his face, curious but also a little scared.

"I'm sorry…did you say *evaporation?*"

"I am afraid I did. I once told James Thompson on that same night that we are related. He did not believe me, and I do not blame him based on the initial visual evidence to which he was constrained. But we are truly related, and further than that we are interwoven. We are different but we are the same. Identical threads woven into a dissimilar fabric. Which is why we are free, and yet you yourselves do not realize this. We have waited for ages, sometimes encouraged, sometimes less so, that the time would come when you would realize who you truly are. But we can no longer wait for that day, even though we remain confident that you would eventually come to it of your own. And so…"

"OK, OK. But here's what I don't get, Mr. Tzz-Phat; you say you and your people are free. But if you're so free then why in God's name haven't you ever left the island until now?" asked the judge.

Tzz-Phat smiled, then took in a deep breath that I thought might make his suit pop open. And when he exhaled, his scales all exhaled too and suddenly I remembered the Big Bad Wolf in that fairy tale. My mind works twisted that way I guess.

The judge smiled again, and warmly.

"It is because Belle Isle *is* Detroit. It is where your heart has been kept beating for all these many years. Your true heart. And Detroit? It is Belle Isle. It is the center of your gravity, the source of your forever.

"We are the keepers of that heart. Because that heart beats for us all."

...

When the trial ended, it was so quiet in the courtroom that if anybody said anything, I'm pretty sure it would have echoed. It was almost like people were afraid to breathe. I mean, what do you say to something like that? I don't think anybody seriously thought there was ever any chance the judge was gonna send those beasts to jail, even if he had found them guilty of anything. But none of this was about that. This was about what was supposed to happen now.

Because when you don't know, and you *act* like you don't know, then that's one thing. That's why they say ignorance is bliss. But once the blinders come off, then all that weight falls on you, whether you ready to carry it or not. All that knowledge, like a ton of bricks. Knowledge ain't always easy, but then easy ain't always right.

Detroit is about to find that out. Because if we can lift a whole damned island into the sky...

The Black Experience Salesman

There was nothing particularly Black about George Jones, and that was a problem.

Because George Jones was a Black man living in Detroit, which happened to be the Blackest big city in America. Which meant (George thought) that if there was any place to be Black as loud as possible, then Detroit should be that place. He had even heard Detroit described as the Black Mecca by some, although he had his doubts about that description. But then, as stated, there was nothing particularly Black about George, so his opinions on the matter didn't particularly matter.

The way he mispronounced his words, the way he walked, the way he fumbled the handshakes. And Lord, what transpired when he tried to dance…

And it was all so strange, because both of George's parents were unquestionably Black, and so was his younger brother, Ali, whose name was considerably Blacker than that of his sibling. Anybody could be a George, but Ali was a name that not only implied darker hues, it implied a certain level of consciousness. Which probably explained why Ali, as soon as he entered his later teen years and with the full blessing of his parents, became full throttle militant and joined a full throttle militant organization committed to the Uplift of the People.

"You should join too!" said Ali to George, not long after he had made his announcement. Ali had always loved his brother deeply, even if he wasn't particularly Black, and thought that maybe participating in an organization that was committed to Black Community Uplift might make him feel more like he belonged.

But George just smiled sheepishly as he sat beside his brother on the couch in the living room, staring at the floor through thick glasses. He shook his head.

"I dunno, Ali. I don't think so. Folks like that usually laugh at me. And that's all right. I understand. But you go on ahead. You'll do great."

"George, you only *think* folks are laughing at you, but it ain't true, man. It's not! You just need to not worry so much about what you think people are thinking and put yourself out there. You're so smart, George! Mom and Dad are always saying that, and if you could just…"

"You'll be great, Ali. But it's just not for me."

That had been nearly a decade ago, when George and Ali were still kids. Ali had since become a lawyer, lauded as Detroit's own Johnnie Cochran, while George, now nearly 30, remained stuck working shifts in a warehouse. He and Ali had drifted apart and hadn't spoken in several years. George still lived in the family house with their father (their mother had passed not long after Ali had joined the community uplift organization), who quietly smiled and nodded at the end of each day when George came home from work on his bike.

"Dad."

"Son"

And that was the extent of it. Day after day after day of near invisibility. Of being Black While Not Black. Until the day George decided to take a different route home, just because maybe there was such a thing as a different route. Maybe taking a different route home might just take him, you know, *home.*

177

And that was the day when George met Dr. Lester, standing right there on the corner wearing a perfectly-tailored dark gray suit and flashing a megawatt Colgate smile that beamed like a headlight from a dark chocolate oval-shaped face. He was squeezing the handle of a Black leather briefcase in one hand, with the other shoved casually inside his pants pocket.

"Well, you finally decided to come my way, I see," he said as George was pedaling past.

George looked over his shoulder with apparent confusion, then fell off his bike.

"Oh dear," said Dr. Lester, before breaking out into a fit of laughter. "I see we have some work to do."

Part 2

Something about Dr. Lester seemed incredibly appealing, is what George thought to himself as he lay sprawled in the street after having tumbled off his bike. The man practically crackled with an electricity, an almost unholy energy, that pulsed outward from him like a forcefield. Any casual observer of the moment when George fell from his bike would have assumed the unfortunate event occurred as a result of

George being caught off-guard when Dr. Lester spoke to him as he pedaled past the sharply-dressed man standing on the corner.

"Well, you finally decided to come my way, I see," is what Dr. Lester had said, at which point George glanced hastily over his shoulder at the source of the commentary, his eyes wide with surprise. And that's when George fell.

"Oh, dear. I see we have some work to do," said Dr. Lester before laughing uproariously, which didn't seem like a very nice thing to do. But that part of having some work to do was actually true, as would be revealed soon enough.

But about that casual observer. What was most likely missed is that it wasn't what Dr. Lester said that caused George to fall off his bike into the street. Rather, it was the impact of that forcefield pulsing outward as George rode by that shoved him like a blast of wind. What any observer most likely would *not* have missed, however, is the fact that Dr. Lester had not been standing at that particular corner – nor had anyone else – until mere moments before George came pedaling along, thinking to himself how strange it was that this street was completely empty. How it looked so out of place in a Detroit landscape in a way that only a longtime Detroiter would have sensed immediately.

But that is only what the casual observer *would have* noticed. Because, as George himself noticed, there was absolutely nobody around at all except for this singular striking individual, throbbing with an otherworldly energy, holding a briefcase with one hand while pointing at him lying there in the street with the other.

"This is funny to you?" asked George eventually, once he had gathered his senses and felt a tinge of anger replacing his initial embarrassment at crashing so spectacularly in front of a complete stranger. To George, it seemed like he was always tripping or stumbling at awkward times in front of strangers, but mostly those strangers didn't laugh at him. They just ignored him.

"You're accustomed to being ignored, aren't you, George?"

"Wait..how did you know my…who the hell are you?"

The man seemed to briefly shimmer and shift, as if he were a hologram of some sort, but then solidified himself once more. He dropped his accusatory finger, and his laughter ceased as if it had been interrupted, like someone raised the needle off the record. But the broad smile remained.

"George, I am Dr. Lester. Over the next month, we are going to become the best of friends in the best possible way. Your life is about to change in incredible and remarkable ways that will set your currently unremarkable and culturally insignificant life on a path of eye-popping relevance. You will never be ignored again, George. As a senior Black Experience Salesman, you have been assigned to me as an emergency case in need of what we offer, and I have never, ever failed an assignment. Although, admittedly, you do pose some unique challenges. *But failure is not an option, George.*"

By now, George was standing back up on his own two feet, his eyes squinted, his rather large head cocked to the side. It seemed he had forgotten all about his bike.

"But assigned by *who?*"

Part 3

It was a while after picking myself and my bike up off the ground when I lost my balance seeing this Dr. Lester guy suddenly appear on the street corner as

I was pedaling by, and then feeling that sudden punch of hot air shove me over.

That was the question, because this whole situation made me nervous and also a bit angry. Who the hell was that out there actually *grading* my Blackness? And then finding my Blackness so insufficient to the point where they decided I needed someone assigned to me to make me Blacker? And what kind of name was *Dr. Lester?*

He never answered. Instead, Dr. Lester just stood there on the corner flashing that blinding smile, the one hand still holding his briefcase, the other still casually hidden inside the pants pocket of his expensively tailored suit.

Wait…was Dr. Lester wearing those shades when I first saw him? Just as that bit of confusion stumbled through my mind, they sparkled like what you would see in a movie if a particularly hot Hollywood star was wearing them in a role that emphasized just how hot of a Hollywood star they were.

Who was this guy?

"There's a time for everything, Brother George, and now ain't the time for that. May never *be* a time for that. Because what matters is *you,* Brother

George. What matters right here, right now is what *I* can do for *you.*"

"But what is so wrong with me that I need a damned ..what is it? A *Senior Black Experience salesman?* Seriously? I mean, what the hell kind of job description is that, for real?

"*For real!* There you go, Brother George! That's the spirit! Keep talking like that, and this might not take as long as we had anticipated."

Dr. Lester looked incredibly excited, as though his favorite football team had just scored the winning touchdown.

"Dude, you're not…serious…"

And just like that, his shoulders slumped, his smile ceased to glow, and the sparkle faded from his shades. He shook his head.

"Then again," he mumbled.

I almost felt sorry for him. I guess getting assigned to me was kinda like drawing the short straw.

"So is there a choice here, Dr. Lester? I mean, just because whoever these folks are decided I'm not Black enough doesn't mean you have to take the assignment, does it? Or that I have to accept you as my Emergency Blackness Instructor? Right? There has to be a way out of this thing, man, because I'm telling you I'm just not feeling this shit right now."

Dr. Lester put on a lop-sided grin as he peeped at me over the top of his shades and winked.

"Brother George, being Black is never a choice. And there is never a way out. It's how we survive. But you keep making progress like that, and you'll be feeling this shit in no time."

Part 4

It was a while after picking myself and my bike up off the ground when I lost my balance seeing this Dr. Lester guy suddenly appear on the street corner as I was pedaling by, and then feeling that sudden punch of hot air shove me over.

That was the question, because this whole situation made me nervous and also a bit angry. Who the hell was that out there actually *grading* my Blackness? And then finding my Blackness so insufficient to the point where they decided I needed someone assigned to me to make me Blacker? And what kind of name was *Dr. Lester?*

He never answered. Instead, Dr. Lester just stood there on the corner flashing that blinding smile, the one hand still holding his briefcase, the other still casually hidden inside the pants pocket of his expensively tailored suit.

Wait…was Dr. Lester wearing those shades when I first saw him? Just as that bit of confusion stumbled through my mind, they sparkled like what you would see in a movie if a particularly hot Hollywood star was wearing them in a role that emphasized just how hot of a Hollywood star they were.

Who was this guy?

"There's a time for everything, Brother George, and now ain't the time for that. May never *be* a time for that. Because what matters is *you,* Brother George. What matters right here, right now is what *I* can do for *you.*"

"But what is so wrong with me that I need a damned ..what is it? A *Senior Black Experience salesman?* Seriously? I mean, what the hell kind of job description is that, for real?

"*For real!* There you go, Brother George! That's the spirit! Keep talking like that, and this might not take as long as we had anticipated."

Dr. Lester looked incredibly excited, as though his favorite football team had just scored the winning touchdown.

"Dude, you're not…serious…"

And just like that, his shoulders slumped, his smile ceased to glow, and the sparkle faded from his shades. He shook his head.

"Then again," he mumbled.

I almost felt sorry for him. I guess getting assigned to me was kinda like drawing the short straw.

"So is there a choice here, Dr. Lester? I mean, just because whoever these folks are decided I'm not Black enough doesn't mean you have to take the assignment, does it? Or that I have to accept you as my Emergency Blackness Instructor? Right? There has to be a way out of this thing, man, because I'm telling you I'm just not feeling this shit right now."

Dr. Lester put on a lop-sided grin as he peeped at me over the top of his shades and winked.

"Brother George, being Black is never a choice. And there is never a way out. It's how we survive. But you keep making progress like that, and you'll be feeling this shit in no time."

The Egg

May 31, 2037

2:13 pm

I've always kept good notes, and it's a good thing. Kept a diary when I was a kid. Started when I was just seven, and made an entry every day until the day I turned 15 on May 1, 2020. As a 7-year-old kid, that was the day I predicted I was going to stop keeping a diary, and I kept my word. Because that's the kind of kid I was. Nerdy, but reliable. Always reliable. My mother said you could set a watch by me, which I thought was pretty funny. My dad only thought I was strange, but at least he accepted me for who I was. Tried to.

Anyway, I had no plans of starting up my diary again until the day it happened. Because once it happened, I didn't feel like I had a choice. There has to be a record, *there has to be,* and it seems like most folks want to act like none of this is happening.

Just last week, I was at Coco's Coffee Shop with Gerry? This is someone I've been friends with since before I started keeping my diary. We were sitting by the window, not really talking about much of anything, just chatting, lookin' out at the gray weather which is always Michigan this time of year in the early part of winter when the sun goes into hiding. Then I looked right at Gerry and asked him what he thought about the egg, if his life had changed at all since it had shown up. Gerry kept staring out the window as if he hadn't heard a thing. So I leaned forward and raised my voice, asked the same question. I could feel his fear more than I could see it, like a psychic warning. The desperation. I looked around the room and noticed some of the other patrons lookin'/not lookin' at me, as their conversations shut down tight like the lid on a mason jar.

"Gerry…"

But Gerry didn't give me the chance to ask a third time. He grabbed his jacket from the back of the chair and walked away quick, like he'd just gotten word of an emergency somewhere else. Anywhere else but near me. I don't think I'll ever see him again.

Today is Day 364. Tomorrow, Day 365, is the day we have been told will be The Opening, when the egg will make itself known to us. One full year to the exact day after its appearance.

We haven't been told what to expect after Day 365. Or whether we should expect anything at all.

May 31, 2036
1:45 pm

I just got back from Belle Isle. I know I said I was giving up the diary because I figured keeping a diary was more like something a kid would do, and I made up my mind I was done being a kid when I turned 15. Maybe the law says otherwise, but I guess I felt like the law can't always be one size fits all. Because people are different, you know? You say one thing to one person, and maybe they interpret what you said in one kind of way. But then you say that same thing to another person and…

Stop drifting.

Drifting is what I do when I try to keep myself from getting to the point when the point isn't a comfortable place to land. Drifting is what I do to protect myself from facing the reality of things that I'd rather not accept. Sometimes it's a good thing; keeps me from just buckling under to things that shouldn't be a certain way even if they are. But most times, if I'm being honest with myself, it's just ducking and hiding. Which can be OK for a kid, so I forgive myself.

I'm not a kid anymore.

"When I was a child, I spake as a child, I understood as a child, I thought as a child: but when I became a man, I put away childish things."

1 Corinthians 13:11

That's that bible verse my father used to quote to me whenever he thought I was spending too much time with my science fiction and fantasy books, imagining other worlds and weird beings not like us. He'd always tell me to come back down to Earth so I could learn more about actual human beings and real life.

"You need to spend more time learning about what *is*, not what *ain't*," is what he'd say.

Well, Dad, today is the day when what is and what ain't changed forever. I only wish you could have lived to see it.

I'm writing this, my first diary entry in over a decade, because I just saw something that I could not have seen. Except that everybody else on Belle Isle saw the same thing at the same time. That means a whole bunch of people across the river in Canada saw it too, because it appeared right there above the Detroit River; something that looked like a huge egg made out of mirrors.

I have my favorite spot on Belle Isle, like most Detroiters who visit a lot. It's an open grassy space about halfway up the drive, near a large tree. What I do is park nearby, grab my folding chair, and then go out and sit facing the river. Sometimes I bring a book, but usually I just sit there in peace, no phone, all by myself. Which is what I was doing today when I saw it happen. It looked at first like the air was splitting open, one long gash as tall as a tower, but there was no sound. Then, real slow, the egg began to force itself through like something being born.

I know. It doesn't make sense unless you were there. But it's the only way I know to describe it. Once it was all the way through, the opening sealed itself closed, leaving the mirror egg hovering above the water.

Then that thing with the birds happened.

June 10, 2036

11:13 am

I guess I was waiting for the egg to at least make some sort of sound, or to open up. Make an announcement. Take me to your leader. *Something.*

But for the first half hour at least, exactly nothing happened. All the cars on Belle Isle Drive, the strip that wraps around the island, had stopped. A few folks bothered to park, but most stopped wherever they were in the middle of the drive and stepped outside to look above the river at whatever the hell this huge egg-shaped thing was that just squeezed itself through a huge crack in midair. There wasn't much traffic on the drive, plus you can't drive more than 20 miles an hour, so nobody got rear-ended that I could see. Folks just stopped and got out with their mouths wide open. Funny thing is, nobody said a word. We all just kept lookin' at the impossible, and wondering what was gonna happen next.

The silence is what got to you, because it was so intense. You don't know what real silence is and the effect it can have on you until you're standing there in the middle of no sound at all. None. Not even from the geese and other birds, and Belle Isle is full of all kind of birds in the springtime. If you've been to Belle Isle even just a few times, then at least one of those times you had to stop the car while a group of geese took their time waddling from one side of the drive to the other, usually headed toward the river. Sometimes you might even see a mother goose with its little chicks following along single file, which always made me smile.

Yeah, even with all the duck and goose shit you had to navigate around (I always thought their leavings looked kinda like off-color Tootsie Rolls, which made it hard for me to eat that candy anymore once I made the connection), Belle Isle was a special place. You hear everybody rave about Central Park in New York, because New York is New York, which means shit is supposed to be better there. But Belle Isle was designed by the same guy, Frederick Law Olmstead, and it's even bigger than Central Park.

But a park isn't supposed to be dead silent like it was today. Peaceful, sure, at least in places. But not this dead silence. Then, after that first half hour, I was talking about? The birds started to fly toward the egg. Not just from the island, but from everywhere. There were hundreds, then thousands of them. But as many

of them as there were, there still wasn't a sound, not
even of their wings beating against the air. No
screeching. Nothing. They just flew right at the
egg…*and then they went through it.*

This lasted for nearly an hour as all these birds
disappeared into that mirrored egg without making a
sound and without complaint. Like they were happy
to go.

Then they were gone.

July 21, 2036
3:15 pm
Mayor Sondra Waymaker

In those science fiction movies, when
something like this happens, there's usually that
scene when the military arrives and saves the day
with all their guns and bombs, blowing the monsters
into a million pieces. Or like that end scene in
Independence Day when the selfless hero flies into
the belly of the beast with the Ultimate Monster
Killing Weapon attached. But in the end, you always
know that, one way or another, humanity is going to
find a way to win. Because we're humans and finding
a way to win is what we do, right? Dinosaurs might
let themselves get extinct, but humans don't lose.

And here in Detroit? Yeah, we take that defiant humanity thing seriously. We've endured just about everything you can throw at a city, from economic ruin to being the bitter laughingstock of the nation as the supposed one reason why you can't let Black folks run anything. And on top of that, we had the worst football team ever, the Lions.

But nobody's laughing now. Now, Detroit is where everybody wants to be. We're the poster child for a comeback story, and everybody *loves* a comeback story. In February, our beloved Lions won the Super Bowl for the third time, and it looks like the Tigers just might have what it takes to go all the way.

Or at least it looked that way until the egg happened. Now, who the hell knows? It's been a day-to-day thing for a few months now. When the egg first showed up back in May, a lot of us thought maybe this was the curtain call, not just for Detroit but maybe even for the world. I have to say, in a perverse kind of way, I felt kind of honored that if this was going to be the end of the world, death by egg, then to have Detroit be chosen as the ignition point could be taken as a point of pride. Obviously, we must have mattered if the alien invaders felt like they had to attack Detroit first. Because in the movies, isn't it always New York or Washington, D.C., where the center of the universe is supposed to be located?

But then days went by. And then, after a few weeks, folks are starting to figure out their own ways of wrapping their heads around the fact that a huge egg-shaped thing that swallowed all the birds is hovering above the Detroit River, and we have no idea what it ultimately wants or plans to do next. We're Detroiters, and in Detroit, we know how to adapt, plus you can't keep us scared for too long.

Still, dealing with something like this really isn't how I had imagined spending my first year in office. Like any politician, I had all these plans and had made all these promises during my campaign. And despite what a lot of folks say they think about politicians, my plan was to execute those promises to take Detroit to the next level and make it an even better city for all. Because I was born here, and I love this city, and I honestly feel like I was born to be mayor of this city. And judging by how wide a margin I won, most Detroiters think so too.

But now, excuse my language, I'm lookin' at the possibility of having it all undone by a fucking giant egg from another dimension.

November 21, 2036

8:16 am

Jason Richards

Reporter, Detroit Free Press

"How long do you want me to stay out here, George? It's cold as hell, I'm hungry, and I've been sitting in this van for hours. I didn't get breakfast 'cause I didn't think this assignment was gonna go this long, and my cell phone is running low for the same damned reason."

"You got another assignment or something? Somewhere else to be? And if your cell phone is so low, then why are you wasting battery power calling me?"

"How damned long you want me to stay out here?"

"All right, all right. Calm down, Jason. We just don't wanna miss this thing if it actually happens, right?"

"It was supposed to happen three hours ago, George. At least that's what you told me. Speaking of which, you never did tell me where you got that tip from, anyway. That this big thing was supposed to happen with the egg this morning, that was gonna blow everybody's mind and explain everything. Who told you that, anyway? Did somebody from the egg call you to give you the scoop? And how did the egg know you were the editor anyway? Why didn't the egg call me? I've been covering this story since it broke, and it's my byline on all those stories, not yours."

"I never said the egg called me, and don't worry about how I got the tip. Just worry about not missing that story. If it happens, this could be a career-maker, like how Watergate made Woodward and Bernstein, only way the hell bigger. I'm just lookin' out for you like I always have. You're welcome."

"Who in the hell are Woodward and Bernstein?"

"Are you serious? OK, never mind. Hey, you still haven't seen any other reporters anywhere, have you? Remember when they were all camped out there on the island 24/7, afraid to go home?"

"Yeah, I do. That was back when the story was interesting, when we all thought some cool-lookin' aliens were about to step out of that egg at any minute. But here we are, and the only half-decent story was when all those birds disappeared inside it. Other than that, it's been…"

"*Half-decent* story? All the birds disappear inside an alien craft hovering above the Detroit River, and months later, they still have not returned. And you call that a half-decent story?"

"OK. Yeah. It was a big deal. But you know how this business is, there has to be follow-up. Momentum. Something to keep it on the front of everybody's…wait. Hold up…."

"Jason? What is it?"

"Holy… fucking…*shit.* I'll call you back."

November 21, 2036
9:30 am
George Lane
Jason's Editor

"The birds are back, but they're not the same birds," is what Jason told me when he called back 15 minutes later.

"If they're not the same birds, then how can you say they're back?" I asked, wondering why he sounded so scared but also, as his editor, wondering how such a good reporter could be telling me something like this without realizing how it sounded.

"Because they're coming out of the egg, George. So it's gotta be them. Ever since all of them disappeared inside of that thing they've all been gone. But now there's hundreds of them. *Hundreds.* But the way they look…something's not…"

"What? Jason, when you say…"

"I gotta go. I gotta go *now.*"

November 21, 2036

9:32 am

The birds that disappeared into the egg on June 10 were ducks, geese, sparrows, robins, hawks, and even a few bald eagles. Birds that a Michigan resident would recognize if they had lived in the state any length of time. All beautiful in their own unique ways. This was why, when they suddenly became absent from the landscape and the skies above, lured away into some mystery of an alien contraption by a promise only they could hear, a growing sense of dread began to exhale itself across the city of Detroit like a poison cloud. Always thought of and referred to as intensely and strictly 'urban', as if those were the only definitions that could fit a location so less-than-white, the undisputed beauty of Belle Isle and its native wildlife insisted on how much more there was to Detroit's chronically misunderstood mythology.

But then the birds were gone. Whatever called to them from inside the egg promised better than their time spent this side of reality, so when given the opportunity to choose, they chose somewhere else. It wasn't long before the slim, bony fingers of self-doubt began to resume their chokehold around the throat of a city that needed nothing less than it needed this. After everything had finally begun to go right, after the corner was finally being turned.

Why would the birds leave us *now?* Was the question no one asked out loud, but that was etched onto grim faces drawn tight, working to resist the temptation and familiarity of failure.

But when the birds returned, sounding like the clarions of an undiscovered hell, their grotesquely twisted forms defining the winged shadows of a rage long-suppressed, that was no longer the question. Now the question was simple:

Why?

November 21, 2036

9:45 am

"Birds, Mommie. Birds outside."

"Huh? Naw, baby. No birds. All the birds are gone. But maybe one day they'll…"

"Birds. Outside."

Something in the urgent tone of her five-year-old daughter's voice made Faye Winston drop the plate she had been scrubbing back into the soapy water in the kitchen sink. She felt a small chill of premonition overtake her small frame as she stood upright. She felt stiff as she dried her hands on a worn blue towel, sighed, then tossed it aside onto the counter. She fixed her face into a comforting smile before turning to look at Simona, her little chocolate heart, who stood beside the breakfast table, pointing toward the glass sliding doors that framed the backyard porch. Simona wasn't smiling.

"Birds."

But the flock of raggedy-winged creatures that were now crowding into the backyard just beyond the porch didn't look like any sort of bird that Faye had ever seen. They were a dirty grayish Black, with eyes as Black and soulless as those of a shark. Measuring a head taller than Simona, their deformed bodies were semi-transparent, flickering erratically in and out of being like a broken electric sign. None of them made a sound as they continued to land on the grass, staring hungrily through the glass at Faye and her daughter as the two moved closer together.

But then Simona did a funny thing.

November 21, 2036
9:47 am

To Faye, Simona's mother, the creatures gathering in her backyard were something that should not exist anywhere outside of a bad dream. She felt herself begin to tremble as she held her daughter close, determined to protect her only child however she could. But then Simona tilted her head to the side as she leaned forward.

Simona was seeing something else entirely. What she saw were large, multi-colored parrots with feathers so brightly colored they seemed electric. Parrots had always been Simona's favorite bird, but she knew enough to know they didn't belong in Michigan – and parrots never grew that big. She started to raise the question, but then…

Comfort…?

Where was that voice coming from? Simona wondered.

"Simona? Baby? What is it?" asked Faye, who hadn't heard a thing.

Simona looked up over her shoulder at her mother, her eyes questioning and confused.

"Simona!"

Simona knew that mother's tone all too well. A reflexive, biological response was in the process of being formed…but then she heard it again.

Are you comfort? We want all of you comfort. Important.

"All of us?" asked Simona, turning away from her mother.

Not alone. You. Mother. All Comfort.

"Yes," she said, then giggled, as if someone had told her a joke.

There came a sound like a roomful of hissing snakes, growing steadily louder until Faye was forced to loosen her hold on Simona as she squeezed her eyes shut and clamped her left hand over her ear. Simona shrugged free of the remaining grip and took a step toward the parrots with their huge wings outstretched in welcome.

"No. I'm not scared."

Faye couldn't hear herself scream as her hands reached out after her daughter, her feet somehow locked in place. But soon the hissing ceased, and Simona was gone. So were the birds.

Faye was still screaming.

This Is How It Ends
Sunday, June 1, 2037
7:18 am
Day 365

My diary from yesterday:

Today is Day 364. Tomorrow, Day 365, is the day we have been told will be The Opening, when the egg will make itself known to us. One full year to the exact day after its appearance.

We haven't been told what to expect after Day 365. Or whether we should expect anything at all.

Yesterday was when I was sitting with my friend Gerry in Coco's Coffee shop over there on 3rd in the Cass Corridor (they're calling it that again), when he got up and practically ran away from me out the door and down the street. All I did was ask him what he thought about the egg, and that's all it took. He got this look on his face like maybe I had just cursed God, mumbled something I couldn't understand, and then took off like a rocket. That's when I noticed everyone else in the place was staring at me, and the first thing I wondered was how in the hell had they even heard what I said. Then I got pissed.

"Don't y'all have conversations of your own?" I asked loudly. "You got nothing better to do than judge me for what I said to somebody else you don't even know and got nothing to do with you, ain't none of your business?"

Real quick, they all turned back around and picked up wherever they left off, like nothing happened. The pause button got unpaused.

It was after that when I went home and wrote in my diary, same as I had every day since the egg had shown up. Because by the time I got home, it occurred to me why everyone was so much on edge, including Gerry, was because we were *all* on edge. Everyone in the city, and probably over there in Canada too, because the egg obviously wasn't just affecting us, hovering over the Detroit River for the past year. We all knew that the next day was when it was supposed to happen, The Opening, except that none of us knew any more than that. We didn't know what that meant, only that it was supposed to be something special.

And special ain't always good.

7:38 a.m.

Faye's Lament

That day when the birds came for Simona, and Faye had been rooted to the floor, unable to stop them from taking her baby girl, she screamed for two days straight without sleeping. That first moment, once the birds were gone and her feet were released from whatever invisible anchor had locked them into place, she ran to the sliding doors and tore them open, aiming her screams at an uncaring and unusually beautiful blue sky.

No one ever came by to see what Faye was screaming about. But no one complained either. Her neighbors just closed their windows tighter until the disturbance wore itself out. Those walking by kept lookin' straight ahead, though sometimes they picked up the pace.

This morning, on Day 365, Faye was on Belle Isle, sitting cross-legged on the ground, staring upward at the egg. She hadn't spoken a word since the day her scream faded away, leaving her throat raw

with a soreness that lived inside her body as both a
guest and reminder.

She was there, surrounded by hundreds of other
speechless women who were also sitting cross-legged
on the ground, staring upward with blank,
expressionless eyes at the alien craft that had called to
them earlier that morning. The message had been
clear, even if broken:

"They return now. Better. Motherlove.
Motherlove."

And at the exact time the egg had promised, the
egg opened itself like a large white mouth, and the
children spilled forth into the open air, seeming to
float more than a hundred feet above the river as they
made their way awkwardly down what must have
been a set of stairs that only they could see. Faye was
the first to stand as she squinted her almond-colored
eyes at the improbable sight unfolding before her on
that clear day when nothing was clear at all.

"Simona…" she whispered. And then, a little
louder, *"I don't see Simona."*

Moments later, a heavyset woman with waist-
length braids the color of storm clouds, who had been
seated nearby, stood up, raised an arm, and pointed
an accusing finger at the stumbling procession of

small beings that continued to exit the mouth of the egg.

"Those…those aren't…what *are* those…?"

Soon, the fearful chorus of anxious mothers grew in volume and rage as the egg's deceit made itself plain. One fled the crowd and dove into the river, determined to deliver her rage directly to the alien craft's front doorstep, but before she made it more than a few yards, something yanked and tossed her backward onto the island like a rag doll. Her breath exited her body in a painful wheeze as the crowd went silent. For the longest moment, everyone stared at the woman as she struggled to breathe normally again, and to make sense of what had just happened. And then the message came:

We make them better. Return to you better. Want make everything better. *Motherlove.*

The thing that had been Simona looked up at her mother through liquid Black eyes, took Faye's hand with long pale brown tentacles, and smiled.

"Home," it said.

The Gerruh

Michael Sees a Thing

"I want you to tell that officer exactly what you told me. He's not gonna believe it, but you need to tell him anyway, hear? Just make it ….different. Like…don't tell him *exactly* what you saw. OK? Just…I dunno. I just don't want them thinkin' you're crazy."

But it wasn't just the police officer who wasn't gonna believe me. Wasn't *nobody* gonna believe me about this shit. *Nobody.* What I saw that day? In the alley behind J's Market? Naw. Only way anybody was gonna believe that was gonna be if they saw it for themselves, and that next sighting of whatever the hell those things were didn't happen until a few weeks later. For now, though, I was on my own. Just me sitting there on the corner, middle of summer at night, still hot like a wet blanket you can't shake off, lookin' down at the street between my knees.

"You need to tell him, Michael! Otherwise, they gonna think you had something to do with this, man. You *know* how they are. You gotta give 'em somethin'. There's a man layin' dead over there, cut clean in two, and you the first one found him. So…"

"So why it gotta be me, though, James? Just 'cause I found him like this don't mean…"

"You ain't never been stupid, Michael, so don't start now. Why you didn't just keep walkin' I don't know. Maybe make an anonymous call later if you so concerned. But you was just standin' there starin' at the body when they drove by! Somebody said you'd been there for like ten minutes just starin'. So what you think was gonna happen with you puttin' yourself in the middle?"

All I could do was shrug my shoulders because I knew James had a point. And as for why all I could do was stand there and stare at those two halves of a body, I really didn't have any kind of answer. Or at least not an answer that would make any sense. Because it wasn't like I hadn't ever seen a dead body before. I'd seen a few, and come close to being one a few times as well. Price you paid for coming up in Detroit the way I did.

But those other bodies came about their end in natural ways, or at least natural for the street. Wrong place, wrong time, or else somebody figured it wasn't the wrong time after all. Most guys I knew had seen their share of shootings and bodies.

Not like this, though. Never like this.

* * *

Wasn't nothing special about J's Market. Just a corner market like any other you saw in the city, had a little bit of what you needed, but mostly not. But J's did have cigarettes, and that's why I stepped inside. Gotta have my Newports. Plus, it was a hot as hell summer day and J's actually had air conditioning. We didn't have AC at the house, so I took my time walking up and down those small aisles, making like I couldn't make up my mind, before the guy behind the plexiglass started knocking and pointing at me, letting me know I needed to get what I came in there for and get the hell out. An elderly lady who was standing in line turned to look at me and smiled.

"Don't pay that man no mind. He be like that to everybody."

I smiled back, wondering why Arletta didn't recognize me as long as we'd both been in that neighborhood. The shades maybe?

"Yeah, I know. Thanks."

Later, after I got my cigarettes, I stood out front for a minute while I tore open the pack, shook one

213

out, and lit it. The first draw made me cough, which for a sec made me wonder if I had somethin' going on in my lungs, but then I shoved that thought oughta my head. I had enough problems to worry about without adding fear of cancer to the heap. I shook my head, then made my way down the street in the direction of the alley. Most times, I wouldn't ever go down an alley because in the city, you didn't know what could jump off, and if something *did* jump off, there weren't that many options direction-wise for you to make any kinda getaway. It wasn't like in the movies, where you could just hop from one backyard to another. People in my neighborhood were ready for that shit; they either had dogs ready to take off your leg, the fence was too high or was otherwise blocked off, or there was somebody on the other side praying you'd jump in their yard so they could fire a shot dead in your ass.

Like I said, not the movies. But what I saw go walking into the alley that day made me wonder if I was having some kinda flashback, because I definitely did my share of certain drugs way, way back in the day. I always thought there was some sort of time limit on how long before you had to stop worrying about a flashback, but what I was seeing I knew I couldn't possibly be seeing, and that was the only explanation that made any sense.

It was tall, maybe close to seven foot, and its skin was bone white. I mean like unnatural white, not like any white person you've ever seen. Not even like an albino. This was something else. And the hair on its head wasn't hair, but more like a nest of skinny white snakes writhing around, but kinda floating too. I dunno. It was…I dunno. And this thing was wearing a long Black trenchcoat. This was a 90-degree day and humid like a jungle, and this thing was wearing a trench coat. A *Black* trench coat.

Just before it stepped into the alley, it looked over at me and kinda smiled, if that's what you wanna call it. Then this long blue tongue works its way past these razor-sharp needle-like teeth and real slow starts licking its lips.

Just before stepping into the alley, it nodded at me. Then it stood there, waiting. I nodded back because I figured I'd better. Then it was gone. I don't mean it walked away, I mean *it was gone.* Turned into some sort of vapor and faded away like steam.

I looked around to see if there was anybody else nearby who might have seen what I just saw, but it was one of those rare days when the street was empty. Wasn't a soul to be seen in any direction. But there was definitely somebody in that alley, because I could hear the screaming. Not close but far away, like it was coming from the next street over. That's when I dropped my cigarette and ran to see what the hell was going on, because that scream wasn't like what you heard when somebody was getting their ass whupped, or even stabbed, because I'd heard all that before. This was unlike any scream I had ever heard, and it gave me chills even with the heat.

When I got to the alley, I didn't register everything I was seeing at first, but I did see that there was a dude, about my height, except he was real muscular. Real dark-skinned brother wearing brown shorts and a sleeveless white undershirt. He was standing with his back up against a wooden slat fence, and he was pushing himself backwards so hard it was like he was trying to push himself through to the other side. There was blood all over his body like he'd been decorated by someone trying to do abstract painting.

Hovering in front of him about a foot off the ground was that bone-white creature in the trench coat, and the snake things on his head was going crazy snapping back and forth like they were mad. There was blood on them, too.

Yeah, I know. I should have run like hell right then and made myself forget about all of it. Just live my life the way it was supposed to be as if none of this had ever happened. But it did happen. So instead, I started walking toward the scene, my heart trying to beat its way out of my chest, not really knowing why except that to walk away would have been a mistake. Something like this needed a witness, even if nobody would ever believe me.

As I got closer, the brother turned his head to look at me. I hadn't ever seen fear like that. Ever. The creature was calm as could be, floating there in front of him.

"Shouldn't be here," he said, his voice croaking.

"It's OK, man," I said, knowing it was anything but.

He shook his head, confirming what I already knew. But then he said something else that caught me off guard.

"Ain't talkin' about me. Talkin' about *you. You* the one shouldn't be here."

"Looks to me like maybe shouldn't neither one of us be here, right? Like maybe both of us kind of in the wrong place at the wrong time. But if we just…"

And then the creature cut him in half. I don't even know how because it happened so fast. It wasn't with a knife or anything like that, and it wasn't with one of those Star Wars gadgets either. I don't know what it was. I heard it more than I saw it, a sort of crackling sound followed by a blue flash and a wave of heat, and then a stench like sulfur and shit. Next thing I knew, half the brother was falling one way, his other half the opposite.

The creature looked over at me and smiled. Again. My heart was hammering so fast I was sure I was having a heart attack.

"Everyone is where they are supposed to be at any given time," he said, his voice sounding dry and flat. "There is no wrong place, and there is no wrong time. Wherever you are, that is where you are supposed to be. Your friend was where he was supposed to be, and what happened was supposed to happen when it happened. Do you understand?"

That was a lot to take in; this thing speaking to me, saying what it said and sounding like it did. I didn't know how to respond, so at first I didn't say anything. I just stared.

"Do you understand?" it asked again, beginning to drift toward me. I figured I'd better say something, and damned quick.

"He wasn't my friend. I never even met him. I only came to see what that screaming was all about. Now I guess I know. Why you have to cut him in half, though? What the man do to deserve that?"

The creature stopped its forward progress in my direction, and I was grateful for that. It cocked its head to one side, then licked its lips slowly with that blue tongue, which now I could see was forked. For some reason, I got the feeling that it was amused by me.

"That is an interesting question. I have noticed this opinion among your kind that bad outcomes are the result of what is - or perhaps is not - deserved. And yet 'deserve' has nothing to do with it most of the time. This man was dispatched simply because his name was on a list. That is all."

"Wait…a list? What kind of list is this? And what are you?"

"We are Gerruh. The list is not your concern."

"We? But…"

"There is more to us than what you are currently a witness to. We are Gerruh."

Then I heard it in stereo, the other voice coming from behind me:

"Yes. We are Gerruh."

I jumped far enough to the side to where I could see both of these things at the same time. What must have been the twin was standing directly behind me, it's hand folded in front, the edges of its serrated teeth exposed through a thin smile.

"OK, now what's this? What do you guys want? I ain't done nothing to you, and I don't want nothing, so you ain't got to worry about me going to the police on this. Don't nobody around here call the police anyway. We pretty much handle shit on our own."

They both nodded, but said nothing. In a way, that was worse.

"You hear what I said? You ain't got nothing to worry about from me, man. You can ask around, and folks will tell you. I ain't the snitching type. Nobody around here is. So if you think…"

If you've ever seen Star Trek, then you would have an idea of what happened next. It was kinda like Beam Me Up, Scotty, except it was different. One minute they were hovering there lookin' at me with those creepy grins, the next they faded away into some sort of mist.

And this is what James thought I should tell the police?

The Gerruh Settle Up

The full, massive bulk of a smiling Rodeo leaned back in his squeaky, large black leather office chair with his arms behind his head, spit-shined Black cowboy boots propped up on the terrain of an expansive antique wooden desk decorated with carvings and designs of a precision and craftsmanship that you simply did not see anymore. These days, everything was all smooth lines and efficiency with no time for detail or any appreciation for art. A sign of the times is the way Rodeo saw it, or maybe a sign that he was getting old and his time was running short.

But his time wasn't over yet, as evidenced by the two strange-lookin' visitors who drifted into his office. Usually, his bodyguard -Truckhead - would accompany any visitor into the room, and whoever that visitor happened to be would most often try not to look as nervous or fearful as they actually felt.

Because that's the way most folks felt around Truckhead, which was why Rodeo had hired him.

With the Gerruh, the situation was reversed. After sticking his head in the door to let his boss know that company had arrived, Truckhead made himself scarce. Because aside from Rodeo, the Gerruh were the only other two beings in existence who actually scared him.

"Good afternoon," they said in unison, their voices creating a strange echo.

Rodeo nodded.

"You guys take care of things?"

"We are Gerruh," they said.

Rodeo chuckled, shaking his head.

"Right. Of course you are. You know, one of these days you and I are gonna have an actual conversation about shit. Maybe even get us a bite to eat somewhere. I mean, damn, after all these years and all the business we've done together, first with my father and now me, I don't think we've ever…"

"Will there be anything else?"

The genial smile faded from Rodeo's face. He felt the heat of his anger simmer just slightly, but he knew he couldn't let it show. With anyone else, he never would have sat still for being interrupted.

Didn't matter if he was rambling on about cat videos, you were gonna listen to Rodeo until Rodeo got through.

But this wasn't just anyone else, and Rodeo knew enough by now to know he had to tailor his reaction appropriately if he wanted to keep his largest business connection intact - and if he wanted to keep breathing. The Gerruh were literally the largest contract killers on Earth, *and* on Planet 10, their home turf, where they had all the critters and misfits scared half to death.

Rodeo was well aware of this, just like Rodeo was aware of everything else he needed to be aware of. This wasn't his first rodeo, so to speak. Rodeo was the son of Big Rodeo, Colorado's most notorious drug dealer, who somehow managed to avoid even a single day behind bars throughout his reign of more than twenty years, largely because few people, except those associates closest to him, even knew what he really looked like. Big Rodeo was a reputation with bodies - and body parts - of evidence broadcasting his fearsomeness scattered from one corner of the state to the other. And yet there was never quite enough evidence to tie him down, and never anyone willing to give a tip on his whereabouts at any particular time. Not even his enemies, which were more than a few. But not stupid enough to snitch on Big Rodeo.

Then came Soames, the cop who could not be stopped. Somehow, through all the roadblocks and scarce evidence, Soames managed to track down a photo of Big Rodeo - or of who he correctly guessed must have been Big Rodeo - and eventually bring him down.

But Soames had underestimated the staying power of family.

It was mostly in Denver where Big Rodeo's son, Rodeo, now ruled the family business, but in a far more flamboyant 'fuck-you-come-get-me' fashion. Ever since his father had been put away by Soames more than 10 years ago, Rodeo had kept a picture of his father's captor stapled to his wall as motivation - and for Soames to see every time he dropped by to harass the crew, so he would know that he wasn't the only one who could make good use of a photo. The first time Soames ever saw the pic, Rodeo could see how it unsettled him, and he used that fear to keep him warm on chilly nights. The picture was of Soames playing with his children in nearby Cranmer Park - and it wasn't taken from far away.

"Where the fuck did you get that?" he asked.

Rodeo shrugged at the time.

"Sometimes things just come my way. Don't really know why. I thought it was a nice shot of a friend, though, so there it is. Really is a nice shot of you, man."

Soames didn't need to say a thing. The look in his eyes said everything that needed to be said between them before he turned to leave, having managed to calm himself back down.

"You have yourself a nice day, Rodeo. Don't let anything happen to that picture."

Rodeo waved happily at Soames, even though he knew the cop couldn't see him as he walked away. He knew enough to know Soames wasn't the type to be taken lightly, but on that day, he wasn't worried. On that particular day, Rodeo knew he was the one on top.

But today, as his eyes focused on the twin Gerruh standing in front of him, hands folded crisply and neatly in front of them, he couldn't be sure where he stood. That was probably the most frightening thing about the Gerruh: you never really knew where you stood. There was no such thing as being in good with them; if you had a relationship, it was strictly transactional, and it involved murder. So long as you were paid up, then your odds of surviving the next day were better - unless someone somewhere paid more to have you erased. Because with the Gerruh, it truly was never personal, just business.

Which brings us back to the Gerruh's business-only question: "Will there be anything else?"

Rodeo shook his head.

"We're good, if you're sure I don't have to be worried about this guy walking around anymore."

The Gerruh regarded each other, then nodded.

"Show him, brother."

"No! No. I trust you guys. Like I said, we've been doing business together a long time and y'all ain't never missed a step. I was just talkin, that's all. And we got you covered with what you need by way of payment. Check with Truckhead on your way out. He's got your goodie bag."

The 'goodie bag' was a satchel full of Roscoe 21, the newest headsqueezer on the street, sold exclusively in the States courtesy of Rodeo, who inherited the contract with the manufacturer from the days when they used to make MayoMadd. Haley was a strange little dude who produced the drug with his son in a town called Justice, about three hours' drive due west. It was the kind of place where nobody asked any questions and everybody more or less minded their own business, so long as everybody was white. It served the purpose, because who would ever look to a small Colorado mountain town to be the manufacturer of not one but two of the most powerful, potent, and popular drugs the world had ever seen - and that hadn't even originated in this world?

The Gerruh grinned slightly, exposing a partial row of needle-sharp serrated teeth. Moments later, they became vapor. Rodeo heard Truckhead curse out loud, sounding more fearful than angry, which meant the twins had made their exit his way.

"Shoulda never got in business with them two," he said quietly to no one in particular.

He was shivering.

Who Was That Guy Anyway?

The day after the incident, I was sitting on the porch with James, still trying to process everything I saw. What are you supposed to do when you see something like that? Who are you supposed to tell? I told the cops some made-up story because James said I needed to give them *something,* and he was probably right. And after asking me a few questions that didn't even make sense - like 'when was the last time you saw the deceased ?' - they let me go. Except for that one cop who asked me the obvious:

"Why were you even here? You see a man lookin' like that, cut clean in half, and we find you standing here. I don't get why you wasn't long gone."

I shrugged, lookin' away from him.

"Scared, I guess. Wouldn't you be?"

I don't think the cops really wanted to know the truth about what had happened to get a man murdered in that way. Because cops are human too, and when you see something like that, all you want is to pray that whatever - or whoever - it is never happens again. That it was just one of those freak occurrences.

Because if it's not…?

But now, today, as me and James sat in a couple of folding chairs on the porch, barely feeling this July heat and humidity like you get in Detroit this time of year, I don't think either one of us believed that this was any kind of freak occurrence. I was the only person alive who had seen what actually happened, and James, as my best friend for more than twenty years since we were kids, was the only other human being on the planet who knew the truth. He knew it was the truth because I told him it was, and he knew I wouldn't lie about something like that. Plus, he knew my imagination just wasn't that big. I couldn't have made up any shit like that even if I had tried. I wasn't the creative or artistic type, and James wasn't either. We were just your average, basic brothers. That was it.

"So who was that guy anyway?"

James and I had been sitting there staring out at the street for close to an hour without saying a word because there weren't that many words to say until then. The one question that could tie it all together, and that might help us figure out what the hell was going on in our city.

"No idea, but I'm thinking maybe we should try and find out. Because whatever he did made some space aliens so mad they came down to Earth from wherever they came from and cut him in half. That's some serious shit."

James nodded.

"No doubt. So where do we start?"

"If dude was from around here, then somebody from around here knows who he is…was. If he ain't got family, he got somebody."

"Yeah, but we don't even have a name yet. How we gonna track a dude down and we don't even know his name?"

"Because he was cut in half, Mike. Folk don't know how or why; I'm the only one knows that. But no way could those cops keep a secret like that about a man split in two. And by now all kinda stories are makin' their way around these streets. Somebody knows who that boy was. We just gotta find 'em."

Shaking the Trees

For the next few days, James and I became 'hood detectives, which had an advantage over regular detectives because folk knew we weren't police. So that made them open up a bit more, especially if somebody they knew said we were all right.

Then again, the disadvantage was the same thing; we weren't police. Which could either mean 'why the fuck should I talk to you?', 'why the fuck you askin?' or the worst: 'who the fuck are *you?*'

Believe me, we got all that, even from some folk we figured would be more inclined to help us out. But that didn't stop us; it just made us more careful. And eventually, we started to get bits and pieces of info that actually led somewhere. Like the fact that the kid's name was Cecil St. James, who, as it turned out, had actually been a few grades ahead of me in elementary school. His face hadn't been familiar at all when I saw him in the alley, but then I guess nobody quite looks like themselves when they're about to get killed by a space alien.

"So how well you know Cecil?" I asked the youngster standing outside the filling station, smoking a cigarette on a gray Sunday morning.

It had been Sam, whose real Arab name I couldn't pronounce, who told me from behind the protective glass that this kid standing outside probably knew more than he did. He said he thought it was too bad what happened, but that from what he'd heard, just from chatter inside the store, Cecil might have been involved in some stuff that set him up as a target.

But back to the kid standing outside, who was trying to act like he didn't hear me talking to him.

"Yo! Nigguh, you deaf?" asked James. I really wished he hadn't come out his bag like that.

The kid gave both of us a slant-eyed look, indicating he was considering a few things that I probably would have been considering too, given a similar situation. I noticed a young brother standing not too far away, closer to the street, who was taking close notice. We needed to calm the waters and close this deal quick.

"Look, we just wanna talk to you for a minute, then we're outta here, all right? You probably heard about that kid got killed not far from here. Got sliced in half. Don't know if you heard that part."

For a moment, I caught that look of fear in the kid's eyes as he took a step back. Then he shook his head as he took a long drag off his cigarette.

"Man, I don't know nothin' 'bout no damned…"

"Yo, I was there when it happened. All right? Yeah. I was standin' right there when that shit happened, and in case you were wondering, this wasn't no normal type shit. Not at all, my brother. 'Cause what I saw was something that couldn't happen, not in the real world. But it did. 'Cause I saw it."

The young brother from farther away was taking steps in our direction when the one we were talking to made a stiff-arm gesture indicating for his boy to slow up. The dude cocked his head to one side,

I guess questioning the decision, but our guy shook his head.

"Nigguh, go back to where you was. I'm good."

His boy shrugged his shoulders, then went back to his post. I took the opportunity to add to the comfort level while I had it.

"What's your name, man? If you don't mind me askin."

The boy gave me a hard look, searchin', before he responded.

"Darius. So what you mean when you say this wasn't no normal type shit? What you see? You see who did it?"

I nodded.

"Yeah. Except it wasn't a who. It was something else."

Right then, I almost lost Darius as he gave me a quick up and down look, then twisted his face up ugly.

"Nigguh, get away from me with that scifi shit. You must think I'm…"

"Yo, you think your boy Cecil deserved what happened to him? You think he coulda done anything that would make somebody wanna do something like that to him?"

"Man, don't *nobody* deserve nothin like that, but I don't even know if you tellin the truth because way I heard it…"

James jumped in.

"You already know the way you heard it ain't the way it was. You *know* this, dude. And you know we ain't making this up. 'Cause why would we? What's in it for us to be out here saying something like this? The reason nobody else is saying what we're saying is because nobody else saw it except for my man here and the police, and they ain't gonna tell you a damned thing. And for sure, they not gonna tell you some kid got sliced in half, right? But I'm tellin' you because I figure this isn't the kinda stuff needs to be kept secret when it's our lives at risk with whatever it is would do something like this, right? So if there's anything you can tell us, man, it would really be appreciated."

Darius was staring straight ahead at something that nobody else could see except for Darius. I could tell he was shook.

"Cecil? Me and him, we wasn't really boys or nothin like that, OK? I mean, we didn't hang. But yeah, we did know each other. Both out here doing what it is we do. I had respect for him actually, because he been doing this way longer than me, or at least until…anyway. You gotta have heart to last in this thing, and he been out here since he was a shorty."

I nodded, kinda hoping he would hurry up and get to the point, but afraid that if I pushed too hard, he might spook and then we'd lose him.

"Yeah, OK. I get that. So you're saying he knew his way around these streets, then."

"Oh yeah. Cecil? Most definitely."

"Um-hm. Yeah, that's good to know. So what you think could have happened for him to get caught up like this? You think maybe somebody caught him slippin'?"

Darius took a long, slow drag on what was left of his cigarette, then flicked it away.

"Word is Cecil made a bargain with the devil, and he couldn't keep it."

"Bargain with the devil? You mean like how when people say so-and-so made a deal with the devil and …"

"I mean what I said; I mean Cecil made a deal with the devil. The devil for real. That's what I heard. Most of us out here just sellin' what we sell; that rock, some weed, maybe some other stuff, but that's mostly it. The dudes sellin' Roscoe makin' three-four times what the rest of us makin' 'cause it's the hottest thing out here. Been that way for a while. But you can't be fuckin' up with Roscoe. You make mistakes, and you disappear. I heard Cecil was startin' to make mistakes. Now I know I heard right."

"So you're telling me that Cecil ain't the first? You tellin me…"

"I've told you all I'm gonna tell you. I tell you anything else, and it's gonna be me split in half, you find in some alley somewhere."

"Wait, lemme ask you just one more thing; when I told you I knew how Cecil got killed, I said it was a what, not a who, and you said you didn't wanna hear none of that scifi shit. Now it sounds like you been knowing for a while something out here hasn't been adding up. So…"

"Man, everybody out here scared, all right? Ever since Roscoe hit the streets, there's been stories about weird shit going on. But I ain't never seen none of this with my own eyes and I been trying not to think about it because that's the only way to keep takin' care of business. You start listening too close to what's gettin' whispered out here, and it will cost you. So if you and your boy wanna dig deep on this thing, then that's on y'all, but I'm done. Now y'all gotta step, hear me?"

The Gerruh Do Another Hit

"What is it that they call a particular brand of disturbance, brother?"

"I believe it is referred to as a ruckus."

"A ruckus! Yes. So I believe the time has come for you and I to commence a ruckus. We have been carrying on our business in the shadows of this city for long enough. It is time we show ourselves. Fear will take care of the rest."

The Gerruh sat calmly inside an impossibly Black Camaro, engine rumbling, that was parked in front of a small white frame house on Detroit's East Side. The windows, equally Black, were rolled up. The twins were smiling.

"It always does, brother. It always does. So what do you propose?"

The Gerruh regarded his other with a broader smile that stretched into something resembling a hideous joker's mask, snake-like blue tongue flicking then caressing the edges of his thin lips. He opened the passenger-side door and stepped out of the car.

"Perhaps you should turn off the engine. I have a feeling this visit may take a little longer than our normal collections."

"I see. And what is the reason for the extended visit? Business or pleasure?"

"Perhaps a wee bit of both."

The Gerruh chuckled dryly as he turned the key, then slid it out of the ignition.

"A wee bit of both indeed."

The weather outside was warm and sticky, the temperature reaching to within a few degrees of 90. A typical Detroit August mid-afternoon in the summertime. As the Gerruh stood side-by-side in front of the now silent Camaro, they placed their hands one on top of the other in front of them and studied the red-painted door of the house they planned to visit. It was one of only three houses on the block. The other two were abandoned, surrounded by sprawling lots covered by runaway waist-high weeds. A young boy on a tricked-out bicycle wearing cutoff jeans and a white T-shirt came pedaling furiously around the corner, at first appearing not to notice the odd couple who regarded him with interest.

Then suddenly he jammed the brakes, not more than five feet away from the visitors with the bone white skin and the thin ropes of writhing hair that hissed and snapped. He was sucking on a lollipop.

The Gerruh bowed slowly in unison.

"Good afternoon, little one."

The boy didn't respond, choosing instead to position his foot on the pedal in preparation to achieve maximum acceleration in a matter of seconds if need be. He took the lollipop out of his mouth. His expression framed a slight frown on his caramel-brown face as he cocked his head to one side, as if to determine the reality of what he was seeing - and to gauge the threat. He pointed a small finger.

"You them, ain't you?"

The Gerruh looked at one another, then back at the youngster, who seemed to be accusing them of something.

"I'm sorry? Who is 'them'? I'm afraid we don't understand."

The finger continued to point as the boy started to nod, his frown deepening.

"Yeah, you is. You *them.* You the Roscoe people. They say ain't nobody never seen what y'all look like or live to tell about it. Damn."

The Gerruh drifted closer to the youngster, then leaned in to where their faces were mere inches away.

The attempt to mask his fear, which had been holding up fairly well, began to melt, distorting the child's facial features like hot wax.

"Well, if no one has ever lived to tell about it, what do you suppose the future holds for *you*, my young inquisitive friend?"

The lollipop dropped to the ground.

"Are you gonna kill me?" he whispered. "But I'm only a kid."

The Gerruh straightened back up, tilted their heads back, and laughed. It was a dry, noiseless laugh that chilled the air.

They shook their heads.

"You will be the first!" they said, their long arms stretched outward and raised in an expression of joyful celebration.

"The first what?"

"TO LIVE!"

Without waiting to ask why he had been spared, the youngster slammed his foot down on the pedal and within moments was speeding away down the street, lookin' back only once over his shoulder, the terror dancing in his eyes.

"Run along now, child. *Run and tell the world.*"

* * *

"So, should we knock, brother? Or should we simply go through the door?"

The Gerruh seemed to consider the choices for a moment before regarding his other as they stood together at the foot of the small set of steps that led up to the white frame house they had been assigned to visit.

"I believe we should knock, brother. That would be best. Although admittedly it would be so much more entertaining to witness the look of fear on Mr. Johnson's face if we materialized ourselves before him inside his own home, knocking is the proper thing to do. I suspect he will raise his voice to a high level once he sees us out here, and this will attract the necessary attention of any passersby."

"But the homes are vacant, and the streets do appear to be empty. The young being has hastily departed."

"A temporary condition. If he screams, they will come. Also, I believe our young messenger is even now spreading the good word of our arrival throughout the land."

The Gerruh chuckled as he reached toward the well-worn wooden door.

"This is most likely true, brother. Well thought-out, as usual."

A few moments after knocking, they could hear heavy footsteps approaching the door, accompanied by what sounded like a flurry of very ugly words.

"I *told* that motherfucker don't never come by this house again, but a nigguh just don't wanna listen, so I'm just gonna have to put my foot up his…"

The door flew open, revealing a fire hydrant of a man with fiery eyes, skin the color of coffee with too much cream, wearing athletic shorts and bare-chested. His mouth was open wide, large white teeth on display, prepared to spew a heated stream of invective designed to melt whatever got caught in its path - except for what he saw standing in front of him.

The invective froze mid-delivery, exactly halfway between the occupant's lips and the highly amused twin faces of the Gerruh.

"Please, Mr. Johnson. May we come in?"

The invective shriveled like dry leaves, then slowly dissolved into the sudden silence before fading away.

Mr. Johnson closed his mouth as he looked from one to the other, then back again. He began to tremble slightly.

"Just Billy," he said meekly. "Y'all can...who...?"

"We are Gerruh. We are here to collect a very important debt. Please, if we can all just step inside and settle the matter."

"Oh, holy Jesus, Father God, and Mary too. Y'all are *them.* I been hearing things, but I ain't been believing. I thought..."

"*Inside,* Mr. Billy. Kindly, of course."

"It's just Billy," he whispered, as he stepped to the side, allowing his odd-lookin' visitors to enter.

Once inside, the Gerruh looked around the front room with obvious curiosity, seeming to take note of every little thing in view, from the large flatscreen TV attached to the wall, occupying nearly the entire size of that wall, to the small sculptures and family photos that occupied the fake wood coffee table squatting uncomfortably in front of the emerald green couch.

"Do you guys wanna.."

"We prefer to stand. But by all means, have a seat, Mr. Billy. Your couch does appear to be comfortable."

Billy nodded as he slowly made his way to ease his compact bulk down onto the furniture, never once taking his eyes off the Gerruh.

"Yeah. I guess. Kinda old so…you know…it's broken in…"

The Gerruh nodded in unison, seemingly sympathetic to Billy's dilemma.

"Indeed. Yes. Perhaps some newer furniture is in your future, Mr. Billy! What do you think of that?"

Billy reached for the large Black mug of coffee on the coffee table, which was half full, and drank the rest in one large gulp. He burped.

"' Scuse me. But yeah. That would be cool, I guess. So y'all gonna buy me…"

"We are not. As stated before, we are here to collect on a specific debt that you owe to Mr. Rodeo. It appears he has been trying to reach you for some time now, and you have been ignoring his attempts to contact you in regard to said debt. So he has sent us as a means to more emphatically demonstrate Mr. Rodeo's determination to settle, as in collect, this outstanding balance."

Billy was beginning to sweat.

"Rodeo sent you? You know, he might have *told* you that he's been trying to get a hold of me, but that ain't true. I mean, how hard am I to find, right? You guys just walked right up to my door, and I even opened it, and here I am! So if Rodeo wanted his money back, all he needed to do was…"

"Stop, Mr. Billy. I am afraid you are embarrassing yourself. To rectify this situation, all you need to do is to produce what you owe, and we will be on our way."

"Yes. We will be on our way," echoed the twin.

"He heard me, brother. There was no need."

"My apologies, brother."

"Noted."

There was a long moment of relative silence, broken only by the overlarge television on the wall where a western was playing. The Gerruh stared at Billy as Billy continued to sweat, his mouth hanging open, waiting for the right words to set him free. Those words never came.

"Mr. Billy? Did I fail to make myself clear?"

Billy closed his mouth. Shook his head.

"It's just that…if you could maybe give me a little more time, right? Or ask Rodeo if he can give me more time. You know what? Why don't we call him? Yeah, we can call him right now and ask him if he can just give me another week, and then if I don't have it by …will you guys *please* stop shaking your heads like that! Just hear me out. See…"

"I am afraid there will be no hearing out. We are the last stop, Mr. Billy. We are Gerruh. We are always the last stop. Those whose ill fortune it is to receive our visit, we are most often the last thing they see. And unfortunately, this does appear once again to be the case in this sad instance. Are you prepared, Mr. Billy?"

"I told you it's just Billy! And hell no, I'm not prepared!"

The Gerruh nodded, once again twisting their facial features into an awkward attempt to appear sympathetic.

"No one ever is, Mr. Billy. No one ever is."

"No 'mister'! I said it's just…

The sound of Billy being sliced in half was a sickening, wet sound that thankfully did not last long before the two halves fell in opposite directions on the couch, which began to thirstily absorb the flood of red into its color scheme.

The awkward look of sympathy had dissolved into a more comfortable expression of calm contempt.

"So who is next, brother?"

* * *

Over the next three weeks, the Gerruh went about their business with a bloody efficiency as they whittled their way through the list of drug debtors who had made the mistake of thinking (hoping, wishing) that Rodeo was the kind of forgetful drug lord who may have overlooked their delinquency, or just let it slide. Where they may have received that impression could be anyone's guess, but in each instance during the course of their visits, the Gerruh made it part of their mission to clarify whatever misconceptions may have led to those delinquencies - followed by their erasure of those responsible.

Also, in each instance, the Gerruh knew it was important that each execution be a message. And the message, quite simply, was *'Don't'*. The Gerruh's calculation was that this approach was merciful, because the sheer terror created by a sudden wave of executions conducted by what appeared to be space aliens in broad daylight provided the required sense of urgency to remaining debtors to settle their debts with sweaty smiles and a begged apology.

"I believe our assignment is done, brother," said the Gerruh to his other as they strolled away from their final execution. The location was a nine-year-old's birthday party on the city's west side in Palmer Woods on a beautiful Saturday afternoon attended by a large crowd of wailing children and their terrified parents. The victim, now split in two on either side of a huge blood-spattered birthday cake, had been the 9-year-old's father.

"No more names on the list then?"

The Gerruh shook his head.

"None for now."

"And you still believe this will work? Sparing the one? Didn't we already spare the child?"

"That was a child, brother. Too easily dismissed by the adults. This will leave little room for doubt of our intention."

The other nodded his head in clear satisfaction.

"Then I suggest we find ourselves something to eat."

"Agreed. Something special for a very special occasion."

Their laughter sounded like an agitated nest of snakes writhing in dry leaves.

What Is A Gerruh?

So where *did* the Gerruh come from? Were they really from the arid Dregs region on Planet 10, their planet of origin, just outside the notorious Vivacious 5 Sector? To date, the only answer seems to be that nobody knows for sure.

There is no record of them as infants, and the first recording of them as being in existence only occurred after they had grown old enough to pin a younger critter against a wall and demanded that he sing the song he hated most at the top of his lungs. According to reports, a few passersby attempted to step in and assist the poor victimized child, only to think better of it once the Gerruh focused their vicious attentions on them instead, simply by each of them wagging a finger simultaneously while shaking their pale heads in warning. The warning was followed by a chilled smile featuring two pristine rows of shark-like serrated-edge teeth.

From that day forward, the Gerruh slowly established themselves as an evil force to be reckoned with - even as children. The one time they were actually taken into custody by a particularly bold keystone (a 'keystone' was a police officer on the Vivacious 5 Sector, and this one later disappeared and was never heard from or seen again), the pair was asked during questioning about who their parents were and where did they live. The questions had to be repeated three times before one of them (according to the report) leaned forward and was said to have uttered the following:

"We are not like you, my brother and I. You must understand this. We don't need the same things, we don't want the same things, and we fear nothing. Where do we live? Nowhere and everywhere. Where were we born? Again, I say nowhere and everywhere. Who were our parents? We came into this world because this is the world we chose, and that is all anyone needs to know. Everything we do is *our* choice. Even our birth. You might say we are the ultimate control freaks."

Gerruh Sightings on the News

"Yo, James, you gotta come out here, man. The news has got this guy sayin' he saw the same thing we saw. And he don't look good."

"What you mean he don't look good? Like he sick or somethin'?"

"Man, finish fixin' your sandwich and come out here. Quick."

* * *

"Thanks, Jennie. As you know, we have been reporting on these mysterious murders over the past few weeks, where each of the victims was apparently cut in half. Police still say they have no leads, not only about the possible identity of a suspect, but they're not even sure about the method of execution. Simply put, and without being too graphic for the sake of our viewers, they just don't know how the murderer is doing what he or she is doing. They have never seen anything like this.

"Well, tonight we have what could possibly be a break in the case with this exclusive report coming to you live from Gordon Park on Detroit's West Side. We are here with Darius Ramsey, who says that not only has he seen the killers, but that he was intended to be a victim himself, except that he was spared for a very special purpose. Darius, could you tell us more about who the killers are? And why were you spared?"

"Ummm…yeah. Well, I guess the first thing I wanna say is that this is gonna sound crazy, and I don't blame nobody for not believing any of it. Because if I hadn't seen it for myself, I never would have believed it either. I also wanna say that, you know, that I'm in my right mind. I used to take drugs, but that was a long time ago so…"

"And Darius, we appreciate your honesty, but if you could just tell us more about why…"

"Yeah…yeah, OK. So you were the one reported that story about that little kid who said he saw some space monsters over on the East Side and that he talked to them? He even described what they looked like."

"Yes, I remember, but…"

"And the way you reported it was like it was kinda cute, and this cute little kid probably had what you called an overactive imagination? Right?"

"Yes…"

"Um-hmm. Well, y'all shoulda listened to that little kid, because wasn't nothing overactive about that imagination. He didn't imagine a (bleeped out) thing. Because what that boy described is what I saw, both of them, and they call themselves the Gerruh. I don't know where it is they come from, they didn't tell

me anything about that. But they (bleeped out) sure don't come from anywhere around here. Not lookin' like that. Skin white as chalk, snakes for hair, and those forked blue tongues, I ain't never seen…"

"Darius, I want to thank you for sharing, but I think we will have to…"

"I knew you wouldn't believe me, and that's OK. That's why I wasn't all the way straight with you the first time you asked me what I saw is because you woulda never come out here. But let me say this one thing, please, because if I don't then they're gonna kill me. And that's for real. And it won't matter to you because I know I don't matter to you, but I'm telling you this is for real."

"You do matter to me, but please make it quick."

"Thanks. Michael? And James? Yo, I don't know y'all, and I don't know why they told me this, but if you're watching this report right now, and I really hope y'all are, then the Gerruh said they know what you're doing. They wanna meet with you because…"

"Thank you, Darius. I hope you'll let us know if anything else develops. Meanwhile, please take care of yourself. Jennie? Back to you."

* * *

"So what you think?" asked Michael.

James shook his head slowly, staring at whatever the next news story was, but not really seeing or hearing any of it.

"Man, I don't know. *Those things know about us.* You know? *Shit.*"

Michael nodded.

"Yeah. It's messed up. But then maybe it's not such a bad thing."

James looked at Michael as if he was one of the Gerruh himself.

"Not such a bad thing? *Not such a bad thing?* Man, what the fuck are you talkin' about right now? Two murderous creatures from outer space who like to split folks in half just sent us a message through live TV that they're coming for us, and you sittin here sayin' maybe this ain't so bad?"

"Except they didn't say they were comin' for us, James. Or at least that's not what that guy Darius said they told him. He said that they knew what we were doing and that they wanted to meet. That's a different thing."

"Oh. Yeah. Right. So like, you thinkin' maybe they wanna pick us up for ice cream or some shit.

Congratulate us on our outstanding detective work. Like that. Is that what you thinkin'?"

Michael chuckled.

"I don't think they can do ice cream with those tongues they got. But I also think that if they wanted to kill us, they coulda done that already. Without making the news. You think they sent messages to those other guys they killed to give them a heads up? Naw. So something else is up. I don't know what, but something."

"So maybe you're right, but even if you're right, that doesn't mean it's something good. Those things do *not* look like the types to be bearers of good news. Plus, they didn't say where it is we're supposed to meet. How are we supposed to know the place or time?"

"Somehow, I don't think they'll have a problem finding us, James. They seem pretty resourceful to me."

Michael and James Meet the Gerruh

Somebody was knocking, and I knew. I just…knew…

It had been nearly a week since that broadcast when the Gerruh had sent their message. Since that time, I hadn't been able to get hardly any sleep, and same went for James. He had his own crib, but I'd been letting him stay with me since the broadcast. Figured maybe we were safer together, but mostly figured whenever they showed up, they were gonna want to meet with both of us. And we really didn't want to have to have a conversation with those things one at a time.

The knock came again. What was scary about it was that normally, if somebody knew you were home, or figured you were, they would knock harder the second time, or yell out your name. But this knock was soft and patient, like whoever this was wasn't the least bit worried that I was gonna answer the door.

James, who had been trying to get a few winks in on the couch, was sitting up ramrod straight in his boxers, staring at the door. It was just starting to get light outside, which you could see through the little diamond-shaped glass at eye level. Normally, when somebody knocked, I went to look through the diamond to see who it was, but this time I just stood back, feeling my heart starting to race.

Knockknockknock.

"We have other ways to make entry, but we would prefer if you simply let us in, Mr. Michael."

I could feel my heart trying to beat its way out of my chest.

"Put your pants on, James. And your shirt."

"Huh?"

"Put your clothes on, man. I gotta let these things in."

"Oh."

While James started putting on his clothes, I walked towards the door. It was weird because I felt like my legs were moving forward with no real direction from me. So when I got to the door, it was like I wasn't quite sure how I got there. But I still opened it.

And there they were, their hands placed neatly one on top of the other, and wearing those smiles that gave me goose bumps the size of molehills.

"Good morning, Mr. Michael. I believe the term I have heard some of your young people use is, 'appreciate you.' For opening the door, of course."

I nodded.

"Sure. So come on in, if you're comin'."

I guess the sound they made was supposed to be a laugh, based on the way their smiles stretched, but far as I could tell, wasn't nothing funny. I wanted to get this overwith as soon as possible - and to stay alive.

"Y'all want something to drink? Coffee? Water?"

They shook their heads.

"Your generosity is noted, but will not be necessary."

"OK then. You want some chairs?"

"Again, this is not necessary, but you and Mr. James may sit on the couch."

"Yo, man, it's just James and Michael," said James, lookin' a little irritated, which I thought was a mistake. "Ain't no 'Mister' in front of it."

The Gerruh exchanged a look with each other that didn't exactly make me feel comfortable. Then they looked at James.

"That is exactly the same thing Mr. Billy said when we paid him a visit not long ago. He was rather emphatic about it, wasn't he, brother?"

"Yes. Emphatic."

"Who the hell is Mr. Billy?" asked James.

"He is dead, Mr. James. He was not able to appropriately settle a debt he owed, so now he is dead. But we can refer to him simply as Billy if that would make you more comfortable.”

James was a dark-skinned brother, but I stood right there and watched him go at least three shades lighter before he sat down on the couch. I took that as my cue to do the same.

“OK. I understand the point you tryin’ to make. But we don’t owe you guys any money, so why you here? What is it you want?”

“Actually, we came to ask you a similar question.”

“You wanna know why we’re here?”

The Gerruh shook their heads.

“We want to know what you want. You both have been following us ever since Mr. Michael bore witness to my termination of Mr. Cecil in the alley. Also, for an unpaid debt, I might add. Rest assured that our actions always have reasons attached. We are not random actors.”

My first attempt to speak came out like a hoarse rattle, so I had to clear my throat several times. Then I looked from one Gerruh to the other.

“What we want is what James just said; we want to know why you’re here. Because it’s obvious you’re not from here, and by ‘here’ I mean Planet

Earth, not just Detroit, although I wanna know how you ended up here too. So wherever you're from, what is it that made you want to take the trip, because I'm pretty sure it wasn't a vacation."

The Gerruh stared for a long time, not moving a muscle and hovering a few inches above the floor in front of us like a hologram. I was starting to think maybe they were ignoring my request - or preparing for an answer that we wouldn't like.

"What harm could it do, brother?" said one, maybe responding to a question the other one asked telepathically. I watched a lot of sci-fi.

The other one sighed, then shrugged its shoulders, which struck me as weird.

"None, I suppose. Proceed."

"Proceed where?" I asked.

"You have questions. Ask them."

James and I exchanged glances. This was what we wanted, but now that it was here…

"You will not get another chance, and you should know that no one before you has been afforded this opportunity. We are the best at what we do, which means we rarely have time to answer questions from a lesser species, but for some reason, you intrigue us. I advise you to proceed with your inquisitive intentions."

"Question Number One," asked James, and I could hear that edge creeping back into his voice. "What the hell makes you think we are a lesser species? Just because you can kill us so easy, or because you so damned ugly?"

"James, seriously?"

"Not to worry, Mr. Michael, we take no offense. The question is a simple one, and fortunately so is the answer; we believe we are a superior species because of our superior efficiency and because we are not tethered to our emotions in the way that you purebloods are. This means we are able to successfully complete our required tasks at a significantly higher rate. Ugly? I advise you to check your mirror."

"Ouch," I said.

"Purebloods?" said James.

"That is what you are called on our home planet, Planet 10. We primarily reside in the Dregs region, although we tend to find more work in the Vivacious 5 sector. The Dregs is similar in some ways to your deserts."

"So then that's where you guys are from originally? Planet 10?" I asked.

They shook their head, and I could feel their mood change. When they walked in the door, they seemed relaxed, probably because they knew they didn't have anything to worry about. But now I could tell they were tense. Those skinny snake things on their heads were starting to make a noise like a field of crickets.

"We were created here. Long ago. Before the critters. Part of an experiment."

"Wait…*what the hell you just say?*"

"We are not surprised you have not heard of this. For obvious reasons, this experiment was not made public. The intent was to create a more servile life form. We were the first draft of that experiment. You might say things did not quite go as planned. When the originators saw what we had become and that we could not be course-corrected, we were dispatched to the wilderness of Earth, and then eventually to Planet 10, where all the rejected and failed experiments have been housed."

"Jesus. This is…*Jesus…*"

"So then, this business that you guys are in. Because you're like debt collectors, right? Is this some kinda revenge thing for that experiment that went wrong? You trying to get back at Earth folks for that?"

"Hardly. We do this work because it is in our nature and because we enjoy it. It is a joyful thing to be feared, and we are the most feared beings on all of Planet 10. It is now our hope to expand our reputation to your planet, and Detroit seemed like a natural place to start. We also have interests in Colorado, but there is something about this place, Detroit."

"And why would you want to start here?"

"Because Detroiters do not scare easy."

You might say that was an ice breaker. For what felt like a long while, nobody said anything. Then we all broke out laughing, us sounding like how laughing is supposed to sound, and the Gerruh sounding like, well, how it's not. But they were laughing is the thing. Because how many folks would ever be able to tell the story about sharing a laugh with the most murderous creatures in the galaxy?

A New Job

Sometimes your life takes the kind of turn that you just can't explain, because maybe you don't want to. Like that kind of job you get after being broke for so long that pays you all the money you ever wanted, but maybe it has some guilt attached. Maybe like that kind of job you and your friend both get. By coincidence, you know. And maybe your friend's name is James.

So James and I were sitting in my brand new little red Corvette with all the toys and whistles. We were both wearing shades, and I was smoking a cigarette with my tinted window rolled down just enough. We were parked in front of a large house in the English Village neighborhood that looked like there ought to be butlers and maids running around inside. The garden out front, all by itself, was probably more square feet than my crib on the West Side, and I'm guessing this individual probably had three or four little red - and blue, and black - Corvettes stored away all polished and shiny inside that mini-mansion garage, right beside the Rolls and the Mercedes.

"So what you think, Michael? You ready?"

"Lemme finish my cigarette. Then I'm good."

"OK. And just so I don't screw it up on our first job, tell me again what it is them Gerruh want us to do here. Because this isn't my kinda neighborhood, and I don't know anybody live in a neighborhood like this, so I'm feelin' kinda nervous, and I don't wanna say the wrong thing."

"Understandable. So let me do the talkin' this first time out. You just stand right beside me, maybe a step back. Hands crossed in front, one over the other, like how they do, lookin' like you ready to crack a neck if you need to. And lookin'' like you belong in that sweet new suit."

"Right, right. OK. I can do that."

"Look, all the Gerruh want us to do is make an introduction. They payin' us so they can step back more in the shadows, which is what they prefer, right? So we're like the face of the Gerruh here in Detroit. Which means that pretty soon folks gonna be steppin out of our way from a block away because of who we represent. Sometimes we may have to do things, but so what? You think Dan Gilbert, that multi-millionaire developer, ain't never had to do things? You don't get that kinda paper without doing things, and we know this. So let's get to work."

James took a deep breath, blew it out slow. Then he smiled. Gave me that look.

"Yeah. Let's get to work."

The Wall

In 1941, the Birwood Wall was built in Detroit. The purpose of that wall, which was built by white Detroiters, was to keep the Black neighborhoods separate from the white neighborhoods. So segregation. But the wall was also built because it was hard to sell those nice homes to nice white families if Black folks were living as neighbors, because nice white families didn't want Black folks as neighbors. So economics.

The Wall is a story that came about when I let my mind wander, and I started to think about 'what if...?' As in, what if the Birwood wall had been built around the entire city of Detroit? And what if the Black people inside, over time, started to tell themselves that they had been the ones to build the wall, and then began to rewrite their own history to make their plight easier to swallow?

Science fiction, fantasy, horror, and alternative fiction almost uniformly spring from the question created by those two little words: what if? Detroit

Stories Quarterly (DSQ), which first began publishing in 2018, was created to explore alternative ideas and visions of Detroit not tethered exclusively to reality. It was the question of 'What if?' that launched our magazine, and that keeps it going to this day. Because sometimes the best way to see what's right in front of you is to view your world through another lens.

Here. Try these on.

"You think Granma's crazy when she says that, don't you? Don't lie. I can see it all in your face, the way it's screwed up tight like a rat. So if you're gonna say it, just go ahead and say it, Marlon. Won't change a thing, 'cause truth don't change. But you gonna believe what you gonna believe, no matter."

I could feel my stomach starting to squeeze, just like it always did whenever my grandmother and I had this conversation. Which is why I wished she would drop it because we both knew she didn't have much time left, and I didn't want us spending our last days, weeks, or months together arguing about whether or not there was some long-lost race of white people on the other side of the wall.

I don't even care, to be honest. But Granma swears it's the truth, and that she saw them – lots of them – when she was a kid growing up in pre-dawn Detroit before the wall got built. She even says that it was the white people who built the wall, not us. But that didn't make sense, because…how? The last recorded sighting of a white person in Michigan was in 2245 way up north somewhere, and that may have been the last white sighting anywhere in the country. We were in touch with other walled communities, and none of them had any evidence of white people appearing anywhere after 2245.

White folks built the wall? Yeah, right.

Granma was old for sure (one hundred years old and eight months to be exact, and she was tiny and reminded me of an almond), but I knew that the wall had been around for way longer than that. According to the municipal history ledgers, the wall has been here for close to 500 years, and was built by the original Detroiters in 2350 to protect against 'encroaching environmental dangers,' is what it says. Even if white people had wanted to build a wall and there had been enough of them around at the time, they simply wouldn't have had the technology or even the energy to pull something like that off. Not if

the ledgers were correct about the bare survival
condition they were in during the last hundred years
or so of their existence. And since the founding
historians were my ancestors on my mother's side
(Granma was on Dad's side), then I preferred to take
it as gospel.

Granma did not take it as gospel. Not even
close.

"Y'all need to know we ain't the only ones
here! You think it's always been like this because this
is all you've ever known. But I am telling you, there
are white people out there, and I am also telling you
this damned wall ain't as old as everybody says! It's
those implants got your heads all screwed up. I swear
I don't know why you let the Council get away with
that."

We were sitting outside in the common area on
a small cushioned bench beneath a large red umbrella
behind the senior facility where she had been staying
for the past couple years. There were several tall
trees, and the grass was a lush, dark green, and was
always cut close. Multi-colored arrangements of all
sorts of sweet-smelling flowers were scattered about
the yard in a random design, and there was even a
bubbling brook that meandered its way through the

postcard beauty. The sky looked almost too blue, as if it had been imagined.

Trail Winds was the most expensive senior home in the state, and it showed. Nevertheless, I felt guilty nearly every day for having had to put the woman who raised me into this facility, even if I didn't have a choice. And hearing her rants about the return of white people didn't make me feel any better.

Not only did Granma insist that there were white people on the other side of the wall, she also said that the final recorded sighting is a false record.

But as old as she is means you can't always believe what she says, or at least that's what I tell myself.

After all, she was one of those who chose not to get the implant once they were made available. Unlike those of us who either chose the implant or were implanted at birth (the implants were offered voluntarily by the Council, not forced on us like Granma seems to think), her memories would sometimes get infected and cloudy. That meant there was no way for her to check her memories for one hundred percent accuracy, like the rest of us.

Which is why most citizens from Granma's generation chose the implants. She was one of a bare handful who resisted. Everyone else was excited to get them because not only would you develop perfect recall with exact detail, you would also experience overall well-being 24-7. Who wouldn't want that?

Folks who didn't trust feeling good all the time, like my grandmother, that's who.

Those from my generation were all given the implant at birth, so we didn't have anything to compare it to. But we had nothing to complain about either because we always felt content, for the most part.

Anyway, there are no records anywhere that give credence to what Granma says about there being white people still in existence outside the wall. The city has been sending out exploratory crews twice a year for as long as I have been alive, which is 34 years, and not once have they ever come back with evidence of any form of life beyond the wall aside from some weird-lookin' plants and animals that never seem to last more than a few days once brought inside the wall.

But she's also my grandmother, so what the hell am I supposed to say?

"I never said you were crazy, Granma. And that's because I'm not crazy. You and I both know if

I was fool enough to call you crazy, you would hop out that bed like you were 50 years younger and beat my ass like a rented stepchild."

I was trying to make her laugh, and normally that line would have worked. But instead, her eyes flashed as if there was lightning inside as she reached over to grab my forearm and squeeze harder than any century-old woman should have been able to do.

"When was the last time you could think for yourself?"

"Granma, come on now, why do we have to…"

"Because you don't even know. Think about that. I'm the last surviving citizen didn't take that implant. The last one who had a choice. Every single member of your generation got that damned implant at birth. And where are those implants made, huh? Who makes them?"

"It doesn't really matter, does it? They were approved by the Council, and the Council would never approve of anything that would hurt us. You know that. You used to be a member of the Council!"

"Yes, I did, baby. And then they kicked me off. And do you want to know why?"

I really didn't, but I knew I didn't have a choice. Might as well play along.

"No, Granma. Why?"

"For asking that same question. And because
when no one would tell me, I found out for myself. I
found out by sneaking outside the wall."

I could feel my heart starting to race.

"But you can't do that, Granma," I said, my
voice sounding weak. "It's not safe! We need to stay
inside…"

"For our own protection? That's what I thought
too, Marlon. Even though I didn't have the implant, I
still believed what they told me. Until I saw the city
on the other side of that wall. Where the implants are
made. 'You're a brave one,' is what they said. 'The
first to see and know. And you will be the last.
Because no one inside will believe you.' And then
they laughed. I never felt so scared in all my life."

She leaned closer and started to whisper.

"This wall isn't for our protection, it's for their
comfort. And this isn't Detroit. We lost Detroit
generations ago. Where we are now ain't nothingbut
a zoo. Detroit is outside those walls."

As I left the facility for the last time, I felt a tear
trickle down my cheek. It wasn't what I wanted, but
the law was clear. And I guess I had always known
that this day would come, sooner or later, when I

would have to sign the papers. The facility administrator assured me I was doing the right thing, but that didn't make it any easier.

She was still my grandmother, and I will miss her terribly.

Where Does That Alley Go?

The Water

So I wanted to tell the story of how the Green Alley came to be—which is amazing, as those of you who have lived through it know. It hasn't been easy, that's for sure, but I think now maybe people are starting to see why we have been pushing so hard on this sustainability thing. I'm sure we've all heard the saying that the definition of insanity is doing the same thing over and over again, but expecting different results. Yeah, well. Look at how that turned out for us, right? It's been five years, and the rain still hasn't stopped. I think it's safe to say that maybe our environment is getting a little fed up with us.

Anyway, I want to thank all of you for coming to the Green Garage this afternoon. As Shakespeare said, "We few, we happy few." I think it will be fun, even if a little painful, for us to view this slideshow together. Because, after all, who else could we experience this with, right?

Who else would believe it?

We've come a long way, and tomorrow we begin the final leg of what has been a very long journey—we will be crossing over to Next Detroit. That's what I like to call it, anyway. I was only there the one time, but perhaps we'll discuss that later.

A lot of us didn't think we were ever going to get this far. And we don't really know how it's going to end. But we can agree that staying here in Detroit much longer—in *this* Detroit—is not a viable option. Sometimes in life, you simply have to take risks for the greater good. Tomorrow, as they say, is promised to no one.

But right now, let's just try to relax and enjoy the show. Most of you here will recognize a lot of what you'll see in the slides, but I think you'll find there are some surprises, too. So strap in!

Peggy? Can you get the lights, please? Thank you.

You know, when Peggy and I got married, I promised her an interesting life. Maybe I over-delivered?

So, Peg's not laughing, which means maybe I need to just keep moving along.

Anyway, in 2008, we were just entering the recession, so things were turning south at that time. We had already acquired the Green Garage and were feeling pretty good about that. As I'm sure you know, that was quite the herculean task all by itself—creating the city's only environmentally sustainable shared working space. You know, when you start this kind of public project, there's all this excitement, and then there's just a thousand details.

So, I'm starting us off about twelve years ago, in May of 2008, before the rains started, and at that time, this is what the alley looked like. As you'll see, it had water in it almost all the time. Not very inviting.

That's the thing about alleys—when you think about it, they were never really meant to be attractive or inviting in any sort of way. They're just… *there.* They're these functional, raggedy little pathways that most people don't pay any attention to—because why would they? It's just an alley. It was no different with ours at first.

What's that, Peg?

Oh, right. I was getting to that, but you're right. It's not quite accurate to say our alley was *exactly* like the others. Our alley had that water that never left. And we had those critters—for lack of a better term—that showed up every now and again. I see some of you nodding your heads, so I know you remember, too. Not one of our more pleasant memories, right? But it's all a part of what got us to this point. That's how I see it, anyway.

I wish I had been able to snap a picture of one of them, just for our records, you know? I even tried a few times, but it didn't work out so well—Peg can tell you. She was there that night, and I guess all of you know that's how I lost part of this leg below the knee. I had no idea how fast those things moved. Plus, I guess I didn't plan for how much they didn't like to have their picture taken, right?

Not everybody wants to be a star! You live, and you learn.

But I'm pretty sure all of you have seen one of them at one point or another, because I saw you nodding your heads. So, I mean, did they look that vicious to *you* at first? I know they didn't look like harmless little puppies, especially not with the size of those pincers, but still…

Oh! Bob! How could I forget our dear friend Bob? I apologize—here I am acting like it was just me out there, but as we all know, Bob paid a much higher price for his curiosity than I did. He was a hell of a biologist—someone who had seen so many unusual things in this world. A true explorer. Honestly, he is the last person I think any of us would have thought could have been caught off guard by those creatures like he was, with all of that experience he had.

But these things—whatever they were—we know now that they weren't from around here. They came up from those deep pools we used to have back there in that alley, remember? Before the rains started? And who knows how far down those pools went. I still remember the time—man, that poor kid—he rode his bike through what he probably thought was just a wide puddle and got swallowed up. He couldn't have been from around here either, because otherwise he would have known to steer clear. I saw him headed that way, but I was watching from inside the Green Garage, and there was no way for him to see me or for me to warn him in time.

After the incident with the boy, Bob took some kind of measuring instrument back there to see how far down that 'puddle' went. When he came back, I'll never forget that expression on his face. When I asked him what he had found out, he just shook his head real slow and said he would have to try again later. Then he went upstairs. I never asked him about it again.

It was springtime, and we went for that unusually long period of time when there wasn't any rain at all. Nearly two months, I think, wasn't it, Peg? The strangest thing, though—and hindsight is always 20/20, isn't it?—was that Bob started taking weekly depth measurements of those pools to see if there was any noticeable change. If the rain had stopped, that should have had some effect on the water level, right? It should have gone down some?

But it didn't. I remember how frustrated Bob started to get by the end of the first month with no rain. It was something he was having a hard time with as a scientist. It was strange enough that there was suddenly no rain for this really long period of time— and during the rainy season, too—but climate change could maybe explain that. But him seeing these deep pools refusing to dry up I think kind of pushed him to the edge. He was fascinated by it, but he was angry about it too, and I think that right there is where Bob may have made a mistake letting this get too personal for him, because it never helps to get mad at Mother Nature. She's gonna do what she's gonna do because she makes the rules. It's kinda like the kids say: it's her world, we just live in it.

I think we all remember what happened that day, even if we'd rather not, right? I remember standing right over there, where the sidewalk meets the alley, watching Bob work. I wanted to see for myself what he was doing. I was curious.

I truly wish I hadn't been. Bob was kneeling beside the largest pool of water, which was about ten or fifteen feet into the alley, and he was facing my direction. He was lowering that measuring line down to see where the bottom was. I remember my stomach starting to knot up after about a minute, when that sinker still hadn't touched bottom. That's when I called out to him, and he looked up. I still feel guilty, because maybe if I hadn't called his name, he would have been lookin' in the right direction—at that water—instead of at me. Maybe he would have had time to jump out of the way.

But that isn't what happened, of course. One minute he was lookin' at me like he was going to ask me, "What the hell do you want?" And then there was that huge splash, like a sound you might hear near a lake or an ocean but not in an alley. Three of those critter things, like they had been waiting for just the right moment, lunged out of the water, latched onto him with those pincers, and dragged him down. There was no scream, no nothing. Bob was just gone.

Some things you'd rather put behind you, but since this is our last day in *this* Detroit, I think we owe it to Bob to remember. Because where we're going, well, Bob should have been able to go with us.

Anyway, we forge ahead.

Next slide, please.

Tokyo Alley

I think you know that Peggy and I lived in Tokyo years before we were even thinking about this green alley. If you want to know what the alleys look like in Tokyo, then that slide you see right there shows you. Tokyo, in my opinion, isn't that interesting a city in the macro. But in the micro? It is *very* interesting.

This is where we would go in the evenings— into alleys like this. I think the difference is pretty obvious between what we here in Detroit think of as an alley and what we're seeing here, right? All the little shops and all those beautiful colors? Especially at night. Honestly, Peg and I wanted to spend more time in the alleys than any of the other tourist spots, because they were each so unique, with their own personalities and quirks, each reflecting the neighborhoods where we found them. Some of those alleys seemed to go on forever, and you could practically get lost in them, which may have been the idea. Because trust me, you don't mind getting lost at all in there—there was always so much to see.

That's when I knew alleys could be a very important part of how a city operates. I could see how every part of a city could be made not only functional but beautiful, you know? In our society, we tend to be so quick to discard things. We don't consider their worth. And the things we do value aren't, as a rule, all that valuable. So our vision becomes cloudy, and we don't allow ourselves to see what is in front of us, and what is open to us, right?

But getting back to our beloved hometown—I don't know if you know this, but Detroit has over 1,000 miles of alleys. Mostly, they're used for access to parking and trash collection—things like that. But after seeing those alleys in Tokyo, I thought there must be something else we can do here.

And then one day, a neighbor of ours, Harold Evian, who you all know, approached me to ask if I would be interested in a project—not just to clean up the alley, but to turn it into something truly special. I told him, though, that I didn't want anything to do with sprucing up the alley *unless* it had something to do with sustainability because that's why we at the Green Garage are here. We agreed.

By the way, I am kind of amazed at how the timing of Harold's request worked out,—almost like he knew what was on my mind without even knowing what Peg and I had seen in Tokyo. The universe does work in odd ways sometimes.

When the neighbor and I were discussing our vision, I decided to show him the Chicago Green Alley Handbook I had. Have any of you ever seen it? I didn't like any of their design concepts, but it did show that a city could get behind a project like this. I saw how certain patterns could bring life to an area and interconnectedness. I began using those ideas to figure out how we might approach our concept, and once Harold saw what I had in mind, he got pretty enthusiastic about it.

After that, we were off and running. Well, maybe not running, exactly. More like run, stop, walk, jog, trip, fall down, get back up, run some more. Kind of like that. It was progress, but at times it was a maddeningly uneven sort of progress.

When I look back at some of the difficulties we encountered trying to make this happen, I have to wonder if maybe we were being warned here and there along the way—warned about what we were getting ourselves into. Because there were more than a few opportunities to get off this train, and I certainly did consider it, let me tell you.

But once it became clear to me—when I started to see those signs of what was happening all around us—I began to have a feeling. I can't really explain why, because it was just a feeling at the time, but I felt that perhaps by recreating this alley in a special way, we would also create an opportunity to help manage the way our world was starting to change.

It really is strange how things can come together in your life like that. I don't know if I have ever believed in God, but I do believe in a higher power—an Ordering Force that I believe sometimes can direct us if we open ourselves up to living more in harmony with nature, moving in the same direction instead of against the grain all the time. Against the grain seems to be what human beings specialize in.

I think that for us, maybe building this alley was one of those given directions.

The Sketch

So we got together with our friend Woody, who began to sketch the plans. If you look at this slide, here's Woody—finishing up the first pencil sketch of the alley. You know, he uses only a stub pencil, about two inches long, and he hand-draws everything.

You can see the basic concept that we had in mind here in this first drawing: the red bricks, the plants, the flowers along each side. And you'll notice you don't see any of the large drains you would normally see in an alley, because we knew then that the only way to keep the water from pooling up was with the help of some very special plants.

We'll talk more about those plants a little later, but I'll just say quickly that if it hadn't been for Bob, we never would have known such plants existed, and there probably never would have *been* an alley.

One of the first things Woody asked me was how we were going to pave over those deep pools. How in the hell were we going to get rid of all that water that wouldn't leave, right? And the things that came out of the water…

I didn't have an answer for him. That was just another dilemma in a long line of mounting dilemmas and challenges we would face while trying to make this green alley a reality.

My father used to say, "Don't ever let anybody tell you that dreams are free." I think he meant that there's always a price to pay for those of us who can't let dreams stay dreams. Because they're free only as long as you're willing to wake up and walk away.

Anyway, Bob had been a good friend of Woody's, so he was hit pretty hard when those things grabbed him. We all were. But Bob and Woody had grown up together. They were always sharing some funny tales—and sometimes not so funny—of what it was like growing up as two white kids on the East Side of Detroit. Listening to them share those stories was about the only time I ever saw Bob relaxed and not so focused on some major scientific dilemma somewhere in the world he felt needed fixing.

All of that was to say that Woody was really sensitive about those pools being there because of what happened, and it made the whole project a lot more personal for him. Getting that alley done wasn't just a beautification project—it was something that *had* to be done. I think he felt like maybe once those pools had been drained and covered over, then it would be like burying a bad memory. Like locking up a nightmare in a crypt.

I should point out that Woody doesn't normally let anyone into his studio for any reason, and that he prefers not to share his sketches until they are done. But in this case, he made an exception, and I owe him a huge thanks for that. I explained to him that I needed to document this project as best I could, and he agreed to let me take this photo of him and get a peek at his sketch in advance.

The Meeting

Eventually, we met with Sue Mosey, who, as most of us know, is often referred to as the Mayor of Midtown because she can get things done like nobody's business. She has invested her life in the revitalization of this neighborhood for years.

A long meeting with Sue is about three minutes. I showed her what we were interested in doing, and she said, "You guys keep going, I'll find the money."

After that, she let us take a quick picture with her—which she almost never does—but you can see it right there on the screen. And she's smiling, which is a good thing.

Skipping ahead to January of 2009, this is what our alley looked like nine months into the project.

So what makes a green alley green? Well, the first and foremost issue is rainwater runoff. If you're going to upgrade an old alley, you need to do something with the rainwater runoff. If you're going to do something with the rainwater runoff, then you gotta build so that water runs off to the side so that it can be absorbed by the plant material below, instead of running down into the storm sewer.

By the way, that storm sewer was built in 1877 and is made of brick. Just imagine.

Anyway, that was another four or five months of work just right there. But it's work we never would have done if we hadn't gotten the go-ahead from Sue Mosey. Well, her and a lot of other good people along the way. But she really was instrumental; she really was.

The Thirsty Plants

What you see right here, these long plant beds lining the alley? These are Michigan native plants. They have deep roots that absorb the water, and after they get established, they don't need to be watered, because the runoff from the alley takes care of their thirst.

Well, at least it takes care of *that* part of their thirst. Because I guess we know now that, come nighttime, it starts to get a bit like *Little Shop of Horrors* back there. But in a good way, right? At least it has been for us. Because those critters with pincers are now a thing of the past.

I still remember the first time Peg and I got a chance to see how the plants work after the sun goes down. As you can see here in the slide, they look perfectly harmless during the day, right? All green and purple with those magnificent yellow stripes down the side?

They aren't any taller than about a foot or so, right? Nice, friendly little plants.

OK, Peg. Next slide.

Great, thanks.

Now, do *these* look like the same plants to you? I can already tell which of you have never worked here much after dark, because you guys are the ones with your mouths hanging open. I don't blame you.

Like I said, the first time Peg and I got a chance to see that transformation up close for the first time, it kind of made my hair stand up—and that's not an easy thing to do with all I've seen. Trust me.

If you take a moment to examine your presentation materials at your seat, there are photocopies of an article that Peg and I submitted to *Wild Detroit*, which we figured was the only local publication that would even consider our story. We even submitted it as fiction—but of course, all of you know this really happened.

Our Green Alley After Dark
by Tom and Peggy Brennan

Normally, Peg and I leave around 4 pm to give us a chance to get back home to Ann Arbor, and Matt locks up at the end of the day. But on this particular night, we had a late meeting.

So there I was in the big conference room—this was later in October after it had gotten dark, so I guess it was around 9 p.m. —and as I was standing up to stretch and gather my thoughts, I heard a rustling sound coming from the alley. I was facing the whiteboard where we had written notes, so my mind was still scrolling back over the discussion. I thought maybe it was a couple of dogs scuffling. Sounded like they were probably pretty big...

Then came a horrible shrieking sound unlike anything I had ever heard before. I whirled around but couldn't see anything outside the windows. Peg came rushing into the room, and we just looked at each other.

"Tom, what was that?"

I just stood there doing quick calculations inside my head; should we drop everything and hightail it to the parking lot? Would we have enough time to get to the car and get out of there?

"Is the parking lot gate closed?" Peg asked, reading my mind as usual. We both knew that getting out that way was no longer an option, because by the time the electronic gate opened wide enough for us to drive out, whatever was out there would have time to reach the lot—and we'd be trapped inside the car.

"Turn out the lights," Peg said, and I remember wondering how she sounded as calm as she did. I also remember feeling very thankful, because so long as both of us kept our heads, we would have a better chance of figuring this out together.

I turned out the lights.

Moments later, another shriek tore the night as we stared out the windows—only this one was much longer and sounded closer. We felt something crash against the side of the building. Whatever it was, it had to be big to shake the building like that. At first, we couldn't quite see all that was going on—because whatever was happening was just outside the view of our windows.

Gradually, we were able to get clearer glimpses of the action as the struggle moved closer. What we saw first was a thick, ropey branch whip itself around in front of us, then raise itself up to where it was illuminated by the lights in the alley. That's when we saw that the branch was wrapped tightly around a large, lobster-lookin' creature that was struggling ferociously to get free. Then the branch kind of flexed and slammed the thing into the ground so hard that it practically exploded.

I recognized the splattered mess of meat and broken shell as one of those critters from the deep pool that had been terrorizing us for so long. I also

recognized that telltale coloring on the branch...
Green and purple with that yellow stripe. I have to
admit that gave me the shivers, because how in the
world...?

But then it tapped on the window, and that's
when my heart started to pump even faster. I felt like
I had been transported to a world my imagination
couldn't even begin to comprehend. Nothing about
this could be happening. And yet, there we were, Peg
and I, forcing each other to witness the surreal
becoming quite real indeed. I almost wished Peg
hadn't come down to the Green Garage that day, not
only for her own safety, but because if I had told her
about my day later that night, she would have told
me, with absolute certainty, that I must have fallen
asleep and had a bad dream. And I would have been
so happy to accept that. To just erase it all and hit
reset in the morning.

Tap. Tap. Tap.

Whatever this thing was, it wasn't going to
allow me to escape back into my comfortable reality.
It was demanding that I recognize its existence. That
_we_ recognize its existence.

Peggy and I looked at each other in the near
darkness of the room, then back at the window as this

massive plant began to gather more of its vastly expanded and distorted bulk into our direct line of sight. I noticed that the way it moved resembled the writhing, coiling movements of a huge snake—but only if the snake was drunk. There was a thick, damp odor forcing its way into the room—a not-too-unpleasant combination of roses and cinnamon, which somehow didn't seem the correct aroma to fit what we were experiencing.

"Do you think it sees us?" Peg whispered.

I didn't answer right away, but then I said, "I don't think the whispering helps."

Peg nodded.

"I think you're probably right."

Tap. Tap.

Where in the hell did Bob get these things from anyway? He swore they were from upper Michigan, but now I was really starting to wonder.

Before I had a chance to contemplate that question for much longer, the plant, or whatever it was, made a beckoning motion with one of its smaller branches—a motion that is recognized literally all around the world. But considering the source of this motion, I simply didn't want to accept that a giant alien plant was summoning me and my wife to come outside.

"It looks like—"

"Nope," I said.

"OK. But doesn't that look like it's trying to—"

"*No!*"

Taptaptaptaptaptaptaptap.

"OK! OK!" I yelled, my voice cracking.

Peg started to say something, but she decided to reach over and squeeze my hand instead. I'm pretty sure that worked better than anything she might have said, because this was one of those moments where there simply weren't any words that could live up to the moment. How do you describe a point in time when your entire world, everything you had ever been taught, was certain and couldn't be changed, begins to fade away right in front of you, and all you can do is stare? What do you do when you discover that Mother Nature isn't an only child after all?

"So I guess we should go outside...?" said Peg, tugging at my hand.

I nodded.

"I guess so."

Tap. Tap.

Another beckoning motion, this time noticeably more urgent. We obeyed.

When we got outside and stood on the sidewalk near the entrance to the alley, we noticed a small crowd had gathered across the street. They were staring and pointing with various and assorted looks of horror and amazement. A tall, lanky young man holding a skateboard in one hand noticed us, and a terrified look came across his face. He must have thought we didn't know what was in the alley. He gestured frantically for us to cross the street to safety.

"Hey! *Hey!* You guys!" he shouted. "Hurry up, you need to—"

I raised my hand calmly and tried to smile.

"You guys stay over there," I called back. "We'll be fine. Looks like things are a little bit out of control over here currently, but don't worry. These are just plants, after all. They've asked us to come outside for some reason, so my wife and I are just going in there to see what the fuss is all about. So, not to worry. We're... we're fine."

The young man dropped his skateboard onto the sidewalk and didn't bother trying to pick it up as it coasted smoothly away. The look on his face told me everything I needed to know about how I must have sounded. But what else could I say? Something more reassuring than what I said, I suppose... But no matter what I said, I wasn't going to sound sane if it ended with me and Peg going into the alley.

Which is what we did.

"Hey..." called the kid again, as we turned to walk away, perhaps never to come back again. The sadness in his voice almost broke my heart.

As we stepped further into the alley, I remember thinking what an amazing difference just a few feet can make. While on the sidewalk, as close as we were to the plant thing, we were still conversing with other humans, and we felt connected to the real world.

But once we began our journey deeper into the alley, stepping around the deep pool and into, over, and around the thick, multi-colored branches and vines that resembled a perverted version of Jack's giant beanstalk, the world as we knew it disappeared.

The pungent, sweet smell that had forced itself into our nostrils earlier when we were standing inside was now more pungent than ever—almost intoxicating. I also noticed a strange, hoarse whisper that was similar to someone breathing while asleep, mixed in with the rustling, writhing sounds of the plant as it moved around.

"My God..." said Peggy.

My heart jumped into my throat.

"What?" I asked.

And then I saw it—up ahead, cracked open and torn, shoved up against the side of the Green Garage. Although it was distorted and broken as a result of having lost its fight against the plant and being smashed against the wall, the oversized pincers made it relatively easy to recognize the limp, hard-shelled body as belonging to one of the critters from the deep pool. It measured at least seven or eight feet in length.

On the other side of the alley lay another crushed critter. This must have been the one we saw raised high into the air by one of the vines before being slammed into the ground. Several smaller branches and vines were busying themselves, tearing the critter apart and stuffing pieces of the body into a row of open mouths that moaned hungrily. The wet, smacking mouths opened and closed, positioned in evenly spaced intervals along each branch. I kept myself from throwing up only by sheer force of will.

"So why are we here?" said Peggy, asking the question we were both wondering. I don't think we expected it to answer, but we had to say something. Plus, we were both nervous and wondering if we were about to suffer the same fate as the two unlucky critters.

Almost as if on cue, we heard a splashing noise behind us. Another of the lobster-like critters came scrambling up out of the depths of the pool and hurtled towards us at a rapid pace, its many multi-jointed legs making repetitive clacking noises as they skittered across the ground.

"Oh boy," was all I could say, as we both turned to face what was headed our way.

Peggy squeezed my hand hard enough that something should have broken.

The critter was within a few feet of us when a flurry of branches and vines lashed together in front of us like a protective shield. Another flurry of vines wrapped around the body of the assaulting critter like a green storm made of bullwhips—and tore the creature apart. Then, slowly, the vines set the gory remains at our feet as the 'shield' untangled itself and slithered away in all directions.

"What are we supposed to do with this?" I whispered.

"I don't think whispering is going to help," she said, mocking what I had said earlier with a slight smile.

"Hey... hey... *look,*" Peggy said, pointing at the twin carcasses of the two critters that had been destroyed earlier.

The one that had been partially eaten was obviously worse for wear, but the vines and branches had gently wrapped themselves around what was left and were dragging the remains in our direction.

"If this is supposed to be an offering of some sort, they really don't have to do this," I said.

"Be quiet," said Peg.

Soon, the shredded, bloody body parts of three dead critters were piled up in front of us. The remains were close enough to us to completely replace that eerily pungent sweet smell with another scent that was anything but sweet. Somehow, I still kept my food down.

"Thanks..." I said, figuring I should express some sort of appreciation, even if they didn't understand me.

Moments later, the plant extended a small pair of vines in our direction, one toward me and one toward Peg. Each vine simultaneously wrapped itself slowly around our lower arms, then squeezed three times. The squeeze wasn't that strong, but you could nevertheless feel that if it had wanted to yank our arms out of their sockets, it could have easily done so, and tossed them onto the pile of body parts in front of us for good measure.

But instead, all the plant seemed to want to do was to reassure us, because after the preliminary squeezing, the vines unwrapped themselves from around our arms and released us, retreating back into the thicket of living, breathing vegetation.

Then, for no reason that I could discern, it uttered several high-pitched shrieks, after which all of the branches between us and the street began to part like the Red Sea.

Once the path was completely open, Peg and I made our way back to the sidewalk. The small gathering of onlookers was still clustered across the street, waiting to see how everything turned out. I'm pretty sure how it actually turned out wasn't how they were expecting it was going to turn out. We waved at them, but none of them waved back. I didn't think they were being rude; I think they were in shock. For that matter, we probably were, too.

We went back inside the Green Garage and gathered our things. That was enough for one day.

Tom and Peggy Brennan are Co-founders of "The Green Garage" in Detroit, Michigan

Well, as I'm sure all of you sitting here can guess, over the weeks that followed, we didn't stay late very often at the Green Garage. But we did let everyone in the G.G. know that things were a little 'different' around here at night, and that they should be aware of that, but that they were probably safe, considering that the plants seemingly weren't interested in hurting humans. Maybe if I had assured everyone that they were *actually* safe instead of 'probably,' my assurances would have carried more credibility. As it was, the only folks who ever stayed late again were me and Peg.

But one thing we all began to notice was how the pools started to shrink in size, day by day, until one day they were just gone. And with it, as far as we could tell, went the critters. In this photo here, you can see that there's barely a rain puddle left. Before the pools had dried up for good, there were a few more instances of the critters surfacing to snatch someone who ventured too close, despite the warning flyers we had posted all around the alley after Bob had been dragged under. But if it hadn't been for the giant plant patrol working the night shift, things could have been quite a bit worse, I'm sure.

It was hard to reconcile how innocent and, well, *plant-like* they appeared during the daytime. It was also hard to imagine that such normal-lookin' plants, not any more than a few feet tall, were thirsty enough to drink up *all* the water in pools so deep we couldn't even measure them. Maybe they only drank at night… that was the only explanation that made any sense at all to us in a world where logic was growing more and more strange. Where else could the water have gone in such a short period of time? What else would explain it?

But in the end, we were just glad. Glad the critters were gone, the pools were gone, and that the plants seemed to be on our side.

It was a win.

The Magic Bricks

OK, so this slide you're seeing now is a photo of our alley after the bricks had been laid—don't they look great?

But the story behind how we got those bricks—well, that's really something. I actually think there's enough there for a short film, no kidding. It's just unbelievable. But this is Detroit, right? And nothing ever comes easy or simple. But somehow this city always seems to make the sacrifices worth it. I see some of you nodding your heads in agreement, so that's good. We're not alone.

So. The story of the bricks. Here we go…

The bricks we got for the alley are about the only part of *anything* attached to the Green Garage that wasn't made in—or ordered from—somewhere in Detroit or Michigan. Because we were very committed to shopping local and supporting our local businesses whenever and however we could while we built this.

But to get *these* bricks, we needed to go to a place in Ohio, close to the Kentucky border. A friend of ours, Marsha, who knows a considerable amount about construction materials and the like, we shared with her that we were having a hard time finding the right kind of bricks. We had seen some that came close enough to what we wanted, but, after all we had gone through for this alley already, it just seemed like selling out to settle for some bricks that didn't look just right.

Marsha has known us a long time, and after we told her what we had in mind—I can't believe that conversation took almost an entire hour—she said she was pretty sure she knew what we wanted. I asked her if she was pretty sure or *sure*.

She was sure.

That was good enough for me and Peg. So Marsha offered to call the owner of the place and tell him what we needed. She said he could be a prickly sort, and it might go easier if she smoothed the way, especially since we weren't from anywhere nearby. I pointed out that Ohio was right next to Michigan for crying out loud, but Marsha shook her head.

"Not close enough," she said.

I asked her if we could at least sit nearby when she called the guy, so we could listen in. Marsha said it wouldn't be a problem, so she took out her cell phone and put it on speaker as we sat around the kitchen table. We sat for more than a minute before someone picked up.

"Marsha?"

The voice was a deep bass that sounded both scratched and torn.

"Hey, George. Yeah, it's me. How you be?" She winked at us and smiled.

There was another long pause. His heavy breathing sounded humid and sticky.

"Alive," he said, finally.

Marsha flashed us another conspiratorial grin and a quick nod.

"That's a good thing, George. Glad to hear it."

"Good for you, maybe. I'm not so sure about it for me. So what do you want, Marsha?"

"Bricks, George. The special kind."

The heavy breathing stopped, and I wondered for a moment if the line had gone dead.

"Someone is there with you," he said, sounding both suspicious and angry.

Marsha gave us both a quick searching look, one eyebrow raised. I nodded, signaling it was fine with me to confirm. Might as well get it out of the way.

"That's right, George. I have someone with me. Two someones, as a matter of fact. They are the someones who need your special bricks. You know I wouldn't recommend just anyone to you—these are good people. I've known them a long time, and what they're working on is truly worthy of your craftsmanship."

"Is that a fact."

"Actually, I believe it is. They are building a very special alley, and…"

"An *alley*."

Marsha squeezed her eyes shut, then mashed her lips together.

"Yes, George. An alley. But this isn't…"

"Let me stop you right there. Because you're about to tell me a lie, and you know how I feel about being lied to."

"Except that I'm not lying to you, George. This *is* a very special alley, for a very special purpose. Nobody else can give them that extra something they're lookin' for—and that I am convinced only you can provide. You are the master, George. The craftsman."

"Impressive flattery, Marsha. But you have always been an impressive flatterer."

"I'm honest, George. There's a difference."

"Is there."

"Yes. Now, if you don't mind, I would like to introduce you to my friends, Tom and Peggy. They're the founders of a wonderful green co-working space called the Green Garage here in Detroit, and now they are in the process of, I would say, *reimagining* the alley that runs behind their building. Personally, I think it's exciting because…"

"Are Tom and Peggy capable of speaking for themselves, Marsha?"

The expression on Marsha's face looked like someone who had just been slapped by a total stranger. I felt bad for her, and I was starting to wonder if this guy George was worth the hassle. If Marsha said he was a genius, then he probably was, but he was also something else that I saw too often in people who were supposed geniuses—and had been told so too often by too many people.

"Yes," said Marsha, her voice sounding tight and brittle. "They know how to speak for themselves, George. Anything else you need to know?"

George didn't bother to answer the question. Despite the many miles of distance between us, I felt like the man was hovering there in the room up above, lookin' down with a frown of disapproval.

"Tell me about the alley and why it's so special," he said, his voice sounding dismissive with a lingering hint of anger.

I proceeded to tell him about the Green Garage as background. Then Peggy and I made our pitch on alleys, and why they did not have to be the discarded pathways to nowhere that they usually were; instead, they could be transformative. We told him about our time in Tokyo, and how the people there recognized that alleys could be *part* of the community, not just an ugly sidenote, and that it was not only possible but imperative to make this happen. It isn't possible to have a healthy neighborhood be compatible with an infected network of alleys full of trash and other discarded items—and discarded people. The only way to upgrade a community was to upgrade every square inch.

After making our pitch, the three of us—Marsha, Peggy, and myself—looked at one another dubiously, unsure if we had made the desired impact. As for George, all we heard from him was the labored sound of his breathing, which sounded more like the inhalings and exhalings of some large beast. I gave

Marsha a look that essentially translated to "WTF?"
And that's when George responded, which made me
even more sure that he was hovering.

"You still there, Marsha?" he asked.

She smiled, lookin' relieved.

"Yes, George. I'm still here. So what do you
think? Are they worthy?"

Marsha gave us a wink. I heard George
grumbling on the other end of the line.

"We should discuss quantities," he said.

"Hmmm. You should probably direct that to
Tom and Peggy."

"I *am* directing that to Tom and Peggy. Unless
you are interested in purchasing a load of my bricks
as well."

I told George about how many bricks we
needed, adding that we should probably purchase a
number of extras just to be on the safe side.

"Today is Tuesday?" he said.

"Yes."

"I'll see you in two weeks. You should come in
person to make sure they are exactly as you wish.
You'll pay me the other half of what you owe me,
and you can take your bricks with you. I am putting

my son on the line now to negotiate the price. Have a good day."

A moment later, a much cheerier voice came on the line that identified itself as belonging to George Jr. But as cheery as the voice was, I wouldn't exactly call our discussion a negotiation. George Jr. informed us what the price would be, then told us that he would be needing half of the cost up front before they even got started on the first brick. The price was high, but I expected it would be. Arrangements were made to send them the down payment the next day.

City Problems

When it came time to inspect our bricks, we were more than satisfied with them. In fact, we were practically giddy. Each brick had a strange-lookin' pair of symbols engraved on both sides that resembled an eye and an hourglass. They gave the appearance of having been forged long ago, resembling those on Michigan Avenue near where the old Tiger Stadium used to be, or on Canfield near the Green Garage. But they also kinda *glowed* from the inside. Just faintly, and not consistently, but enough that it caught your attention if you held one of them in your hands.

When I asked George about it, he smiled. George was an exceptionally large man, even bigger than his voice suggested, with a thick mane of unruly gray hair and an equally unruly beard that framed his fleshy face.

"Don't you worry about that," he said. "Special bricks for a special alley." Just how special they were was something we wouldn't find out for a few more years. Lookin' back, I'm proud to say that in the face of all that we were up against, we still managed to create a safe and walkable area that is accessible by all. Even with all the rain that we've had for the past five years, it has remained something very special that the entire community has come to love and appreciate. I view that as a major accomplishment.

But in 2008, when this odyssey began, that was hardly the prevailing perspective of the powers-that-be. Back then, if you were doing anything with an alley in the City of Detroit, the first question they asked was whether you wanted them to vacate the alley. What they wanted to do was get out of maintaining the alleyway, simple as that.

But we believed it had to be accessible by all. So we went to the City and told them that we wanted this to remain a public alley, and that whatever we were doing would be open to the public, always. That was not a minor point in 2008.

One of the key parts of this project you have to keep in mind is that if we were going to have the water run away from the storm sewer inlet, the water had to go somewhere. That meant we had to have this foundation under the green alley that allowed the water to seep in and be stored there, and then slowly percolate into the water table below. So this was a whole design concept that had to be figured out.

And even when we had the design figured out, we then had to get approvals. So who needs to approve this thing, right? Originally, we were thinking it's the City of Detroit that needs to approve it—but turns out you have to have the OK from the City Engineering Department, the Department of Water and Sewer, the Traffic Department, and the Fire Department. The Fire Department had to make sure its trucks could get down there.

But the biggest problem we had was that no one could accept the idea that we could build a road where the water was not going to the water outlet or to the storm sewer inlet. So, for about five months, the plan was sitting in City Engineering and not going anywhere because of that. One person told us, in a kind of secret way, that they wanted to see it happen, but they were afraid that if they approved it and it didn't work out, then they could be fired. We even took Sue Mosey down to talk to top management, to tell them it would be good for Midtown. They still weren't enthusiastic.

Eventually, after all that time going back and forth on how to get this done, we came to an agreement that satisfied both sides: they agreed that this would be a demonstration project only, and would *not* set a new standard for alleys.

Finally, the project got through.

If I had known about all this trouble when I had that first conversation with our neighbor, I think I would have said, "I'll pass." But we were too far down the road by then. Or maybe I should say too far down the alley…?

The Sinkhole Creature

So that brings us to construction in March of 2010—about five years before the rains began. Time flies when you're having fun, right? Anyway, all construction projects have a problem somewhere—that's just the way it happens. Can you see that hole? In this slide, here? That was the famous sinkhole in the alley. I think maybe it had something to do with when those pools dried up. I don't know for sure—how could I? But I know it wasn't there before.

So then the question became, how do you build an alley on top of a sinkhole? We called the water department and had them come out—they probably came out four or five times. They looked down the hole, and nobody could quite figure it out. So we started trying to figure out for ourselves. What *is* under the Green Alley? I think I mentioned before, we found out we had a brick storm sewer from 1877 down there, for one thing.

What I didn't mention was that you could write a sci-fi story about the creatures coming out of that storm sewer. Nothing quite the size of the pincered critters that took Bob, but nothing that fit any category of normal animals I had ever seen. There were snake-lookin' things with webbed feet and bird wings, five-foot-long worms as thick as my arm with eyes all down their sides. A few other species I won't even try to describe. Let's just say that if Hell had a zoo, these things could have been the main attractions.

Marcus, who owns Kareem Market on the corner, had a running joke with me long before we started work on the Green Alley that there were actually dinosaurs in the sewer, and that they got out from time to time to run down Second Avenue. It was a great joke until I saw the critters from the storm sewer and invited Marcus to come take a look for himself.

"Those aren't dinosaurs," he said.

"Not at all."

We haven't joked about dinosaurs since. In fact, we haven't joked much at all.

Anyway, the brick sewer isn't the only thing down there under the alley. There's a four-inch water main, a DTE underground transformer main, telephone lines, Comcast lines, trunk lines, and gas lines. All under the Green Alley. So how were we supposed to solve the sinkhole problem?

Well, we prayed to our angels and the Department of Public Works. They have a guy over there they call 'Junior' that Stu asked me to call in. Junior said that he could help solve the sinkhole problem.

And then they started digging—the Water Department and the Department of Public Works—at the same time. And this photo here is the Water Department guys trying to figure out what the heck is going on down there. They noticed that the 1877 sewer main was in rough shape, and so they ended up scoping it and realizing that they had to reline it. It was amazing.

They put a liner down there so it wouldn't leak anymore. This was a major, major undertaking by the city. But I don't think that leak could explain those deep pools we used to have. None of us mentioned those to the city department folks downtown, for obvious reasons.

I think it was $200,000 worth of work that had to be done just below ground here.

Now, do you have your notes? Do you see this guy right here on the slide? That guy—his name's James—went down into that brick sewer, and no, I'm not kidding. I saw it with my own eyes. They tied a rope around him, and he went in headfirst. See the rope? He inched his way down there, and he had to connect the whole thing—the liner—by hand. He was a little guy, only like 4'11" or something, and he's in this hazmat suit—you see where he has that light on his head? He also showed up with a few extra tools—weapons?—ready-made for those critters that were squirming and squiggling down in the sewer.

"Looks like you knew about those things in advance," I said to James, just before he started his descent.

"Yep," he said. I thought he was going to say more, but when he didn't, I felt like I had to push him.

"Can you tell me how you knew? I've never seen anything quite like some of these creatures before. Have you?"

"Yep," he said again, a little irritated.

"Look, I'm not trying to hold you up or give you a hard time. We appreciate what you guys are doing more than you know. We really do. We couldn't move forward on this project without you. But I think you can guess that by now we're not the only ones who have seen these—and some other things—and I think people may have some questions that they need answers to. Right?"

He looked at me hard.

"You said something about some *other things* you saw? Besides these sewer animals?"

I nodded.

"Some big lobster-lookin' things," I began. "One of them took part of my leg... And some *really* big plants—well, they only get big at night—that *eat* those lobster things. It's been pretty interesting around here lately."

James chuckled and shook his head. I looked around at some of the other workers, and a couple of them were grinning as well. But not all of them.

"I think I better get ready to do this job," he said.

"So then you've seen them before, right? Please, James, c'mon. If you have, I would really like to know... I need to know I'm not crazy."

James paused, staring past me into the distance.

"Yeah," he said finally. "I've seen 'em before. Seen those plants, too. And the lobster things. Detroit's an old city, and sometimes old cities have things buried underneath, you know, like the catacombs. Those things you've been seeing lately haven't been seen by anyone for a long, long time. But something's happening, and, for whatever reason, it's bringing them up to the surface. I'm not any kind of scientist or anything—I don't even know if this has anything to do with science—but I'd say Detroit's about to go through some kinda change... That's about all I can tell you. But now I gotta get to work, OK?"

I nodded.

And then he was gone.

The Permit

Before I get too much further down that road, we had to get a permit for the Green Alley, right? So you should probably hear *that* story. This one particular person, who I'm not going to name, is literally the Lord of Permits for public right of ways in Detroit. I would guess that he's retired by now, but in his time, he was famous. So, my friend Bruce and I went in to talk to him, and well, he kinda chewed us out. So, we went back into the hallway, and somebody else who worked there said to us, just as we were leaving, "Did he talk to ya?"

"Yeah."

"Did he yell at ya?"

"Yeah."

"Well, just bring Lorna Doones next time. 'Cause he loves Lorna Doones."

This is Detroit as a big small town, right? So, the next time we went back in, we picked up a pack of Lorna Doones, and sure enough, we got approved for our permit for public right of way. In fact, he was able to get us an even better deal on occupying the public right of way. So Lorna Doones are now officially part of the Green Alley story.

Sorry, I had to back up there a little bit to get that part in, but obviously, without the permit, we couldn't have done a thing, and we probably never would have known about all those strange-lookin' creatures that were crawling around inside the sewer in the first place.

But we did get the permit, and construction moved forward from there. Here's all the guys working without shirts on, which was very popular with the women at the G.G. They would always go out and make sure that everything was 'under control.'

Pathway to New Detroit

Before I move on to the next slide, there's more to the story of those bricks that I wanted to tell you about.

As I was saying earlier, these bricks were a bit more special than we knew at the time we went to inspect them. To put it mildly, 'special' was quite the understatement. I'm not sure why George thought that we should be the recipients of these unusual bricks with the strange twin insignias of the eye and the hourglass—except that maybe he somehow knew what was coming, about the rains and all that. Maybe George was a kind of Noah, and the bricks were an ark...

Let me explain.

When the bricks were delivered, I remember asking one of the guys driving the truck if he had noticed any of the bricks glowing at all. Now, why in the world did I do that? This was a man roughly the size of a bear, and with the same disposition. He looked at me like I was a fly that needed swatting. Instead, he just grunted and shook his head. Then he turned and walked away, mumbling something under his breath that I probably didn't want to hear.

Two days later, when the crew arrived to begin laying the bricks, I couldn't help but smile as I watched our alley taking shape. I thought about everything we had been through to get to this point, and I grabbed one of the bricks from the pile and took it inside the Garage to the space I use for my office. One of the great things about the Green Garage is that everybody knows how to respect each other's space, even when there aren't many walls.

So nobody bothered me or gave me any funny looks as I stared at this brick. It took longer than that first time I held one in my hand, but sure enough, after several minutes had passed and I was about to give up, the brick started to glow—just barely. This time, up close, I noticed a steady pulse to the glow, like a faint heartbeat. And then, the meaning of the symbols dawned on me…

An eye and an hourglass. My God…

I dropped the brick onto the floor and shoved my chair back from the table, making a loud screeching noise across the floor. This time, I did get a few inquisitive looks. I think someone may have even asked if I was OK, but the voice sounded muffled, as if it was coming to me from the other end of a long, padded tunnel.

In time, you will see.

An Alley Takes Shape

Next slide.

Here you can see the latticework guys going in. Then we got the Green Garage garden club to come out, and we got the topsoil in. That's when the wild plants started coming in. Not quite as wild as the Little Shop of Horrors plants, but still very nice. Finally, we got a Detroit artist to go in and do some really nice work—a mural on the alley wall.

Lo and behold, our finished alley. We're now in August of 2010, and all the newer plants are coming up.

So now let me tell you about the response, which has been just great. While we were in the process of opening it up, here are the first two non-worker residents just admiring the alley. I took it as a sign that this was a nice place to be. A place you might take your dog for a walk, and maybe bring your baby. At least during the daytime hours—maybe not such a good idea when the sun goes down, and the plants rise up, but that's OK. I've made peace with the Shop of Horrors plants—I think they're actually more about protecting us than anything else, but I don't know that anybody who didn't have our experience with them would ever believe that.

Anyway, there was another woman, a longtime resident of the neighborhood, who was also an artist. And sometimes she and I would stop and talk whenever we would run into each other, which, for some strange reason, was always somewhere along Second Avenue. This one time, I saw her at the Bronx Bar right up the street—this was right around the time period when we were just finishing construction–and I asked her how she liked the alley. And she said, 'Well, I can't go in the alley.' So I asked her 'Why can't you go in the alley? Why is that?' That's when she said that it was just too overwhelming for her—that she couldn't believe something this beautiful could happen in an alley.

That story has always stuck with me. We just don't know the weight that is placed on people when they have to navigate areas in their lives that are cluttered and dark. So, to think that our alley has brought some light is, I think, a really good thing.

Postscript

What are green alleys good for? Well, we've had movie nights there, we've had dinners in the alley, and weddings. People even get professional pictures taken in there.

People do walkthroughs all the time. Some G.G.ers used to use it as extra office space before the rains started. And there are now four more green alleys in the area. So, you could say that our alley has had a ripple effect. In fact, I've heard whispers of an alley *district* or something like that planned for the area.

One final comment—there's a young man, who was sponsored by the American Institute of Architects to travel around the world lookin' at innovation in alleys, who actually came to Detroit and spent 2 ½ days with us. He published a book called *Tight Urbanism,* and we're proud to be recognized as a part of that.

And, you know, this alley is a lot of work to maintain. There's maintenance, like weeding, and then more maintenance, and *more* weeding. Plus, a new DTE transformer substation has been put in there, a new Comcast trunkline, an AT&T complete upgrade, and a new gas line.

So here's what it looks like today with the G.G.

One more thing: you all remember August of 2014, right? Many of you were caught in areas of the city that you couldn't get out of, because everywhere was flooded.

But our alley was not flooded at all, which means it works just like it was designed to work. We're ten years into it, and it works, which has turned out to be a really good thing with the rains these past five years. Turns out we were preparing ourselves for something we didn't even know was coming.

You know, I think of that one young girl who came on Day One to the Green Alley. And it occurs to me that, when we're thinking about this work, we have to think about what kind of relationship to the Earth we're building for the next generation. I think it's a big deal. That doesn't mean we can do everything, but we can, I think, do our small part.

Post Postscript

The first time it happened, I wasn't sure how I was going to make it back to the present day, because I was even less sure how I had stumbled upon that other Detroit. It happened a few days after the bricks were laid. I was taking a walk just to enjoy everything we had managed to accomplish on a nice fall day in 2010. A nice day in fall was a rare thing that year, with all the cloudy days and the excess rain, even though the forever rains hadn't started yet. That was still five years off.

I'd just had a meeting with the Detroit City Council about the plans we had for the El Moore—a beautiful old building down the street, we intended to renovate as a hotel and residence. Once the meeting was concluded, I decided to take a break and get some air. I exited through the south side into our brand new Green Alley, and I noticed Fred, one of our more recent G.G.ers, sitting at a small table to the left of the door, typing on his laptop beside a half-eaten sandwich. He didn't even look up once I stepped outside, so I figured I wouldn't disturb him with one of my patented 'hellos,' which, I'm proud to say, force even the angriest of Detroiters to smile against their will.

I turned left down the Green Alley, heading away from 2nd Avenue, and noticed a young lady up ahead walking her dog. It clicked that this was Jenna, a friend of mine, and I called out her name. She turned around, looked right at me, and frowned. Then she started lookin' around as if she didn't know where the voice had come from. This didn't make any sense, since I was in plain view. I said her name noticeably louder, but this time the sound of my voice sounded foreign to me. It sounded flat, and thin…

And then, like dust into the wind, she faded away.

"Jenna…?"

I stared at the spot where Jenna had been for a long while before I noticed that she wasn't the only thing missing. A few yards past where Jenna had disappeared was where there should have been another, more traditional alley, running perpendicular to our Green Alley heading north to south—but instead all I could see was a large green park with a water slide in the middle. And there were so many kids, laughing, playing, and yelling as they ran around on ridiculously lush green grass, as they lined up to take turns on the slide.

Hearing the sounds of children playing was something that always made me smile, and for a while, it made me forget the twist in the universe that I had somehow stumbled through. I took a few steps closer to the park to get a better look at all the joy, but then I realized…

Where were the adults?

Feeling the parent in me starting to activate, I picked up my pace toward the kids as I kept lookin' around for any sign of a grownup. No luck. When I got within a few yards of the kids waiting for the slide, I wondered if I was letting myself get too close to the situation. The last thing I needed was an angry parent noticing me getting too close to their kids and running out to accuse me of something.

But somehow I knew that wasn't going to happen. Not one of these kids was lookin' around for the reassurance of mom or dad. Even though kids tend to lose themselves in the enjoyment of play, there is still that invisible bond where it's not long before they know when they've strayed too far. That's when the crying starts, and it's how kids get lost as they run screaming through unfamiliar surroundings in search of their parents.

But none of that was happening here. A little bronze-skinned boy with long, sandy-brown dreadlocks looked over at me, then smiled and waved. I smiled and waved back. He broke away from the line for the slide and came closer to inspect me for a moment before reaching out his hand to hold mine.

"You should come sit down," he said. "There's a nice picnic table over there."

I looked over to where his other hand was pointing and, sure enough, there was a red wooden picnic table—lookin' as if it had been freshly painted.

I didn't remember seeing it there before. I noticed that he had an extremely strong grip for one so small.

"What's your name?" I asked as we strolled toward the table.

"Nathan," he said. "But we really don't have time for that right now." He sounded much too serious for a kid.

"Time for what?"

"Small talk. We knew one of you would show up eventually. We've been waiting for someone from the other side to find us."

"If you don't mind my saying so, you speak especially well for someone so young."

Nathan smiled, but his smile seemed somehow forced and impatient.

"Let me guess. We don't have time for this either, do we?"

He shook his head.

"OK then. So help me out here, because right now I'm not sure if I'm dreaming, or losing my mind, or if maybe someone dropped something in my milk. Where am I, and how long have you been waiting? And where are your parents?"

I noticed the other children had stopped playing on the slide and were watching us. They were all sizes and colors, but they were also a mixture of human and… something else…

"But you already know where you are. You're in Detroit—just not the Detroit you know. We've been here a very long time. And there are no parents here. No adults at all. Only us. Which is why we've been waiting for contact."

"Waiting for…"

"I'm sure you have noticed that in your Detroit, things have begun to change. There are some things that are no longer like they were—and some new things that don't belong."

"How do you know all this?"

The boy shook his head sharply, brushing off my inquiry like a pesky insect.

"The rains are coming," he began. "And once they come, they will never stop. As the rains become heavier, the Detroit you know will eventually be washed away.. *We* are kind of like an insurance policy. Because Detroit must not be allowed to die."

"I would agree with that... But how did I get here? I was out for a stroll in our Green Alley, and then next thing I know, I'm sitting here talking to someone who appears to be a very small adult that only *looks* like a child."

"There are bricks paving your alley, right? Bricks that had two symbols on them? The eye and the hourglass?"

I felt a chill run through me with the force of an electric current.

"In time you will see…?"

The boy smiled, this time excitedly, and nodded his head. He reached over and squeezed my hand again.

"When the time comes, you'll need to bring as many of your people here as you can. Many probably won't want to come. The familiar, no matter how horrible, will be far more preferable to them than the unknown. But you will have to convince them. Let them know that they are not *leaving* Detroit, because we're aware of how loyal Detroiters are to their city. *We* are Detroiters, too. So let them know they will be *coming* to Detroit, not leaving it. You must make that clear."

"But what kind of Detroit will it be if all the kids are acting like grownups? Won't that be kind of hard for folks to adjust to?"

Nathan smiled at me as if I were the child.

"You are the first, and you are the messenger. It's your job to tell the others, to bring the others, and that will take time, even though time is something you really don't have. But you will know when the hour is getting late. And when you return with the others, then what you see here will be different. It will be the Detroit you know once again."

"But how?"

"By your memories of Detroit. The *true* Detroit lives in the memories of Detroiters. And it will be those memories that create the future."

Nathan's Song

The small, golden-brown boy with the ginger-colored dreadlocks that hung halfway down his back sat across the picnic table from Tom, who had placed his phone between them to act as a video recorder. His hands were folded calmly. It was Tom's second visit to New Detroit (there would have to be a new name for this place at some point, he thought), and he required proof of what he had seen during his first visit. Several months earlier, he had accidentally (or maybe not so much) stumbled into this new territory during a stroll down the Green Alley, somehow passing through dimensions without even making an effort. Without the small being who looked like a child named Nathan, Tom probably never would have made it back to the Detroit he recognized, where the forever rains had been falling for five years now and showed no signs of stopping. It was Nathan who showed him how he could return at will.

Nathan had eyes the color of burnt copper, and they were eyes that shouldn't belong to anyone who appeared to be as young as he was. They were not the eyes of an innocent—trusting and anxious to witness new things. Instead, they were wary and intensely observant, not missing a thing. Tom got the sense that Nathan was not only paying attention to his every move, but also somehow managing to see deeper. They were the eyes of a survivor, and Tom could only imagine what it was that Nathan and the other children had been forced to survive that could produce eyes like the ones that were scrutinizing him right now.

He decided to smile. It was a nice day after all—the first one he had seen in years—and they were sitting outside in a beautiful park that did not exist in this same location back in the Old Detroit. In Old Detroit, this would have been a worn parking lot with stubborn weeds pushing up through the cracked asphalt. There were tall trees all around, and the sound of the leaves rustling mixed with the sweetened smells of abundant, multi-colored plants and flowers (some of which Tom didn't recognize at all and appeared strangely more conscious than any plant should be) made him feel relaxed despite the intensity of Nathan's stare. In fact, come to think of it, Tom felt more than relaxed. He felt…*exuberant.* Was that the right word? Close enough, he thought.

His smile stretched wider as he reached up to remove his glasses and wipe them briefly with a corner of his shirt.

"So are you ready?" he asked Nathan. Tom slid the frames back onto his nose, leaning forward across the picnic table as he did so, squinting his pale blue-green eyes.

Nathan said nothing for a noticeably long moment, but then made an attempt to return the smile. The effort suggested someone who had never tried to smile before, or never had reason to.

"Yes, Tom. I am ready."

For the record, what is your name?

My name has been Nathan for as long as I can remember.

Where are your parents?

There are none like you here, no adults. We have been in this Detroit all our lives. There are other Detroits, like the one you come from, but we believe yours to be the most compatible with ours. We believe that your Detroit and ours have a lot to offer one another. In truth, we believe that we need one another. It may even be critical that we join together.

How did you get the name Nathan?

No matter how hard I try, I cannot remember who it was that named me. I am not even certain how I know my name to be what it is. I only know, somehow, that this is my name, and that it is a good name to have. As far as I know, I have always been this same size and age, which is twelve years old. All of us here, we are all twelve. None of us have last names.

You said that there are other Detroits? How do you know this? Have you seen them?

There have been visitors over the years. You are not the first, although you are the ones that we have been waiting for. Not all of the visits have been pleasant. On occasion, we were forced to take measures.

What do you mean we are the ones you have been waiting for? Aren't I the first one from my Detroit that you have met?

You are the first, yes. But we always knew there would be a first. We even had some idea of how you might look. The description we received was close, but some things about you are different than what we expected.

Different how? And who or what gave you these descriptions?

Perhaps another time. There is too much for me to explain that you would need to know in order for you to understand. Let's move on.

Explain what you mean about not all the visits being pleasant. What was unpleasant about

some of those visits? And what measures did you have to take?

Not long ago, another group of Detroiters showed up. They seemed angry, and unlike you, they came here with malicious intent. It was obvious that their visit was planned and that they somehow knew how to find us. They accused us of things which were false and...

But didn't you know they were coming? Like with me?

Something went wrong. We should have known and been able to prepare for their arrival. It is something we are lookin' into. There could be a problem if this happens again—but not just for us. I assure you.

Were these visitors adults like me? Or were they...

They were not adults. They were nine.

There were nine of them?

They were nine years old. There were seven of them. We think that may be why they were able to sneak into our Detroit, unidentified. They are the most like us, and yet they are also very unlike us. They are a problem. Or, they could be...

And the other visitors? Have they all been children, too?

All the other visitors have been adults.

What was it that the other children accused you of?

They say we stole their Detroit. They claim that they should be the ones who are living here and not us. But they brought nothing to add truth to that claim—only their anger and their accusations. They say they intend to return to take what is theirs. We will see.

So that's why you want us to join together? So we can join a group of 12-year-olds to win a battle against some angry 9-year-old kids?

No. We want you to join us because we need you to build and grow. That is the only way we believe we can be released from our current age and allowed to grow older like you and the others who come from your Detroit. We are stuck because nothing here ever changes. Everything stays the same. And you cannot grow older if your life stays the same.

Tom in Old Detroit

Maybe these kids had all been stuck at 12 years old for who knows how long, but no way were they just kids. Because kids don't talk like that, and kids don't think like that. Nathan was beautiful, and so were the rest of them, but they were also scary as hell. I had kids of my own back in the Old Detroit, and if any of them had ever started talking like Nathan, I would have driven them way up in the woods somewhere, dropped them off, and never looked back. I saw *The Omen,* and that's not the kind of child-rearing experience I need.

On the other hand (I hate that saying, but I don't know another way to say it), I really did feel a sense of obligation to these kids—or whatever they were. However they got this way, and however they got here, they were all alone with no way that I could see of protecting themselves. But more than that, as I turned off the recorder on my phone and got ready to head back home, I thought about the last thing Nathan said before I stopped the recording:

"Everything stays the same. And you cannot grow older if your life stays the same."

Like I said, kids don't talk like that. But that didn't mean what he said wasn't true. And if there was something we could do to help, then maybe that's what we were supposed to do. Besides, our time in Old Detroit was ticking like an explosion as the forever rains got worse every year and the carnivorous plants got more unruly. We didn't have many options.

"So," I turned to Nathan. "I follow the same steps that you showed me last time to get back home, right? I just start walking through the big tree?"

Nathan nodded as he stood up from the table, but I could tell by lookin' at his face there was more he wanted to say.

"Something on your mind, Nathan? You seem a bit troubled."

Those burnt copper eyes stared at me hard. I didn't know how long I could maintain my composure under the intensity of that gaze, so I looked away.

"Do you really think you can convince your people to come here?"

Nathan's eyes may have been unsettling, but the voice belonged to a scared child seeking reassurance.

"I'm going to do my best, Nathan. Like I said I would. I wouldn't lie about that, plus it's not only in your best interest, but probably ours too. This is for all of our sakes."

Nathan nodded again, then made another semi-successful attempt at a smile.

"That's good. Then you should also know that the pathway between worlds won't last long. They never do. And you finding us the last time wasn't an accident. The pathway found you for us. But you need to tell your people that there isn't much time. Once the pathway fades, there is nothing more we can do. We will be lost to one another forever."

"How much time do we have? And if the pathway found us, then doesn't that mean the pathway found those others that you're so worried about? Why would it do that? Sounds to me like this path doesn't have your interests in mind as much as you think it does."

Nathan's semi-smile faded.

"None of us can understand the path. It chooses, and we adjust our lives accordingly."

I started to say something, but then I noticed how much closer the other kids were standing around me in a tight circle. Maybe I hadn't been paying attention, but I could have sworn they weren't standing so close a moment ago. They all wore the same solemn expression as Nathan, and they were all staring at me.

"Right. So I guess it's time to go," I said.

"Convince your people this is the best way. The *only* way."

"I said I'll do my best, Nathan. But people have their own minds to make up, so in the end it will be up to each of them to decide what they want to do. But I'll make my best case. You have my word on that."

I stood up, and the crowd of children parted, clearing a way toward the large tree that was taller than any tree I had ever seen anywhere in Detroit or anywhere else. The other trees were all sizable, but this particular one appeared to be the size of a redwood. It made me think of the fantastical overgrown plant from *Jack and the Beanstalk.* The closer I got, the more hazy it appeared, like a mirage you see above the pavement on a hot day.

And then I was back. The rain was pouring down harder than when I had left several hours ago, sending streams of restless water down the Green Alley in front of me. It was daytime, but we never saw the sun anymore because of the constant presence of clouds, so it was usually hard to tell the difference between morning and afternoon. It was either more gray, less gray, or dark, which I suppose accurately reflected everyone's mood these days. It was difficult to feel cheery when it was raining all the time, the sun never shone, and plants the size of giant squid raged all through the night before shrinking back to normal size during the daytime.

I looked around at the changed scenery, not caring much about how soaked I was getting, and thought about what it would mean to leave everything behind for another dimension. As bad as things were here, at least it was familiar. Well, maybe not as familiar as it used to be (the giant plants had not always been here), but still more familiar than where we were headed.

On the other hand (there I go again), if we decided not to leave, then we would likely die sooner rather than later, and not in a pleasant fashion. When the rains first began five years ago, it started as a sprinkling, with heavier storms coming through occasionally but not enough to worry anyone. We thought it was unusual that it never quite stopped, but as long as the sun still peeked through to check on us once in a while, most of us didn't suspect anything beyond global warming. But after several months passed and the rains got heavier, and the sun faded from sight, we started to get worried.

Especially when we heard that this was only happening in Detroit.

As things got worse, some folks started to pack up and leave. Some went to the suburbs (again), some moved further out, and some left the state altogether. But most of us stayed. That's just the way we Detroiters are. When things get rough, we get stubborn. Nobody and nothing is gonna make us leave our homes.

At least that's the way I felt then, and I was proud of it. But now I had to admit how much all of this was wearing on me. I knew how much it had been wearing on Peggy, my wife, and everyone else in the Green Garage (a co-working space that we own and manage). Nearly everyone in the G.G. was a diehard Detroit enthusiast and lived in the city, which was why I thought this option with Nathan and his crew of strange kids might actually have some appeal—because we wouldn't *really* be leaving Detroit. Right? Instead, we would be trading one Detroit for another. Scouting out new territories, like how they do in Star Trek.

The point, I realized, as I stood there with my hands on my hips getting completely soaked in the rain, was that we weren't going to get a better option. For those of us who had been secretly longing for a way out besides suicide, Nathan's path was the only direction.

I started walking toward the G.G., which was about fifteen yards ahead of me down the alley. As soon as I stepped inside, clothes dripping all over the floor, Fred looked up from the greeting desk where he had been reading something on his iPad, and immediately his expression shifted from a welcoming smile to shock and confusion.

"Tom! Man, where have you been? Everybody's been worried sick. We've been calling your phone for days now, and all we get is that stupid recording of yours. We even called the police because…"

"Call them off."

"Well, we can let them know that we found you, but you're still probably going to have to go in and make some sort of report because…"

"Just call them off. We'll worry about what to tell them later, but for now, just…please…call them off. The last folks I want to be bothered with right now are the police. We have more important things to deal with."

Fred raised his eyebrow and sat back in his highchair, which was what he liked to do just before he made a smart-assed remark.

"Oh, really? Would you mind telling your wife that? She's upstairs in the library. Because I'm sure she'd like to be reassured that there are more important things than finding her husband, who suddenly decided to come in from the rain after refusing to answer his phone for three days."

Smart-assed remarks like that. All I could do was sigh.

"Fair enough, Fred. And I'm going to talk to Peggy in just a minute. But remember when I was telling you guys about that experience I had with that kid Nathan and those other kids in the other Detroit?"

Fred's eyebrow dropped back down to normal as his shoulders slumped and he began shaking his head.

"I thought we were done with this, Tom. Didn't we already have this discussion? And didn't we finally manage to convince you that what you thought happened couldn't have happened?"

"And maybe that intervention would have lasted a bit longer if I didn't start thinking about the fact that six years ago, we could still see the sun. Six years ago, plants didn't transform like the Incredible Hulk every night and roar like movie monsters as they went to battle with the other sci-fi-looking critters none of us had ever seen or heard of. And that got me to thinking, why is it nobody wanted to believe me when I told you guys about Nathan and the other Detroit when all of you don't have any problem settling in with all this madness we see taking shape around us each and every day? Was what I said about Nathan really all that crazy when you compare it to that?"

Fred's facial expression told me he knew I was making sense, but if he admitted it, then he would have to admit something he didn't want to admit. So instead he said nothing, and we stared at each other for a prolonged moment.

"Fine. Don't say anything right now. But after I go talk to Peggy, I want to round everybody up because I have an announcement to make. And when I'm done, we'll see if everybody still thinks Tom Brennan is crazy."

The best way to describe Peggy's reaction when she saw me enter the small upstairs library is a brief moment of love and relief, followed by a chill so deep I could almost see my breath clouding up in front of me. I tried to smile, then shrugged my shoulders. She was sitting at military-style attention on the edge of a large, brown, comfy sofa with her hands folded tightly in her lap.

"I'm back."

"So I see. Did you have a nice trip?"

I squinted my eyes, bobbing my head back and forth indecisively.

"Wellllll…yes and no."

"Hmmm. Yes and no?"

"Good and bad. I haven't made up my mind yet whether it was more good than bad, but I'm leaning toward the more good version."

"I see."

And then we were back to staring at one another, exchanging volumes of unspoken communication that can only take place between two adults who have been married as long as we have. And all in the space of less than a minute, I understood that Peggy wasn't likely to believe a word I had to say if it had anything to do with a small brown kid with dreadlocks in a parallel universe.

But I had to try.

"So, I'm sorry I was gone for so long. I really didn't know it had been as long as it had. To me, it felt like just a few hours or so."

"Right. Because when you left, you just said you were going to the market on the corner. You said you would be right back. Isn't that what you said?"

I nodded.

"Yes. It is. And I admit I didn't exactly tell the truth about…"

"You lied, Tom."

I put my hands up in surrender.

"OK. OK. Maybe I lied, but…"

"No. Not maybe. Because you never planned to go to the market in the first place. And now you're going to tell me that you've spent all this time in some galaxy far, far away. With…what is that child's name again?"

"Nathan. His name is Nathan. And no, I didn't plan on going to the store. You're right. Because I knew if I said I was going back to the other Detroit, then that would have caused all kinds of problems."

"Really? And why would you think that telling me that you planned to return to an imaginary land in another dimension would cause all kinds of problems? What good wife in her right mind wouldn't believe her husband when he says he's going to another dimension?"

"But what if her husband could prove it?"

Peggy closed her eyes and put her face in her hands. It hurt to know she thought I was crazy, but that wouldn't last for long.

"Tom. Please."

I stepped closer and reached out to squeeze her shoulder.

"I made a recording, Peggy. So that you can see for yourself that I'm not making all of this up. The others, too, but mostly I took that video recording for you. Because I want you to see and hear. You have to see this, Peggy."

Slowly, her face appeared from behind her hands, and I was heartened to see from her expression that she at least wanted to believe me. She was willing to try.

"So you have this video with you now? When can I see it?"

I nodded, trying for an even bigger, more encouraging smile. A smile that would get me out of the dog house.

"Yes, I have it with me all right. I used my phone, can you believe that? As much as I hate to use cell phones for stuff like that because I can never figure it out, I actually used the video function on my phone."

"Congratulations, I guess."

"Right. So what I'd like to do in the next few minutes is make an announcement, OK?"

"An announcement? What kind of announcement? Why?"

"Because I want everyone to see this video, Peggy. It's that important. This can't be a private thing just between you and me, where you're the only one who knows I haven't lost my mind."

"I never said I thought you'd lost your mind, Tom. But what if maybe you need help? There's nothing wrong with that if you do. We both know these forever rains have been affecting folks in a variety of strange ways, and then there's the night creatures that have started to show up. It's a lot, it really is, and maybe if you…"

I was shaking my head as hard as I could without twisting it off.

"No. No, Peg. I don't need any help. I get that you're worried, and if I was in your position, I guess I would be worried too. Once you and the others see this video, it will make everything a lot clearer."

"Tom, I don't think this is a good idea. I really don't."

"How long have we been married?"

"Oh my God, Tom, you are not going to use that!"

"Long enough for you to trust me on this, Peggy. You know I wouldn't say it like this if it wasn't that important and if I didn't think it was something that I really had to do. But this isn't just for us; this is for everyone. Because we're going to need to leave this place. We're going to have to move to this New Detroit."

I'll be honest: as angry as she was, I thought Peggy was going to just get in the car and leave. And if she had, there wouldn't have been a thing I could have done to stop her, and there's no way I could have shown my video to everyone else in the Green Garage while trying to explain why Peggy had just stormed out.

But she didn't leave. Instead, before we left the library, she said, "You better not embarrass me with this, Tom. And we're not moving anywhere. We're staying right here in reality with the rest of the real Detroiters who actually exist."

"Sure. OK."

Once I had gotten everyone together, I had Julian, one of the younger G.G.ers, show me how to project the video on my phone onto the screen in the common room. Peggy was sitting beside me with her arms folded, wearing a stiff smile.

"So I suppose you're all wondering why I've gathered you here today," I said.

There were a few chuckles, but mostly I could sense a bit of tension mixed with curiosity. Aside from our normal Friday community lunches, we rarely had full group meetings like this, especially not on the spur of the moment. And after I had disappeared without a trace for several days and then suddenly reappeared, I suppose they had a reason to wonder what in the hell was going on.

"Look, I know you have a lot of questions. And after I show this short video of where I've been, believe me, you'll have more. I don't want to take up too much more of your time with any long preamble because the video will speak for itself, but I'll just say that what you're about to see isn't made up. You all know me, so you know I don't have the technical ability to manufacture or doctor a video, and I wouldn't know where to take it to have it done. What you're about to see is another Detroit, and the young man I'm interviewing lives there with a group of children his age. There are no adults in this Detroit. It is also not raining there, and the interview takes place where the parking lot is located behind us—except that in this other Detroit, it isn't a parking lot, it's a park with a lot of really tall trees. And some wonderful playground equipment. So with that, let's watch."

When the video was done, it was so quiet you could have heard a pin drop. I looked around the room, but it seemed no one wanted to look me in the face. I wasn't sure if that was because they were in shock or because nobody wanted to tell the crazy guy that this didn't prove anything. But when I looked over at Peggy, her arms were no longer crossed, and that stiff smile had faded. Unlike everyone else, she was staring at me directly, and she was nodding just barely. Then she spoke.

"It looks like nobody else wants to be the first to speak, so let me start this off and say that Tom came up to the library earlier and told me about where he had been and what he had seen while he was away. When he said he had a video to prove it and that he wanted to show this to everyone, my stomach started twisting up in knots because I was afraid of being embarrassed. But more than that, I was afraid that this could hurt Tom when he realized that what he thought he had seen didn't actually happen at all. I imagined a blank screen, or worse.

But as we all just saw, this is something else. Maybe it's not 100 percent proof, but, at least to me, it's something that we need to take more seriously. Because if this place really exists, then…"

"Then *what*, Peggy?" asked Marian, a longtime G.G.'er who looked as upset as Peggy had before she saw the video. Tall and willowy with dusty brown hair and freckles, her dirt brown eyes were practically shooting sparks.

"If this place really exists, and this Nathan boy is real and all his little friends are real and existing in another dimension in a galaxy far, far away without adult supervision, exactly what are we supposed to do about it? Are you seriously proposing that we rescue them? *They're not even our kids!*"

Peggy and Marian had been friends long before she decided to bring her small business to the Green Garage, and I could tell that her barbed attitude had inflicted a wound. Peggy shook her head slowly.

"No, Marian. I'm not proposing anything. Not yet. For now, this is just a video of an event that is hard to explain. But it does need an explanation."

"Why? We're not scientists. Why do we need to…"

"Because Detroit is dying and we need somewhere to go," I said. "That's the first thing. We can't continue to exist here in denial, chanting, " Rain, rain, go away." It's been five years for crying out loud! And we have seen what five straight years of rain can do, just like we know we can't hightail it to the suburbs or to Ohio and start anew. Nobody out there wants us, and we need to face that. They all want to *be* us, but nobody actually wants us living right next door to them. Why do you think that barrier is around the city? Who do you think voted to build that barrier?"

"Who do you think let them?" asked Henry, a caramel-colored man built like a fire hydrant, who always wore a Black baseball cap with a worn Detroit-style Gothic 'D' logo on the front. "This is an indictment of all of us, right? We let them do it, and now here we are."

"My point exactly," I said. "Here we are. And it doesn't really matter the mistakes we may have made or who let who get away with what. Here is where we are right now, and we can't stay here for too much longer."

"So then you *are* suggesting that we go rescue these kids," said Marian, the icy tone of her voice dropping the temperature in the room to near freezing.

"No, Marian. What I'm suggesting is that we rescue ourselves."

Tom and Peggy in New Detroit

It was Peggy who uttered the first words after the video was over, and it was Peggy who closed out the discussion when she said that she intended to go see the New Detroit for herself. This was a complete surprise to me, and may have been a bit of a surprise to Peggy herself, even though it was her idea. I think it was one of those things that came to her suddenly, and she didn't question it. Neither did I. She gave me a look after she said it, and I smiled.

"We'll go tomorrow," I said.

Just that quickly, Marian went from pissed off to worried.

"Peggy? Are you sure you want to do this? Just because Tom wants to go chasing after these kids who live in another dimension doesn't mean…"

"Tom is my husband, Marian. OK? Tom is my husband. I appreciate your concern, but I'll be fine. Besides, I don't think Tom is chasing after these kids, as you put it. This is something that could benefit all of us. Even you. So even though they're not our kids, it might do us some good to care what happens to them. Sometimes you help yourself when you help others."

Marian shrank down into her seat, her face turning bright red. I had to bite my lip to keep from smiling.

"We'll be fine," I said. "And if you're here in the morning, then we'll get to see you before we head off down the alley."

No one said a word.

* * *

The next day, as Peggy and I stood in the Green Alley, it looked like the entire G.G. family had come to see us off. We were thinking maybe a handful might show, but the area was crowded with anxious and smiling GG'ers.

"Wow," I said. "I'm not sure what to say."

"Just say you'll be back," said Marian, who was standing near the rear of the group and was now actually smiling.

"We'll be back sooner than you think," said Peggy.

I took a long look at everyone standing there, trying to freeze-frame the image in my mind, and then I grabbed Peggy's hand as we turned around and started walking. Peggy squeezed my hand hard and whispered, "What if this doesn't work this time and we don't disappear? How are we going to look then?"

That was the last thing she said before we crossed over.

"Peggy…? My hand, you're about to break it…"

"But *look! And it's not raining!*"

Then she looked behind her.

"There's no Green Garage…"

"Yes. I know. But please…my hand…"

"Oh. Sorry."

Slowly the pressure from her squeeze eased up as she ogled the tall trees and blue sky before noticing the playground in the distance. But there weren't any children. I felt a cramp forming in my stomach.

"Where are they?" I said, barely able to hear myself.

"You mean the children?"

"That's exactly what I mean. Something is wrong. They shouldn't all be gone like this."

"Tom, they're just kids. You and I both know kids don't always stay in one place, especially if there aren't any adults around to keep watch. Maybe they found themselves another playground somewhere else. We can just go find them, right?"

I did a full 360-degree turn, lookin' for any sign. Not only did I not see any of the kids, but it was silent in a way that made no sense in a city, not even a city with no adults. There were no voices, no dogs barking, nothing. Just the sound of the breeze as it blew through the trees. I shook my head.

"I'm not so sure it's that easy, Peggy. Where would we start lookin'? Do we just start wandering around shouting, 'Is anybody here?"

"Why not?"

"Peggy, I'm telling you, something is wrong, and this is not just a matter of some kids getting bored and searching out a new playground. Can't you feel it?"

"How would I feel it? I've never been here before. But…hey. *Hey.* Look over there, isn't that a kid coming our way?"

I looked toward where she was pointing, and sure enough, I could see Nathan running towards us. Why I hadn't seen him earlier, I had no idea, but I wasn't going to worry about it now. I was just glad to see the kid.

"Nathan! I'm so glad to see you." I called out. "I brought my wife Peggy so she could see everything for herself. But where is everybody? It looks like a ghost town."

"You and your wife must come with me *now,"* shouted Nathan, sounding winded.

As he got closer and I saw the fearful expression on his face, I stepped back and reflexively put my arm in front of Peggy to push her back.

"Wait...what? What's going on, Nathan? Come with you where?"

Once he was standing in front of us, I could see he wasn't *asking* us to come with him; he was *telling* us. The firm grip of his small hand around my wrist confirmed that.

"There's no time right now. I will explain everything once we're safe. But we're not safe out here. The others didn't even want me to take the chance to come get you, but I knew why you came back, and I couldn't allow anything to happen to you. So please come. Now. Before it's too late."

"I think we better listen to the boy, Tom," said Peggy, who sounded much calmer than I would have expected, this being her first time in another dimension.

I nodded.

"I suspect you're right about that, Peg. So where is this that you're taking us, Nathan?"

He pointed back the way he had come, then tugged hard at my wrist.

"Hurry. Please."

Moments later, we were standing near another huge tree that was much taller than the others, and that was saying something. I was about to ask Nathan why we had stopped when an opening appeared in the side of the trunk that was about five feet high and maybe a couple feet wide. One minute, the trunk was solid, and then…it wasn't.

"What the…?"

"No time," said Nathan, sounding impatient, bordering on angry. "The two of you go first. I will follow to make sure no one comes behind us."

"But there's no one else here, Nathan. What are you talking about?"

Now he was full-blown angry and started pushing me. He was definitely stronger than most kids, but he was still a kid. And I didn't like being pushed around by a kid.

"*Nathan.* There's nobody else out here except us, and now you're telling me and Peggy to jump inside a tree before anybody else sees us? Do you know how that sounds?"

There's that saying, "if looks could kill." Nathan was giving me one of those looks.

"I risked my life to come get you. The others warned me not to. They begged me. I am the leader of my group, and they need me, but I couldn't allow harm to come to you. And now you're asking these stupid questions and putting all of us at risk. If you cannot trust me, then why did you come back? Why didn't you just stay where you were in the other Detroit?"

That's when we heard it—an echoing explosion that sounded like something had blown up in the distance. Moments later, we heard it again, only this time the sound was noticeably closer.

"What is…"

Nathan shoved both of us inside the tree, and the next thing I knew, we were staring at a roomful of kids staring back at us with angry eyes. The room was the size of a high school gymnasium, but hardly a uniform shape. It was, after all, the inside of a tree.

"We *told you* not to go after them!" one of them said, after which all of the heads nodded in unison. I have to admit I felt pretty guilty, like the classic ugly American who insists on taking selfies next to the Mona Lisa while the museum is burning.

But as I stared around the room, which smelled like a forest after heavy rainfall, I also found myself marveling at our audience, who, although angry, were also kind of adorable. That probably wasn't the most appropriate way to be thinking about them at that moment, but I couldn't help it. They were all about the same height, approximately five feet tall, but they were so many different colors and shades, not just in skin color but in the color of their eyes as well, and their hair. And the variety was much more striking than the more "normal" human variances you would see on our side of the alley. Standing not two feet away from me was a boy who looked so white and pale that he was practically transparent. He had a head full of equally pale-colored hair that tumbled down past his small shoulders in ringlets and waves, and the irises of both eyes were so light that at first glance it appeared he had none at all. Standing next to him was a girl as dark as he was fair, yet her hair was the same color as his, and her eyes were aquamarine.

All I could do was smile, which I doubt was the reaction they wanted. I waved.

"Hi," I said, then was surprised by a slight echo.

"I'm Tom, and this is…."

"They know who you are, and they know why you are here," snapped Nathan.

"Really? And why is that?" said Peggy, sounding irritated.

As if to answer Peggy's question, there came another explosion from outside the tree, only this time the sound was heavily muffled. Nevertheless, the room shook, and the look of anger on the kids' faces shifted to fear.

"Because of *that*," said Nathan.

"And what exactly *is* that? And what is it you think we can do to help?" I said.

"More importantly, if you need our help with whatever this problem is that you're having, then why didn't your young friends here want you to come rescue us? If we're the only ones who can help you, then why would they want to leave us to die?" said Peggy, lookin' at Nathan as if he were an errant schoolchild.

But he wasn't. None of them were. Maybe they needed our help, but I knew it would be a mistake to treat Nathan and his… *tribe…?* as if they were the same as our children back home. They were something else.

"We didn't want to leave you to die," said the pale boy with the pale eyes as he stepped closer. "We just didn't want Nathan to be taken from us because he is important. You two may be important as well— at least that is what Nathan says, but we don't know that for sure. We will see."

I nodded.

"I can understand that."

A moment later, Nathan tapped my shoulder and motioned towards a space where Peggy and I could sit down. It was a smooth knot of wood, part of the tree, that had naturally formed to resemble a bench that looked as if it had been designed by Salvador Dali.

"So I guess I'll get right to it then. The last time I was here, Nathan told me there were other Detroits in the universe, or wherever, but that ours is apparently the most compatible with yours. He also said that there was another group of young people from one of these Detroits who are angry with you because they think you stole this version of Detroit from them, and that they planned to return and take it back. So, is that who is making all that noise outside?"

"Yes," they said in near unison.

Nathan continued. "Only this time, they brought more. Many more. The first visit, there were only seven of them. Now we don't know how many there are, but we know they are well armed."

"We are not," said the dark-skinned girl with the aquamarine eyes. "We have never been fighters."

"But aren't they just nine years old? And aren't all of you guys three years older than that? When you're my age, three years doesn't make much of a difference, but I don't know too many 12-year-olds who can't handle a 9-year-old. Plus, wasn't I just here a few hours ago? How did they get themselves together to fly across galaxies and declare war on you guys in that short a time?"

"Time works differently here, as it does across all Detroits. Time here is flexible."

"Meaning what exactly?"

"Meaning sometimes minutes can be one period of time, but at other times a minute can be something else. Time itself makes the decision as to when these changed calculations are made. I am sure this is difficult to understand, but it is the best I can do. Except that I can say much more time has passed than a few hours since the last time you were here."

"How much time? I mean, if you had to guess."

"Approximately five years."

"Whoa! So what does that mean for when we go back to our own Detroit to try and convince our people to come here? If we even agree that's what needs to happen? Last time I went back, it was only a three-day difference on our side. But if five years have passed on this side of the alley this time, then what…Jesus…"

Nathan shrugged, as if this were nothing more than a minor glitch.

"I don't know, but I'm sure you will figure it out. After all, you both are adults, right?"

"What, is that some kind of a joke?"

"In a way. Yes."

Except that he wasn't smiling, not even in the eyes. None of them were. I was beginning to think none of these kids had ever smiled a day in their lives, which was both sad and scary.

"Right. So then what about the age difference between you and the youngsters outside who have all of you so scared that you're hiding inside of a tree? Because I have to tell you that if you can't stand up to a bunch of angry nine-year-olds, then I'm not sure there's much we can do to help."

There was a low, dry hissing sound like rustling dry leaves in autumn that began to spread through the room as the kids whispered back and forth to one another, occasionally pointing at us. Definitely not a positive development, but all we could do was stand there and watch it play out, hoping that we managed to get out of this OK. I was starting to question my earlier conviction that we should all move here and live happily ever after. The absence of 24-hour rains was a plus, but these kids had some issues that I'm not sure we needed to get tangled up in, especially if it involved declaring war on an army of angry nine-year-olds from another dimension.

"They have been nine a long time," said someone from the back of the room who I couldn't see.

Nathan was nodding his head.

"What's that supposed to mean? How can you be nine years old for a long time?" I asked. "You're nine years old until you're ten. And then you're eleven. And so on until you look like me and Peggy. That's the way it works."

"But that's not the way it works here. I told you time is flexible here, it is not the same. I can't tell you why it's that way, only that it is."

"Oh my God, you're saying age really *is* just a number over here," said Peggy, who looked as if she couldn't quite believe what she was saying even as she was saying it.

"I have never thought of it that way, but yes," said Nathan. "How did you come up with that?"

"I didn't. It's just something…something we say sometimes. But it has a different meaning."

"Different how?"

Peggy shook her head. "Nevermind. I would have just as hard a time trying to explain that to you as you were trying to explain how time is flexible. But you need to tell us why it matters that the nine-year-olds have been that age for a long time. Because so have you, right?"

"We were simply trying to get you to understand. You seemed to think that because our attackers are nine years old and we are twelve, that somehow we should automatically be able to defeat them. This difference does not mean anything at all in our Detroit. In truth, it is our belief that they have probably been nine for a longer time than we have been twelve. That would explain why, in some ways, they are clearly more advanced than we are."

"So I'm not even going to try and understand what you just said because I'm pretty sure my brain would twist up like a pretzel but…"

"Pretzel?"

"Never mind. Just let me ask you this: did you guys take this Detroit from the nines? Is it even possible that they may have any sort of claim on this place?"

Why did I have to say that? Peggy didn't bother lookin' at me to register her disapproval, but we had been married long enough that there was no need. I could feel it, and that was worse.

As for the kids, their whispers and pointing escalated to yelling and shouting. Eventually, Nathan managed to quiet everyone down, and I started to thank him, but the look on his face indicated it might be in my best interest to speak when spoken to.

"I think you had better explain yourself," he said in a voice that was both quiet and tense.

"Yes, I think you had better," said Peggy.

I cleared my throat.

"Right. So first of all, I'll take that reaction as a no, you guys didn't take this Detroit from the nines, which is a good place to start. Secondly, I'm sorry I asked the question, but I felt like I had to get that out of the way. It wasn't meant as an accusation, nor was it meant to indicate I questioned your integrity in any way. But for me, I just needed to hear you say it. You did that pretty loudly."

"So now that we have passed your test, what are you going to do?" asked Nathan.

"I brought Peggy here so that she could see this for herself. When I went back with the video I took of Nathan, too many of my friends in our Detroit still did not believe me. They thought I was stringing them along, making all this up. The others, maybe even more of them, thought that I might be telling the truth, and that only made them more afraid. Because, as bad as things have become in our Detroit, it's still familiar. And asking them to leave behind what they know to come to another Detroit that they never even knew existed is a tall order. And that was *before* we knew that the nines had decided to declare war on you guys. But I knew if Peggy came back here with me and actually saw what I saw, then the chances of the others agreeing to follow were a whole lot better. Because even though Peggy wasn't one of the ones who doubted me—heck, she was even trying to convince them to come—I knew she would be more persuasive than ever once she had witnessed this place and seen all of you for herself."

"So what are you going to do?" asked Nathan again.

"How long before you figure it's safe to get out of this tree?"

"Hopefully not long. Now, will you please answer my question?"

"We're going to get as many recruits as we can. OK?"

Nathan stared at us for an uncomfortably long moment, then sharply nodded his head. I could feel the tension begin to seep out of the room like air from a balloon.

"How many do you think will come?" asked the dark-skinned girl with the aquamarine eyes.

"I'm not sure. I wish I could give you a better answer, but I'd rather not make you a promise of any specific number and then turn up short-staffed. But I will get as many as soon as I can—or as soon as I can, depending on how this flexible time issue of yours works."

"Thank you," she said.

Soon, I heard others murmuring the same. I felt like we were doing the right thing—if we could pull it off.

Back to Old Detroit

As soon as we crossed over, Peggy and I knew that a lot had changed. For one thing, the winds had picked up speed, and it was noticeably colder. Ever since the rains had started five years ago, the temperature had stayed between 75 and 80 degrees, no matter the season, night, or day, but now it felt closer to 60. What we didn't know was how much time had passed.

Maybe it wouldn't be so hard to convince our colleagues to return with us after all.

"Oh, my God. What happened to the Green Garage?" asked Peggy, pointing approximately twenty yards away toward the end of the alley.

What had been a sturdy, red brick building with large triple-pane windows lookin' out from three sides was now a crumbling wreck, and at least one of the windows was boarded up. But I couldn't see the full extent of the damage because it was nighttime and the plants had grown to their nighttime size of Jack's fairytale beanstalk, and they were writhing and growling as they snaked their way over the top of the Green Garage. I wondered if anyone was even inside, and if they *were* inside, what kind of condition would they be in?

"We at least have to see," said Peggy, as if she were reading my mind while we stared at the nightmare unfolding in front of us. "If we approach real slow, then I think maybe we'll be alright. Remember, they have always recognized us, and they haven't hurt anyone yet—at least I don't think so. They just kill the night critters, which is actually a good thing since it was one of the night critters that took part of your leg."

"Maybe you're right, but don't they seem different to you? I mean…did they growl before?"

Peggy didn't respond right away, and I was starting to think maybe she hadn't heard me over the noise of the rain and the restless plants. She was just staring.

"Peggy…?"

"They do seem different. But we still have to see. We have to try. Maybe someone needs our help. That's still our building, and those are our people."

"Are you sure? We can both see this isn't the way it was when we left, so who knows how much has changed?"

I was thinking we might be better off going back to the other Detroit, even if we had to go back empty-handed. Then maybe if we crossed back at a later date the problem would have solved itself. Perhaps not as brave a move, but definitely a whole lot safer.

But Peggy was already forging ahead, and as it turned out, she was right about the plants. As menacing as they looked and sounded, they slithered aside and cleared a small path toward the Green Garage. They even dialed the growling down a notch, which I thought was considerate. There was a powerful stench that came from the vines, something like rotten eggs mixed with something long-dead, but I did my best not to flinch or say something ugly because, as crazy as it sounded, I didn't want to offend the plants. We needed them on our side, and it probably wouldn't help to make a big deal over how much they reeked.

Once we were inside the Green Garage, our questions were answered about how much had changed. When Peggy and I had crossed over to the New Detroit, what felt like only a few days ago, the structure still resembled the marvelous creation we had designed and that had managed to hold up remarkably well even throughout the rains and the dramatically increased humidity. Other buildings around the city began to show increased signs of wear and tear after only a couple years of the changed weather, but five years in, the G.G., which was created and upgraded from the bones of an old automobile showroom, still looked as if we had just finished construction. The hardwood floors had maintained their polished appearance with no signs of buckling, and there was no flooding or even dampness in the basement.

But however long ago that encouraging vision had been, things were different now. I felt something like a large stone form inside my stomach as Peggy reached over and took my hand. The floors had not merely buckled in places, but looked hacked and torn, as if someone had assaulted them with a hatchet and whatever other sharp tools they could find. Greenish purple vines, which I assumed were related to the more gargantuan versions crawling around outside, stretched themselves up the full height of the two-story walls and were wrapped lazily around the sagging crossbeams. As Peggy and I forced ourselves to walk deeper inside, hearing the echo of our footsteps as we went, I noticed a number of the vines following along behind us.

I felt an almost unsustainable burden of guilt weighing me down like an anvil strapped to my shoulders as it occurred to me how everyone probably assumed we had abandoned them. I couldn't bear to consider what they must have thought of us as day after day crept by and we didn't return.

But exactly how much time had it been? There was still no way to tell without an actual calendar or a phone able to mark the days accurately. Not surprisingly, our phones only registered the *actual* number of days and hours we had been gone. There was no way for them to calculate two sets of time zones simultaneously, especially when one of those time zones was "flexible" and from another dimension.

"Where do you think everyone went?" I asked.

Peggy shrugged as we stood in the middle of the building lookin' around.

"I don't know, but can you blame them? This isn't even their home, Tom. This is where they work. Or where they used to work, I guess. Sure, we were a community, or I'd like to think so, but this still wasn't home, and it wasn't their responsibility. It was ours. If things were getting as bad as it looks like they were, they probably stopped trying to maintain the place once they had accepted the fact that you and I weren't coming back anytime soon. Because if we didn't care enough to come back and help save it, then why should they?"

All I could do was sigh and shake my head.

"So after all that work, all those years of planning, the G.G. is back to what it was before we even arrived. It's like we never even set foot in here."

"What are we going to tell Nathan and the other children?" she asked.

"If we can't find the others, then we don't tell them anything because we're not going back. It's hard enough trying to handle how much we let down our own people. I don't think I could handle crossing back over to disappoint a bunch of kids who were counting on us. If this is going to be the end, then let it be the end here in the Detroit that we know."

But then someone started knocking at the door. *Hard.*

One Last Time

"Whoever that is banging on the door isn't planning on stopping," said Peggy.

"Maybe not, *but how in the hell do they even know we're here?*"

Not even an hour ago, Peggy and I had been in a Detroit from another dimension where there were no adults, the forever rains had either stopped or never existed, and all the children were twelve years old but acted as if they had lived through an eternity. Now we were back in the nighttime of the Detroit Peggy, and I knew, the city where we had spent most of our lives, and where we should have felt more comfortable.

Home sweet home.

But it wasn't. It had been raining for five years straight, with the rains getting progressively worse over time. Those were the conditions on the day I had taken Peggy with me to see Nathan and the New

Detroit. I wanted her to know I hadn't been lying about what I had seen and where I had been when I had left for what I thought was a few minutes that turned out to be a few months.

It was during our trip to the other side that Nathan tried to explain how time worked in their dimension, which was, as he called it, "flexible." That partially explained why the kids over there had been twelve years old for as long as they could remember, or why the kids who had launched an attack against them on the day we had arrived were all nine years old - even though some of them were somehow older than the ones who were twelve in some way that I could never hope to understand.

It also explained why what had only been a few days in New Detroit had been far longer here at home. Peggy and I stood in the ruined center of what had once been our beloved Green Garage, now seemingly abandoned and broken with greenish purple vines - extensions of the monster plants outside - climbing the walls and wrapped around the beams above our heads, following our every move.

But what it didn't explain was that persistent banging at the door.

"So why don't they just come in like we did?"
asked Peggy. "The door is hardly locked anymore."

I hadn't thought of that until she mentioned it. I
shrugged.

"Maybe they don't know…?"

We looked at each other with uncertainty.

"Yeah. Maybe."

We didn't have to guess much longer once we
heard the door's hinges squeal as if in excruciating
pain. Peggy and I took several steps back, and I
reflexively placed myself in front of her so that
whoever - or whatever - was coming through the door
didn't get to her first.

"Hello…? Is anybody here?" came a familiar
voice. "Actually, I saw you guys come in. I don't
want to…"

"Marian?"

It was exactly who it turned out to be. The same
Marian who had been so grumpy during the last
group GG meeting, where we had discussed Peggy's
decision to go with me to New Detroit, and watched
the video I had shown them featuring Nathan. Last
time we had seen her, she was wearing her standard
weather-worn jeans and lumberjack shirt, a uniform
she wore even in the more miserable days of a

Michigan summer in August. Oh, and those horrific Black boots that looked as if they had experienced at least two wars on the front lines. Wars that we couldn't have won.

In normal times, I have to admit Marian wasn't the person I would have chosen to be our welcome-back-to-your-home-dimension party, but in this case, I was glad to hear the sound of any familiar human who wasn't homicidal. The fact that Marian still wore her same uniform made me feel more relaxed - but not enough to ignore our current situation.

"Marian, what are you *doing* here? It's not safe at all!"

Marian chuckled as she shut the door behind her.

"Is that a fact? And whatever would make you think that things are not safe right now? I simply can't imagine."

I had to smile. I really was glad to see her.

"OK, you score a point. But seriously, I mean, *why?* This whole place is a complete and total wreck, and it's after dark, so how is it that you just happened to be in the neighborhood?"

"Fair enough. Can we sit?"

"Sure, but where? This isn't quite the comfy GG we used to know and love. What the hell happened? How long have we been gone?"

Marian pointed to a table and chairs shoved into a corner across the room. I hadn't noticed them earlier, but then why would I? There had been other things demanding my attention, and my head was still reeling from what I'm sure was some form of PTSD caused by the stress created by time travel between worlds.

Once we had pulled the table and chairs out of the corner and cleaned them off as best we could with some rags that were nearby (they were also dirty but I guess we were pretending), we sat down and looked around at each other, as if confirming that each of us was really here, in this time and place, experiencing the same twisted reality.

"So what happened, Marian?" I asked.

Marian leaned back in her chair, raised her arms above her head, grabbed both elbows, and closed her eyes for a long while. Then she sighed.

"First of all, I didn't just happen to be in the neighborhood. I live here now, in the building across the street. I'm sure you didn't have time to notice it there because you had enough going on inside your heads trying to wrap your mind around what you were seeing. But that mini-mall that used to be there isn't a mini-mall anymore. A group of us repurposed it for what we figured made more sense in the current environment since it's obvious that nobody will ever rebuild the Asian restaurant or the laundromat."

"So…you guys are squatters? And they're letting you get away with that?"

Marian smiled, but not really.

"I know it's not something that you would approve of, Tom, and I understand. Normally, I wouldn't either."

"It's not that so much, Marian. I know things are different now. But…"

"I'm going to interrupt you right there. Because you asked how long it is that you guys have been gone, and I think the answer to that might help you better understand what it is you've come back to. You and Peggy have been gone for over two years, Tom. OK? *Two years.*"

Peggy slapped her hand over her mouth as she inhaled a frantic gulp of air.

"Oh, my God."

All I could do was shake my head.

"He said time was flexible, but still… I thought the difference would only have been a few days or weeks, like what happened before. Months at most. But *years?* This just doesn't make any sense."

"I'd say you're right about that, Tom. But who told you that time was flexible? That sounds like some kind of science fiction-y thing you'd see in one of those movies."

"Nathan. The kid you saw in that cell phone video I showed you guys the last time I was here. Peggy met him, too. He was trying to explain to us how the time difference worked between worlds, but he did say we wouldn't understand it. I guess he was right."

"Whoa. *Between worlds?*"

I nodded.

"But where is everyone else?" asked Peggy. "And what happened to the Green Garage? Even if it's been two years, it looks to me like some of this damage had to have been intentional. I mean, look at it!"

A small tear trickled down her cheek as she gave a sweeping gesture encompassing the ruins of what had been our dream. I reached over and put my arm around her shoulder. Peggy wasn't one to cry easy, so I knew how much this hurt. Marian looked pained as well.

"It may look that way, Peggy. Like somebody purposely ripped this place up. But I'm telling you this is what two years can do to a place in this strange new world we're living in when nobody's tending to it. All the humidity and so much water, plus you can see the plants have taken over just about everything. It used to be they only stretched out at night, like I know you remember, but now they're this size all the time. And the plants aren't the only thing; the critters are back, plus some other things that…well…you'll see. Or maybe not, if you're lucky."

"But where is everybody?"

The Meeting

Marian's rather expansive abode was an industrial-style loft on the second floor above what used to be the Chinese restaurant that once-upon-a-time had some of the best egg rolls you could find anywhere. Now it was stuffed with mismatched furniture odds and ends, scattered books on a variety of topics, news magazines, and an impressively large collection of glass elephants that were stationed at numerous outposts guarding the domicile; some with trunks and tusks raised defiantly, others appearing calm and majestic, while still others were more cartoonish wearing suits and wild colors, tap dancing and playing instruments to a silent melody as they gave the middle finger to reality.

Then again, reality had become a fond memory of the way things once were.

"I thought it might be easier for us to ask everyone to meet here rather than trying to deal with the GG in the condition it's in now. Too depressing, right?"

I nodded. We sat around a circular wooden table in the center of the room that appeared to be an antique.

"Right. So how many were you able to reach?"

"Well, we lost Matt to an accident in the basement. He never should have gone down there in the first place, but…anyway…"

"Anyway, *what?*" asked Peggy.

Marian shrugged helplessly.

"You know Matt always was one to make sure everything was tidied up like it was supposed to be before he locked up to leave. It was just him and me at the end of the day, about a year ago …? Anyway, he thought he heard something in the basement, so he went to check and…well…there really was something in the basement."

"Isn't that where we kept the worms?" I asked.

"Umm…yeah. And that's kinda what happened."

"Marian, what do you mean that's *kinda* what happened? You're not saying…"

"I'm saying those worms got a whole lot bigger and a whole lot meaner. And that's all I'm gonna say about it because what I saw after I heard Matt screaming and I went to look down those steps is something nobody should have to see. Not ever."

None of us said a word for a long while, and then I cleared my throat.

"So is there anybody else we need to know about?"

"Marsha got attacked right out front by a herd of those lobster-lookin' critters with the tentacles. She was heading for her car and didn't see them behind her until it was too late. At least that's what I heard. Thank God I didn't have to see that, too. But everyone else is pretty much accounted for, except for Fred. He kinda disappeared off the map, but we don't think anything necessarily got him or anything like that. We think maybe the stress of, you know, everything. Yeah, you see that a lot now where folks can't handle it anymore. Remember how it was during the pandemic? That COVID thing? Remember how we all had to try and stay inside and not go anywhere or visit anybody for all that time? And that was only for a couple of years, and folks started going crazy, kids acting out in school, and all else. So I don't guess we should be surprised when anyone we know kinda fades away. Matter of fact, I'd say we ought to be surprised when they *don't.*"

Peggy had her face in her hands and was shaking her head. I reached over to stroke her back.

"Sorry…" Marian said. "I thought you'd want to know."

"We do. It's just a lot."

She nodded.

"Everything is, I guess."

"Yeah. So I guess that gets back to our original question: about how many do you think will show up?"

An hour later, Marian's flat was about half full with twenty-three GG residents, most of whom we recognized, but some of them were new. That surprised me in a near-hopeful way because I wouldn't have thought anybody else would have wanted to join after the world - or at least the world in Detroit - had gone mad. Most seemed glad to see us as we ambled around the room making acquaintances, chatting, and occasionally exchanging hugs. I could tell a few were withholding judgment, hiding behind smiles that seemed to be plastered on. I couldn't blame them, although I did wonder what had motivated them to come. Curiosity, I guess.

"Hey, everybody! Hellooooo!"

The conversations faded into an amiable silence as everyone's attention focused on Marian, who had decided to go a bit dramatic and stand on a chair. For some reason, her pose made me think of a ringmaster in a circus.

Marian took a deep breath, stretched her smile a bit wider if that was even possible, and looked around the room.

"Thanks for coming. Really. Before you guys got here, we were remembering the good old days of what it was like during COVID, right? Remember that? How we thought that was going to be the end of us, and how for nearly two years we barely saw one another except on screen? And now we've been dealing with these rains for what? Almost seven years now? Now it's not any crazy disease that keeps us apart, it's us. And you know what I'm talking about. A lot of us here tonight haven't been in the same room or been in any kind of contact for a long, long while. Not because we couldn't, but because we just didn't feel up to it. We're watching the world die, and we're getting worn down, right?

"Which is kind of why I asked you guys to come over tonight, and why I'm so glad you did. Obviously, Tom and Peggy showing up from beyond the void after all this time gave me a hook, I guess you'd call it. But it's also about getting us together to talk about what happens now."

"What do you mean, what happens now?" asked George, a heavyset Asian man who had been a long-time Green Garage resident.

Before the rains, he had been involved in spreading the gospel of urban gardening around the city as a form of healing from the Earth is how he liked to phrase it. But then it seemed like the Earth turned on us, and he took it more personally than anyone else at the GG. Lookin' at the expression on his face and hearing the strain in his voice, I could tell not much had changed since we had left. In fact, he might have gotten worse.

"Do we want to keep living like this forever, or do we want to try and do something about it? Do we sit by until we drown, pretending that's not gonna happen, or do we take some sort of action?" said Marian.

George made a dry hissing sound as he shook his head.

"What kind of action are we gonna take against nature? She broke her agreement with us, and there's nothing we can do about it. Might as well get used to it."

"Agreement? What the fuck agreement are you talking about, George? You act like nature is a landlord who lives right down the street."

That would be Helen, who had issues with George long before the rains began. The group had formed a raggedy circle around Marian as the center of gravity, who was still standing on top of her chair and beginning to look distressed because she could see what was coming. Helen, who had been standing farther outside the circle toward the rear, was now pushing her way toward the center so she could get closer to confront George, who was standing not far from Marsha. If there had been any chance this could turn into a physical confrontation, it would have been over in a finger snap, because George was 300 pounds of flesh compacted into a 6-foot frame, whereas Helen was half sparrow and half hummingbird.

George sighed.

"All I'm saying is…"

"No! You're saying we shouldn't even try for better, and I don't wanna hear it. You used to believe in all this healing power of the Earth, and now you think every day is Armageddon. You're like Eeyore from *Winnie the Pooh*."

"Guys! Please! Shut the hell up!"

I had no idea that Marian could yell that loud, and judging by the reactions around the room, we weren't the only ones surprised. But if she hadn't taken charge when she did, I'm certain that entire evening would have turned into a dumpster fire we couldn't put out.

"Damn, Marian," said George.

There was a brief silence, and then some folks started to chuckle. Pretty soon, nearly everyone was laughing, which was a good sign. That had been close.

"OK, Marian, you have our attention again. So what's this really about?" asked Helen.

There were murmurs of assent scattered throughout the room. I felt like folks *kind of* wanted to know, but then weren't sure, because after all this time, nobody wanted to get their hopes up. George may have caught the sharp end from Helen, but he was hardly the only one who was skeptical of any reason for hope.

"I'm glad you asked, and with that, I won't delay this any longer. No need for suspense. I'll turn this over to Tom and Peggy, who all of you know have been gone for a really long time. They have something to share with us that could be our one shot. It's a risk, but…well…I said I'd let them tell you, and I will. Guys?"

Peggy and I glanced at one another, then stepped forward into the center of the circle and looked around at everyone. I wore my best smile, probably more for me than for them. I figured this must have been close to what it felt like for those unlucky Romans who got thrown into the coliseum to face the lions.

"So thanks, Marian. And again, Peggy and I really do want to thank you guys for coming. We know you all have things to do, and more than that, we know we've been gone quite a while and kind of left everyone here hanging in the balance. I hope you know that wasn't our intention, and we really had no way of knowing so much time had passed on this side. But that doesn't make this any better for how we left things."

"I think you'd better explain what you mean by time passing on *this side,*" said Marian, one eyebrow raised.

"Yeah, that would be helpful," said someone toward the back whose voice I couldn't quite make out.

"Good point," I said. "I'm already assuming you know things you couldn't possibly know. So I guess let's just start from the beginning."

And for the next half hour, I ran through the entire history of what had happened, going back way before I took my accidental trip to the New Detroit to when the rains first started, because that's when everything started to change; critters we'd never seen before, huge, meat-eating plants that only reached full size at night, things like that. I was sure it was all connected, going all the way up to the impending battle on New Detroit between the twelve-year-olds we had gotten to know and the nine-year-olds we never actually saw. Then I tried to make the case for why we should move there, which began to sound more and more implausible the more I heard myself talk. It seemed to make so much sense when we were in New Detroit, even with the drawbacks, but now I found myself struggling to justify something so far-fetched.

"So any questions?" I asked once I was through, trying to sound humorous. Not sure it worked.

"If what you're describing is for real, I guess I'm trying to understand how that's supposed to be any better than where we are right now," said Helen. "It's nice that there's no more rain, or at least not every day, and a return to somewhere sunny would be lovely. But do we really want to be responsible for a city full of children? A city full of children who are at war with another group of children from still *another* dimension? And even as I'm speaking, I can't believe I'm saying this, because it all sounds like an episode of The Twilight Zone."

"And you're saying that what we've been living through these past years hasn't been a Twilight Zone episode? Seriously?" asked Marian.

"OK. Fair enough. Which brings me back to my original question: how is it any better for us trading in one Twilight Zone episode for another? At least the episode we're living through is one we're familiar with."

"Sure. For now," said Peggy, who could already feel the sentiment of the room leaning towards Helen. Partially because of what Helen was saying, but also because she had always been a very strong personality who everyone respected and listened to.

Helen raised an eyebrow until it looked like the outline of a teepee.

"For now?"

"Yes. For now. Just look at how fast everything has changed around here in no time at all. You say we're familiar with all this, but are we really? Or have we just gone numb because it's all becoming too much to process? You're right, we know the names of the streets and where this and that building or store used to be, but is that familiarity enough to say we should be comfortable staying here?"

The room was silent, without so much as a whisper. The only noise you could hear was the sound of the rain that never stopped beating against the windows. I figured maybe it was my turn to say something.

"Look, we're not saying that there would be no risk involved with what we're proposing, and we're not trying to say you have absolutely nothing to worry about. Your fears make complete and total sense, and, to be honest, you'd be crazy not to be at least a little bit afraid. But we can't let that fear cripple us, or keep us from at least considering some options for survival before it's too late. And judging by how much everything has changed since the last time we were here, too late may be right around the corner."

"The other thing I think it's important to make clear is that we never said we would be responsible for these kids," said Peggy. "You need to understand that they have been surviving just as they are without any help from adults. At least not any help that we know about or that they remember. The other thing, and this is going to be hard for most of you to understand or believe, because it's still hard for us, and we were there, but the age of these kids isn't really their age. And I don't think they're really kids."

You could hear the sound of frustration rising quickly in the room, going from near total silence to a steady, angry chatter.

"Now just hold on one damned minute," came a deep bass voice from off to our right. I didn't need to look to know it was Billy, who was short and weighed maybe a third of what George did, but who had the vocal cords of James Earl Jones and the skin tone to match.

"I was trying to hold on and maybe give you guys the benefit of the doubt, but now doubt is damned near all I got. What the hell is this you're talking about, kids who ain't really kids? What kinda sense does that make?"

The chattering continued to get louder and angrier until Marian yelled at the top of her lungs for everyone to shut the hell up. Again. And they did. Never in a million years would I have suspected this woman had leadership qualities, but sometimes you just never know. Disasters bring out the worst in people sometimes, but they can also bring out the best.

"This isn't why we called the meeting, you guys. If all you want to do is scream and shout at Tom and Peggy, then this ends right now, and we can all go back to enjoying this wonderful life we're living. Because Tom and Peggy aren't our enemies, and you know that. They didn't just up and decide to leave us behind for all this time. Most of you remember how it was when Tom came back from there the first time and how he was gone for way longer than he even knew. Sure, it's hard to understand, and maybe it wasn't meant to be understood any more than all this other crazy stuff we got going on, but we can't be blaming them for a time zone change, or for what they saw in that other zone. All they're trying to do is help, so we can take it or leave it. And judging by how hot the temperature got in here tonight, I say maybe we let this sit for a while. Maybe come back here and reconvene in a week?"

There were slow murmurs of assent, and even a few mumbled apologies to me and Peggy. Billy even made his way over and gave us a hug, which I considered a good sign.

"It's just a lot, you know?" he said. "I mean…*a lot.*"

I nodded.

"Believe me, Billy. We know."

The Car Ride

When we woke up the next morning, the only difference I could see lookin' outside was that the dark skies from the previous evening were now slightly improved to a dark gray. Marian had been gracious enough to let me and Peggy take her bedroom for the night while she moved to the large overstuffed sofa that squatted against the wall beneath a large factory window. But I could tell she was already awake as I overheard her talking to someone on the phone while the television blared what sounded like a sitcom. Lots of canned laughter. Must have been one of those nostalgia oldies stations, which I guessed was better than listening to anything that talked about what was really going on. There does come a point when you can only take so much.

"You awake?" I asked Peggy.

"For at least an hour," she said. "You know how hard it is for me to sleep anywhere that's not my own bed."

I nodded, making a mental note that we hadn't been in our own bed for quite some time.

"So I hear Marian is up too. Might as well make our way out there and see what's ahead for the day. See if she still wants to do this road trip thing she was talking about just before we went to sleep."

Peggy sat up and swung her legs over the side of the bed, still not lookin' at me. Her shoulders looked small as she planted her hands on either side of her on the mattress.

"Last night was pretty depressing, wasn't it?" she asked.

She wasn't really asking a question, so I didn't know the best way to answer. I thought about the brief discussion the three of us had engaged in last night after everyone else had left. Marian had been trying her best to cheer us up, especially Peggy, who we could both tell was dispirited by how the somewhat of a reunion had turned out. I'm pretty sure it was what had prompted her to suggest the road trip. Not that taking an up close and personal view of how much worse everything had gotten was the best way to brighten the mood, but it might go a long way toward explaining the infection of ugliness that was so evident in the overall mood.

"Of course it was. It surprised me, too. But I don't think it should have surprised either one of us, really. Because I think people are starting to go crazy, to be blunt about it. People are tough, and the human mind is an amazing thing, but there is only so much it can take before it starts to overheat. And when it does, is when we start the meltdown."

Neither of us said anything for a long while before Peggy issued a heavy sigh and then stood up, staring at the closed door.

"Think we ought to make our entrance?" I said.

She turned to look at me and smiled. Maybe those clouds weren't so gray after all.

"Sure," she said. "Let's go."

* * *

Marian's car, a small gold Toyota with a noticeable dent in the front passenger side door, was parked about a block away on 2nd Avenue. I couldn't quite figure out why she chose so far away when there were hardly any cars in the parking lot or on the street, but I figured it wasn't worth asking about. She had always been a bit quirky.

"I know it doesn't look like much, but she's never quit on me, not even after all these years in the rains. Not a lotta people can say that. You know that saying about silver linings? Well, the rains have been a silver lining for auto mechanics, I can tell you that. All this water and rust, stuff like that. But I haven't had to take her in one time, can you believe that?"

I nodded as she thumbed her key to open the car doors.

"Pretty impressive, I have to agree," I said, as I looked up and down the street, wondering where the rest of the world had gone.

"So does everybody around here sleep late now, or not have jobs, or what? It looks like we're the only ones out here."

Marian gave me an uncomfortable look that I didn't quite know how to read as she walked around her vehicle to the driver's side.

"Get in. There's some things you should see."

"Is everything OK, Marian?"

"I'm fine. Just…please. Get in."

I started to say something else, but Peggy squeezed my hand. I got in the back seat so she could take the front.

"So where are we headed?" asked Peggy, as the car pulled away from the corner.

"I think we should probably go to Belle Isle first. Hit two birds with one stone."

"What two birds is that?" I asked.

"That way you can see what's been happening with the river too."

"Wait…there's something going on with the river?"

Marian didn't answer; she just drove. I guess she figured once we got there, that would be answer enough. We made our way toward Woodward and then took a right toward downtown. Still, not one single person on the street. Most of the buildings along the way were deteriorated and discolored, all of them some shade of gray. Some were still close to their original height, while others only rose up several stories; the view resembled an unending row of bad teeth in the mouth of a giant.

"Is there a reason why we're not taking the freeway? Wouldn't that be quicker?"

Marian shook her head.

"Not really, plus the freeways are all overrun now. They're not safe. The only way you can get anywhere is over the streets, and not all the streets go through."

"What is it about the freeways, do you think?"

"No idea."

Just then, I noticed a mother making her way slowly down Woodward with two small children in tow. The kids were huddled closely beside her as if they were afraid to let go of her soaked garments. She stopped to watch us drive by, and I waved.

"Don't do that!" shouted Marian.

"Whoa! I just waved, Marian. What…"

"Please, OK? We don't want to draw attention. Things are really different now. Especially during the daytime."

"So is that why you had everyone come over during the evening? I wondered about that," said Peggy. "I thought the evening would have been more dangerous."

"The last time you were here, it would have been, but now the plants have evolved - all of the plants, not just the vines - plus there are some different sorts of critters that I'm pretty sure weren't here before you left the last time. The plants around the GG still seem to remember you, so you're probably OK there, but if they don't recognize you, it can get dicey. But it's really not the plants or the critters that are the biggest thing to worry about anymore. It's *us*, the humans. We're starting to change, and not for the better."

"Then why doesn't anybody leave?" asked Tom. "I mean, this is still just happening in the city, right? People can leave if they want? Go to the suburbs or wherever?"

"Not anymore, Tom. Now it's everywhere. And I have to be honest here; I'm kinda not sorry. Because of how they were all saying those things about us, like they always have, mocking us for refusing to leave and saying we were getting what we deserved just for being Detroit. But now? Yeah, now they have it too, and I mean, they got it bad. And they don't have any idea how to cope, because they aren't used to coping."

I smiled, and I noticed Peggy was smiling too.

"Yeah, you may have a point there."

And then I saw Belle Isle. Even from a distance, before we had reached the bridge, I could see that something was radically different about the park that I had practically grown up in as a youngster. Belle Isle had been the most beautiful city park anywhere in Michigan, and it had everything: a zoo, an aquarium, tennis courts, basketball courts, beaches, paddle boats, woods you could get lost in, hopefully with a girl. It had *everything*.

But now, as we got closer to the bridge, Belle Isle didn't look so much like an island as it did a huge, pulsating green creature tethered to a leash, which was the bridge. It looked like a jungle brought to life, and I could start to see what looked like grossly misshapen limbs reaching out from the tangled mass of vines and whatever else was growing and breathing inside of there toward the water, waving slowly back and forth as if it was trying to summon something.

We parked at the edge of the bridge, with the motor running. Not more than a minute later, I could see two large purplish fins making their way toward the island from farther down the river. The closer they got to Belle Isle, the taller the fins got until a submarine-shaped body broke the water beneath them. Both fins, attached to this one single body, stretched at least twenty feet above the river. Behind it formed a churning V-shaped wake large enough to belong to a sizable speed boat, and it was headed directly toward those misshapen limbs, which now seemed to be anxiously encouraging the approach.

"What the hell is going on, Marian? This couldn't possibly be Belle Isle. It may be located in the same geographical location, but…"

"Watch."

She said the word with such finality that I didn't feel like we had an option, so we quietly watched a creature the size of two Moby Dicks racing toward Belle Isle with enough speed and mass to fracture my childhood playground into bits. But then, just as it neared the coastline, the water bubbling and foaming near its misshapen head as it crested the surface, its gigantic mouth opened wide enough to swallow two or three Cadillacs whole simultaneously with room to spare. At the same time, several more limbs shot out from the roiling green mass of the island as if they were being launched from a giant spool. They were noticeably thicker than the ones that had done the beckoning, and they seemed far too anxious to greet the beast as they shrieked with an ear-splitting cry and headed straight for the open mouth.

"Marian…? What the…"

"Watch."

A massive, restless tangle of vines suddenly exploded out of the water behind the creature, writhing, coiling, and hissing like a den of angry snakes. But the beast didn't seem to notice as its grotesquerie of a mouth opened impossibly wider, even as the crowd of limbs and vines racing toward it from the front hungrily poured themselves into the expanding maw like a stream of forest. We watched as the beast was pried apart by its jaws in slow motion, even as its hindquarters began to spray fountains of blood in response to the hook-like claws that the vines had begun to fasten into its glistening flesh. The combined sounds of the shrieking vines, the echoing enraged roar of the creature, and the thrashing of the river waters surrounding the entire event were enough to make me nearly come unraveled. It was all simply too much.

And then it was done. The creature was floating lifelessly in the water, an island unto itself, while the vines began the process of what I assumed was preparing it for a big meal later on. Slowly, almost tenderly, they wrapped themselves around the body as they rotated it round and round as if it were on a spit. Once that process was done, the vines fell away, and I could see the creature was covered in some sort of grayish-white cocoon-looking substance as they dragged it toward the island, which opened up like a horseshoe-shaped mouth, inhaling the body into its depths.

None of us said anything for a while, because what could be said? But then I had to ask, "Why did you bring us here? What was it about this you felt like we had to see?"

Marian looked at me with a tired smile that made my heart ache.

"You said that this couldn't possibly be Belle Isle."

"I did, yes."

"And yet you have to know that, in fact, this really *is* Belle Isle. You may not want it to be, and neither do I, but that doesn't matter because we have just seen the truth of things together. This is what we have. Where we are."

I stared at Marian for a long moment before allowing my gaze to drift back to the river.

"OK. I think I understand."

"Do you?"

"I'm trying," said Tom. "How did you know this was going to happen once we got here, though? How did you know this wouldn't be a quiet day, and then what would we be saying now if things hadn't gone according to plan?"

"That's more honest, and thank you. But Tom, there was no plan. I didn't know what would happen once we got here, only that something was bound to happen. This was a bigger something than what I normally have seen before, although there have been times… never mind. The point is that there is never a quiet day here anymore, because nothing is the same. Everything has changed to a point where a lot of us can't accept it. And that includes some of us from the GG. That's why it looks the way it does now, because

things got to a place where none of us could keep
pretending; we couldn't pretend we didn't hear and
see what was going on right outside our windows. Or
when folks went missing. The screams. For the
longest, as long as we could make it work, the GG
was our refuge, our place to come together and get
away from it all. Our last hope for community. But
then it simply got to be too much, even for us. And so
we just walked away. I'm sorry, Tom. And Peggy. I
know how much the GG meant to both of you, how
much of your lives you put into it."

I shook my head.

"The GG was always about the people, not the
building. It's the people who made the GG what it
was."

Marian smiled again, only this time not so
wearily. She nodded.

"I would have to agree."

The Last Meeting

Belle Isle was only supposed to be the first stop
on a much longer tour of the city that Marian had
planned for us. But why she thought what we
witnessed from across the bridge wouldn't be enough

to get the message across is a mystery to me. Because I certainly didn't need to see anything else if it was any worse than that. She laughed without amusement when I expressed that sentiment, and we motored our way back through the empty streets to her apartment, chatting about not much in particular but mainly to keep from thinking too much about…well …everything.

"We should have another meeting," she said after close to five minutes of silence, which caught me off guard.

"Really? Why would you think it would be any better than the last time?"

"There's never a guarantee of anything, but it occurred to me that part of the reason why some of them acted like they did was that they were scared. It's as simple as that."

"OK. I get that. But what else can we say to get around that and make them *un*-scared?

"This whole thing is gonna have to be handled as a work in progress, figuring it out as we go. But remember, at the end of that last meeting, I said we should all calm down and then meet again in a week, and everyone agreed to that. Grudgingly? Yeah, probably. But the point is that they agreed to come back and hash this out some more. That means they're still willing to listen."

"You sound like maybe you think this is important, getting them to go to New Detroit. Risks and all," said Peggy.

"It's more than important, it's practically non-negotiable. Going to New Detroit isn't as much of a risk as it is a chance. At least that's the way I see it. But if we stay here, in a city that's dying faster and faster every day, then all we have to work with is risk. Because here there's not only no chance of things getting better, there's no *hope*. And once you've lost hope, you've lost everything."

* * *

We held the next meeting one week to the day after the first, and I was so pleased - and surprised - to see that Marian's intuition about the group had been right. The week apart had given each of them the time they needed to wrestle with their fears, but also to face the reality of where they were right now and what that meant for the future - or lack of it. There were even some new faces, including several who didn't belong to the GG. At first, I had a bit of an issue with that, which I expressed to Peggy, and to which Peggy responded that if we were only here to help people from our own little group, then we deserved whatever bad karma we had coming our way.

"So here we are again, and that's a good thing. I know we all agreed to meet again at this time, but that agreement wasn't a guarantee. A lot of us could have decided over the past week that this wasn't worth revisiting and just not show up, so this makes me feel good to see that our GG bond is still holding up despite all that we've been through," said Marian.

There were smiles and nods, as well as rippling murmurs of appreciation throughout the group. The noticeable warmth of response was a welcome relief. Peggy and I had decided that we would let everyone sort through their feelings this time around without us weighing in one way or the other. Everyone already knew where we stood, plus our status as co-founders of the GG still carried a little gravitas that we didn't want to use in the wrong way. Best to hang in the background and see how everything played out; if they were coming, then they were coming. If not, then they weren't. It would be harder to explain to Nathan and the other children once we got back, obviously, but hopefully they would at least appreciate that we had returned and hadn't chosen to abandon them. And who knows? Depending on the randomness of the timeline, maybe we'd get lucky, and the battle between Nathan's group and the others would have resolved itself by then. It didn't seem likely, but even the outside chance that it was possible was something worth holding onto.

The meeting stretched on for more than three hours into the night, coming to a close around a quarter past ten. Other than a few minor eruptions, the conversation and debate were relatively civil and considerate, but at the end, I still couldn't say I knew for sure which way this was going to go. Marian must have felt the same way, which I suspect is why she asked for a vote by show of hands.

Slowly, she smiled.

"Well, I guess that's everybody then."

Back to New Detroit

Nathan sat quietly at the picnic table, watching his friends play on the swings and the slide, laughing and giggling in the ways that only children can do - even children that weren't quite children. He smiled as a slender girl with dark blue skin and silver hair beckoned to join her on the swings.

"Why are you just sitting there? Come *on,* Nathan! This is a great day!"

Nathan shook his head.

"I'm fine, Sonya. Knowing they won't be coming back is all I need right now. Or at least not as our enemies. I never thought…"

Nathan's words caught in his throat like fish bones as he watched Tom and Peggy walking toward the playground from the alley, hand-in-hand, followed by what looked like at least thirty very confused-lookin' adults. Sonya hopped off the swing to trace the origin of Nathan's stare, and soon all of the children had stopped their celebration to stare at the strangers that had suddenly appeared in their midst.

"I believe we made you a promise, Nathan. I hope we're not too late."

www.ingramcontent.com/pod-product-compliance
Lightning Source LLC
Chambersburg PA
CBHW070847160726
48004CB00003B/956